The Mother Of All Things

by
Gabriel Blake

The Mother Of All Things

First published in 2018 by DRF Publishing.
Copyright © 2018 by Gabriel Blake

Print ISBN: 978-1999663612
eBook ISBN: 978-1999663605

Cover art by Farrukh Bala
Gratitude to Alexandra Haynak
Edited by DRF Publishing
Written by Gabriel Blake

www.gabrielblake.com

For Kathryn

This inhuman place makes human monsters.

Stephen King
'*The Shining*'

1

Sunday, 13 August

Elaine's eyes laboured to open, dazzled by the glare from the chandelier above. She blinked several times to shake off the haze and regain focus. Her distorted vision lingered on the wavering webs of dust that dangled from the fake crystals before drifting to the split paintwork on the ceiling and the tattered wallpaper curling from the tops of the walls. Cobwebs oscillated high up, born in the corners they'd extended along the coving over time.

Elaine took a huge gulp and followed it with a frown. Pain flared across her face and she reached up to identify why it hurt so much. She pulled her hand away; a blend of sticky and dried blood covered it and layers of red ran all the way down her arm, concealing her pale skin. She raised her head from the floor to take in an even more disconcerting sight. The white towel around her body was a montage of bloodied shades. Where had it all come from? It couldn't be hers, the only discomfort was on her face.

Her breathing intensified and she became aware of an unpleasant metallic smell. She pulled a face as her taste buds burst to life with the salty and bitter aftertaste of – blood. The coppery tang brought back memories of her childhood when she used to suck on the chain of a necklace, a much-loved gift from her best friend.

The towel stuck to the encrusted skin of her bosom as she rolled off the worn rug near the foot of the stairs. Weary, she raised herself onto her hands and knees. Her hair, discoloured and matted with blood, drooped over her face as she fixed her eyes on the faded varnish of the floorboards. Disorientated, she took a couple of deep breaths, so many thoughts vying for first place in her mind. Of late, and more in control, she'd had more confidence, more strength. Was this a step backwards in her recovery? She hoped not.

Failing to dredge up an explanation, Elaine paused to collect herself. Compelled to look to her right, her eyes settled upon the body of a masked man lying a few feet away, his torso encircled by a pool of semi-congealed blood. She gasped and moved a hand to cover her mouth. What made her look? Was it nothing more than impulse or did she know a dead man lay in her hallway?

A tall, muscular man by the look of him. Could he be the intruder she'd encountered once before? The wide eyes of the dead man behind the mask stared through the peepholes; his accusing gaze directed at her. She wondered how this could have happened but her mind in chaos, she drew a blank. A long black knife handle protruded from the side of the man's neck, the serrated blade embedded beneath the surface of his skin. She recognised it as one from the block in her kitchen.

Elaine endeavoured to stand, her whole body straining to function. She swept aside the bloodstained strands of hair stuck to her caked face. Unable to think straight and increasingly agitated, she stood still, kneading the ends of her hair between her thumb and fingers, surprised to discover it was damp. With a glance at the towel around her, she presumed she'd been in the bath at some point. She cast her eyes over the body, the severity of her circumstances sinking in. She needed answers; answers that weren't exactly forthcoming. Was her mind playing tricks on her? It wouldn't be the first time.

'Come on, woman! *Think*, damn you, think,' she said, her frustration boiling over, desperate to understand her predicament.

She was in the long hallway of her house. The shabby front door was wide open to the night. At the other end of the hall, the kitchen light spilled under the closed door. Opposite Elaine was the darkened living room where she recalled an angry exchange of words with her mother earlier that evening: the reason for her taking a bath in the first place. A good soak usually helped her to relax. She revelled in the comfort of hot water and bubbles until there was a knock at the door, a rude interruption of her peaceful moment. She chose to ignore it. After the second knock, her anger resurfaced and she stepped out of the bath. Wrapped in a towel, she stormed down the stairs in a huff and opened the door. That was the last thing she remembered.

Elaine assessed the burly figure, the man's unclasped belt, the button on his jeans – undone – and the fly at half-mast.

Had she prevented this man from carrying out an appalling act on her? She shuddered at what could have taken place.

Hesitant, Elaine moved closer to the body. Keeping her distance, she crouched, stretched out an arm and took hold of the black material. Consumed with a yearning to see his face, she was afraid; afraid it might be one she'd recognise. With caution and a grimace, Elaine peeled the balaclava upwards to reveal the hidden features behind the hostile mask.

An incredulous shriek escaped as she let go of the balaclava and shot to her feet. Elaine staggered back until she smacked against the bannister, shocked to learn who the dead man was – and it wasn't good. It wasn't good at all.

'Well, this doesn't look great, does it, my girl?' a voice spoke from behind her.

Elaine glanced over her shoulder at the unexpected intrusion. Her mother stood at the foot of the stairs.

'I don't know what happened, Mum, I really don't,' exclaimed Elaine.

'Pretty obvious if you ask me. He's dead, you're alive and your kitchen knife is stuck in his neck,' said Margaret. 'It doesn't take a genius to work out you killed him.'

Nothing was real to Elaine. She wanted to run through the entire incident in her mind but everything after opening the front door … obliterated from memory. Not knowing what to do, she stood, frozen to the spot, her body trembling. Her mother walked forward and placed her wrinkled hands on her daughter's cheeks.

'Calm yourself, child. You know what you have to do.'

'I don't, Mum. I don't know what I'm supposed to do,' she whimpered, tears filling her eyes.

Margaret gave her daughter's cheek a short, sharp slap. 'Now stop! You do know.'

The clock on the console table ticked loudly as she re-evaluated her situation before going through a complete shift in her manner.

'You're right, Mother – I do,' said a calm and dispassionate Elaine.

2

Wednesday, 8 August
5 Years Earlier

The day had been long and eventful. Now, well into the evening, the sun had removed itself from view as dusk surrendered to the night. Robert and Elaine had taken their three children to the circus in Finsbury Park. They'd enjoyed performances from the trapeze artists, a strong man, jugglers, tightrope walkers, watched a brilliant horse show, and let's not forget the clowns, oh – so many clowns. Charlie was amazed at how many fitted inside a Mini Cooper.

As they left the big top, the boys argued about which was the best performance, an argument that soon ended when they were greeted by the clowns, waving goodbye and having photos taken with children. A photographer bumped into Elaine.

'Sorry, my love,' he said, gesturing a single-handed apology. 'How about a photo of your boys with one of the clowns?' he was eager to add, which alerted Elaine to the bump being intentional to get her attention.

'They're reasonably priced,' he continued.

Before Elaine or Robert could respond, Charlie and Michael were either side of a dishevelled clown waiting for their picture to be taken. Out of nowhere, Elaine's chest tightened. The camera flashed – searing pain raced behind her eyes, shockwaves surged through her head. After many years, she knew the signs and sometimes had the strength to suppress her anxiety. She closed her eyes to focus and took a few deep breaths. Of late, she'd been practising mindfulness, and on this occasion, managed to put it to good use. Busy holding Emily and watching the boys have their separate photos taken with a clown, Robert hadn't noticed her attack. Elaine's breathing returned to normal and she opened her eyes as the boys approached, smiles aplenty.

An enchanting vintage fair accompanied the circus. Typically, the children couldn't resist and mum and dad gave in to their requests. As well as the children, Robert and Elaine were equally impressed to see the ornate and refurbished antique rides restored to their former glory. As the evening progressed, they all went on one attraction or another but soon got hungry and stopped for a bite to eat. Robert chose a hot dog while Michael and Emily opted to share a cone of chips. As for Elaine and Charlie; there was no way they'd pass up the opportunity to have their favourite: hot, sugared ring doughnuts.

Robert had spent most of the evening carrying Emily. Her two-year-old legs were only willing to take her so far before her arms stretched out to daddy. They all agreed the carousel would be the last ride of the evening. Emily sat with her mother in an elegant looking carriage, decorated white and gold with beautiful red leather seating. Dad joined the boys in riding the magnificent shiny white steeds. With grace and poise, they rose up and down on the elegant golden poles, etched with smooth spiralling curves.

Elaine took great pleasure in watching her family. The days when they spent quality time like this together were sadly infrequent. The childrens' faces were a pretty picture of innocence, hope, and smiles that brought a delightful warmth to her heart. As for Robert, he looked handsome and set an example as a great father. What more could a wife and mother want? She wished this moment, this fleeting feeling of happiness, love and pride would last forever, but she knew that would be too much to ask. Robert would ruin it, somehow – he always did. It was unlikely to be tonight, but he would, and she'd be stupid enough to forgive him – as she always did. Elaine didn't know if she truly loved him anymore. He'd done so much damage already. Her life – caught in a snare. Robert would cheat on her and she'd find out about it. Then would come the quarrel, followed by his apology, his tears of not wanting to be away from his children, her tears of being alone, her weakness, followed by her forgiveness.

Despite knowing she was a fool to keep forgiving him, her fear of fighting her mental health problems single-handed was too much to bear. He knew her better than anyone. When she plummeted into an abyss of emptiness, Robert took the time to piece her back together. Sometimes he would see the warning signs and do his best to keep her from being consumed by her depression. Not that it always worked. On the flip side, he also fed her dark days with his philandering. She knew he didn't love her, how could he? Their marriage had an expiry date, and they both knew it.

*

Mounted on the horse in the middle row, a son either side of him, Robert's attention strayed to a strikingly beautiful young woman stood close to the carousel on the grass. Wearing a long grey trench coat, she smiled as she watched him. He recognised her immediately and by the time the carousel completed a full turn, any trace of a smile on his face had faded. When he caught Elaine staring at him, he pinned on another grin. The woman turned and strolled away. As the carousel slowed down, Robert took note of which direction the woman wandered.

The family left the carousel and Michael and Emily were quick to point and plead for the Ferris wheel to be the last ride. It was a definite no-no for ten-year-old Charlie, who was afraid of heights. Two years younger, Michael seized the opportunity to mock his brother, the likeliest reason he was so eager to go on it in the first place. On this occasion, Elaine quickly shot down their pleas, but Robert sided with the children.

'Oh, come on, El. Let them have a go on the big wheel,' he said, before turning to the children, 'This is the last one, okay?'

Michael and Emily raced to join the queue in response to their mother's conceding smile. While they were to have their fun on the Ferris wheel, Robert said he'd take Charlie over to the hall of mirrors.

'Dad, when can we pick up the photographs?' Charlie asked as they walked towards the attraction.

'If they're ready, we'll collect them on the way to the car park,' said Robert.

As they approached the booth, he glared towards the shaded gap between the hall of mirrors and the coconut shy, where the woman who'd drawn his attention before, waited.

'Hey, Charlie! How would you like to be a big boy and go into the hall of mirrors on your own?'

'Yeah, cool,' Charlie answered, excited and pleased at the show of trust.

Robert paid the attendant as Charlie went up the steps towards the entrance.

'I'll be waiting for you right here,' he called out as he watched Charlie disappear through the lightweight swing door.

They'd all been inside the hall of mirrors earlier, so Robert knew he had around ten minutes before Charlie would get bored and find his way out. He glanced back at the Ferris wheel. Elaine might see him, but he'd take the risk. Robert slipped down the side of the attraction, snatched the woman's hand, taking a firm grip, and led her around the back, out of sight.

'Chloé, what the hell are you doing here?' he asked, regretting he'd mentioned the family night out when they spoke earlier.

'I know how you like the danger,' Chloé replied in her soft French accent.

She leaned in to kiss him on the lips while her hand wandered down to his groin, bringing a smile to his face. Stepping backwards in a slow and alluring way, Chloé unbuttoned her long coat. Her back pressed against the large lorry as she opened the coat to display her nakedness. His smile widened as he gazed at her beautiful pale skin. Swept up in a deluge of passion, he moved towards her.

Their lips came together, heavy breaths, out of control, fervent murmurs released. Robert's hands moved up, over the soft skin of Chloe's hips, finding their way to her pert breasts. All thoughts of his family eclipsed. He caressed and forced the flesh together before his mouth dropped to her hard nipples, his lips tight around them, sucking and pulling while his fingers eased across her soft skin to between her legs. High-pitched moans of pleasure escaped as he caressed her. Their eyes locked. Robert put his moist fingers up to Chloé's lips, which she drew into her mouth, one by one – slow and tantalising. Their tongues clashed. He could taste her. She reached down and unfastened his belt and the button to his jeans, easing them down a little. Chloé moved her legs apart and he reached a hand down to help enter her. He grabbed the backs of her thighs and lifted her upwards. He loved how it felt to be inside her. The forbidden lust. An irresistible need to be desired by another woman, particularly this woman, and she craved him with as much avidity.

Robert stepped out of the shadows into the light of the fairground and waited next to the hall of mirrors. He stared at the stationary Ferris wheel. People disembarked and boarded the capsules. For a split-second he wondered if Elaine had already left the ride, but then, right at the top, he saw her and the children. They appeared to be exploring the magnificent view below. He saw Elaine pointing into the distance and guessed she was likely pointing to the tower block that loomed over their neighbourhood. Robert turned his attention to the exit door of the hall of mirrors, his patience wearing thin. Surely Charlie should have found his way out by now. As the seconds passed, his agitation intensified. He rubbed a hand across the back of his neck, his go-to stress reflex.

After another minute, Robert stepped forward to speak to the man in the booth, trying to remain calm. 'Is it okay if I go through and fetch my son?'

In an East European accent, the attendant pointed to a scrappy piece of cardboard in the window with the price marked in felt tip pen and said, 'You must pay to enter.'

'I'm not going in for the fun of it, mate. I just want to get my son.'

Without saying a word, the man once again pointed to the card.

'Fuck's sake!' said Robert, and reached into his pocket. He paid the man and entered the hall of mirrors to find Charlie. Calling out Charlie's name as he searched, his concern grew more frantic by the second, bumping into the mirrors as he rushed through.

The exit door flew open as Robert stormed out. He raced back to the booth and persuaded the attendant to help him search the attraction again. They failed to locate Charlie. Flustered, Robert spotted Chloé standing a short distance away, a look of confusion about her. The tension in Robert's behaviour and the guilt on his face was there for all to read. His eyes burned into hers. Chloé stepped forward but a slight shake of Robert's head brought her to an abrupt stop. The stare off continued, and though reluctant, Chloé backed slowly away and vanished into the crowd.

From her vantage point on the slow-moving Ferris wheel, Elaine caught sight of Robert. He looked harassed, and there was no sign of Charlie. Something was wrong. She called out and waved her arms in a desperate attempt to attract the attention of either her husband or the attendant below, who was busy looking at his phone. Robert charged around in no particular direction. It wasn't normal to see him act this way. Elaine's heart raced, her stomach churned and sweat broke through the skin on her reddening face. Her body screamed panic.

Michael tugged at her cardigan and pointed towards the big top. Seconds later, Elaine caught sight of Charlie in his blue coat, approaching a clown. Two helium-filled balloons floated above the clown's head, one red, the other yellow. The clown offered the string attached to the yellow balloon to her son, who took the gift. A white-gloved hand then reached out for Charlie to take, which he did.

Elaine presumed the clown would take Charlie to an office or meeting point and again, attempted to signal Robert, who continued to rush around, accosting people. At last the Ferris wheel stopped at the bottom and she burst out of the capsule with the children. Elaine raced towards the big top where she'd last seen Charlie.

Under immense pressure, Robert's thoughts fluctuated between panic, guilt, and fear as he asked every stranger if they'd seen a ten-year-old boy in a blue jacket, his efforts futile. Who would remember one particular child in such a large crowd? It was his fault Charlie had wandered off. There was no way he could tell Elaine how he'd come to lose their child. He needed to find his son, and he needed to find him fast.

Robert's heart skipped a thousand beats as he watched Elaine run across the fairground, holding Emily and pulling Michael behind her. She must have seen Charlie from the top of the Ferris wheel. Selfishly, he hoped that was all she'd seen. He raced to catch up with them and when he did, they talked over each other and bickered. They asked the clowns about their son but nobody had seen anything.

Elaine watched Robert run off in a desperate bid to find Charlie. With Emily on her hip and firmly holding onto Michael's hand, she did her best to keep up. She looked down the shaded sides of stalls and attractions looking for any sign of her eldest. Then she saw it; in the sky above the visitor's car park, a yellow balloon, floating away, onwards and upwards – into the darkness. With Emily clutched in her arms, Elaine's heart withered and her legs gave way. She slumped to her knees, hypnotised by the balloon. Call it a mother's instinct but somehow, she just knew it was the one she'd seen her boy holding.

A complete wreck, all colour drained from her face, Elaine stared up at Robert. Confused and frightened, Michael held onto Emily's hand as a wilting Elaine had let her go. The world stilled and fell silent around her, seconds that lasted an eternity. Elaine vomited in front of her children and the gathering crowd. Horrendous emotions taking control. With a hand covering her mouth, she looked up and pointed in the direction of the car park. Robert set off in haste and two men standing close by were quick to follow. Little did they all know; Elaine's finger traced the yellow balloon as it drifted far up into the night sky. Her mother's instinct tacit that it was too late. Her boy was gone.

3

Monday, 31 July
Present Day

The American style porch ran the entire length of the house, the front door centred with two large windows either side. Elaine relaxed on the swing bench in front of the left window, staring across the vast amount of recently cut grass, both hands clasped around a mug of coffee, her first of the day. Wearing thick white slippers and an old blue dressing gown she'd purchased for the day she went into hospital to give birth to Charlie, she gently rocked back and forth. The slanted porch roof below the upstairs windows provided a diagonal line of shade, masking her face from the beams of the early morning sun. Ahead of the bench were three steps leading down to the gravel drive.

Suspended by chains from the ceiling, the bench squeaked every time her feet pushed backwards. Elaine found the gentle swaying motion soothing. She had sat on this bench as a little girl – lifetimes ago on those delightful late summer evenings seated next to her mother, who always said it reminded her of those old Hollywood movies. This type of porch was unusual in the UK. It made Margaret all the more determined to convince her husband this was the house for them. Not that he needed much persuasion, he liked the place; he loved the idea of the seclusion even more.

The paintwork, once all white and majestic, now looked dismal, weathered and decayed. In poor condition, the rendered wall under the porch had faded to a drab, dirty grey. When Elaine returned to Sablefall Farm, she was sad to see the house in such a sorry state. She'd already put the porch at the top of her to-do list, along with many other critical refurbishments.

Three days ago, she'd come back, a move her mother would argue should have happened sooner. With far too many things to take into consideration, it was a tough decision for her. Elaine had thought about moving away from London before she and Robert divorced two years ago. Granted, it took her a while to decide, but relief embraced her when she moved back to where she'd grown up: a small town called Helmsley in North Yorkshire.

Her mum and dad had moved there from North London when she was four years old. She knew it had something to do with her father, though she never learned the reason. Memories were hazy before her father died of a heart attack, and she didn't remember much for a short time after, either. Now life had gone full circle and she'd repeated history: left her previous life behind to start over. Elaine sipped her coffee, appreciating how isolated and peaceful it was here. Plenty of distance lay between the next houses and farms. Just what she needed.

An enormous lonely oak tree shaded the front right of the house. The huge trunk covered in ivy. Two long ropes hung from one of its thick branches. Attached to one of them, the plank of wood fashioned into a makeshift swing seat flopped ungainly and dejected, resting on the patchy, dirt-covered ground below. The other rope dangled free and forlorn, swaying in the gentle breeze. Elaine had spent many hours on the swing, either having fun or out of pure boredom. Now it would be Emily's turn to enjoy the experience.

The old two-storey farmhouse with five large bedrooms, surrounded by roughly two and a half acres of land, sat a few miles from town. There used to be more land but over time, her father sold it off for a tidy profit. The only other buildings remaining on the property were a long dry-stone shed to the left and an old dilapidated barn about three hundred feet to the rear of the house.

At this stage, she had no idea if she'd settle here on a permanent basis, but she would use her time here to restore the old place. Elaine and Robert had spent years refurbishing properties and had built up an excellent portfolio. Getting her hands dirty didn't bother her; she'd relish a project to immerse herself in for now.

Elaine sought to find some comfort in the solitude. The last few years hadn't been kind to her. An attractive woman with a face that belied her age, the strain and suffering of the last five years were irrefutable. An extreme sadness cloaked her, recognisable only to people who'd been through a prolonged period of pain. Behind her melancholic eyes lay something else. An unwelcome desolation that had stalked her from as far back as she could remember, haunting her dreams and sometimes dominating her every waking hour, a determined and unforgiving destroyer of anything positive.

Since she was a child, psychiatrist Dr Graham Walker had been part of her life. He helped subdue her various conditions and find the right course of medication and treatment. Albeit there were spells when she was fine, without warning, her darkness would descend once again. Each time Elaine thought she'd defeated her depression, surreptitiously it returned, stronger and more indomitable than ever. Over time she came to the conclusion Dr Walker was right: it would never be conquered, only managed.

Moving so far from London meant a change of psychiatrist and this morning, she had her first appointment with Dr Neville Brown. She'd already been awake for a while; difficulty sleeping was a common occurrence for her. Elaine rose from the bench to go inside to change as her mother stepped out of the house. She had a kind and friendly face, etched with life's experiences.

'Morning, Mum.'

Margaret turned, not surprised to see her daughter already up this early.

'Good morning, dear,' she replied. 'I take it you're off to get ready for your meeting?'

'It's not a meeting, Mother. It's an appointment.'

'I know, but I don't like to think of them like that. Makes it sound like you're unwell or something.'

'I am unwell, I've always been unwell.'

'That's not true. You were a happy child. It was only when we moved here things changed for you, which makes me wonder why you bothered to come back?' Margaret said.

'Are you trying to tell me you didn't want me to come

back?' In Elaine's mind, she was convinced this was what her mother wanted her to do. To return to the farm and find the peace she had sought for so long.

'Of course not. I think you should have come back years ago, you know that.'

'The time wasn't right.'

'And now?' Margaret's tone softened as if to placate her daughter.

'And now, something tells me it is.'

Margaret took her daughter's hand in hers. 'Look, I know things have been terrible and harsh for you. No child is deserving of what happened. I wish there were some way to turn the clock back. All I ever hoped and dreamed was that you would learn to manage and deal with it in some way.'

'I want to, Mum. That's why I've come home. As I said, the time feels right.'

Elaine knew it had taken far too long to accept the loss of her child had torn her world apart. Life had been hard enough on her; losing her boy had weakened her defences further. She needed to regain control, to find new strength from within. Elaine planted a kiss on her mother's cheek.

'I'd better get ready or I'll be late.'

The journey to York for the first session with her new psychiatrist took just over an hour. These appointments, although intended to help her, never stopped her from feeling anxious right before one. Over the years, she'd had countless sessions. In the waiting room she fidgeted in her seat, picking and peeling skin from the edges of her fingers, legs crossed while her foot shuffled up and down.

She thought about how she quite liked her previous psychiatrist Dr Walker, but seconds later she dismissed this as total bollocks. She respected him at first, way back when, but he was the first and only psychiatrist she'd seen until now, so she didn't have much to base her opinion on. Over time, she'd developed a hatred of his craggy, ageing face and his old-school posh accent droning on, telling her what would and wouldn't be good for her. Condescending old tosspot! Lost in contemplation, she failed to hear her name the first time but snapped back into the here and now when the assistant called it again.

Doctor Neville Brown greeted her at the door and closed it behind her.

'Please, take a seat,' he said in a mellow and reassuring way as he gestured to a comfortable red leather armchair.

Settled, Elaine examined her surroundings. Dark wood covered every wall with large book-laden shelves either side of her. Apart from the redcurrant shag pile carpet and two matching leather chairs, there wasn't much else in the room other than a side table with a large, expensive-looking gold lamp with a green shade. She viewed with awe the high ceiling with intricate white mouldings that formed nine squares. There were small sculpted roses in the centre of every square with three different background colours applied to each line of three.

'It's beautiful, isn't it?' said a beaming and obviously proud Dr Brown.

'Yes, it certainly is. Victorian! Looks like original Victorian colours as well,' Elaine replied.

'Why yes, it is,' he said, surprised and impressed. 'Crimson, French grey and—'

'Mid Brunswick green,' she jumped in.

'Wow, very impressive, Ms Bennett.'

For some reason, Elaine had decided to use her maiden name.

Dr Brown took his seat. 'Tell me, how do you know about Victorian decor?'

Elaine smiled, looking more relaxed. 'I used to run a property developing business. Sometimes we acquired old buildings in need of restoration, so I had to learn about Georgian and Victorian design and colours.'

'What happened to the business?'

'Oh, it's still running, I've just taken more of a back seat these days.'

'I see, interesting to know. Anyway, I suppose I should introduce myself.'

Dr Neville Brown was somewhere between his mid to late forties, clean-shaven, suave, with an air of sophistication about him. The introductions over, he began to ask questions. These sessions were always more like interrogations than therapy; she hoped it might be different here.

'Is this your first time seeing a psychiatrist?'

'Yes, it is,' she lied, raising a hand to cover the faint blush forming on her neck.

'And how do you feel about coming to see one?'

'I don't know, yet,' Elaine replied.

'Well, many people loathe being in a room with one, airing what can be extremely sensitive issues or personal problems.'

'I do feel a little nervous, but I've come to accept I need professional help.'

'Being nervous is both natural and understandable.'

Uncomfortable, Elaine resisted squirming under his scrutiny, conscious he observed her every involuntary movement, searching for answers to questions he hadn't yet asked.

'What have you accepted you need help with?'

She paused, already fighting to hold back the tears. An indication of how punishing this subject was for her.

'The loss of my eldest son – Charlie. Five years ago, he was abducted from a fairground. Teenagers found his body nine days later.' A solitary tear escaped and rolled down the crease between her nose and cheek.

'I'm so sorry to hear that, Elaine. May I ask how he died?'

'He was strangled.'

'And you've been dealing with this alone for five years?'

'For the most part, yes. I mean, there was my husband, Robert, but we didn't deal with it well together. We divorced a couple of years back.'

Dr Brown adjusted in his chair. 'It must have been tough for you. How old was Charlie?'

'Ten.'

'Do you have any other children?'

'Yes, two. Michael, he's thirteen and Emily is seven.' A warm smile broke through her barrier as she mentioned her other children.

'Is Charlie's death the reason you moved away from London?' Dr Brown asked, making continuous entries into his pad.

'One of many.'

'And Michael and Emily, are they living with you or their father?'

Elaine took a breather and composed herself. 'They both moved here with me,' she said.

On her way home, Elaine made a couple of stops to pick up some groceries, paint, tools, and various other supplies, ready to make a start on the house. Thinking about her appointment, she was pleased. Dr Brown appeared to be a decent man and she was comfortable enough talking to him. All in all, it had gone so much better than she expected: she'd chosen well. He wasn't as snooty as Dr Walker.

Elaine turned off the main road through a large unattached wooden swing gate that rested against an old stone wall. Attached to the side of the gate was a rusty red metal post box. She drove up the incline on mixed gravel and dirt that led to a large parking area to the left of the house. Elaine opened the boot of her grey Vauxhall Insignia and carried some shopping inside. She put all the decorating materials in the dining room that, for now, was a storeroom.

When Elaine came back through the front door to fetch the grocery bags, a man stood down by the gate. He remained still, watching either her or the house. He was too far away to make out a face. She supposed it could be one of the locals checking out the new neighbour.

'Hi, there!' Elaine called out and waved. There was no reciprocation. As she made her way down the steps, intending to introduce herself, the man turned and walked away.

'How rude,' she mumbled, watching him stroll onto the main road and out of sight.

Evening came and Elaine had fallen asleep on the sofa in the living room. Sessions with therapists always knocked the stuffing out of her, not to mention the two hours on the road there and back. To the side of where she lay was an impressive fireplace. Every so often the kindling snapped. She loved the summers here in North Yorkshire. The days might be sweltering, but come the evenings, the temperatures often took a drastic dip, meaning you could have a cosy, roaring fire despite the season.

The constant flicker of light from the fire illuminated the dark room with a warm glow. An enormous Gothic-style mirror hung above the fireplace with a few small framed pictures scattered about the smoky beige walls. Overlong dark green curtains hung at the windows and rested on the floor. The lacklustre reflection of flames on the floorboards exposed how the patina had diminished over time. This room was no different from any of the others; the ceiling and walls shedding both paper and paint, yet more evidence of how unloved the house felt. It was plausible to believe nobody had lived in it for years. She wondered why her mother had let it fall into such a state of disrepair.

Elaine stirred and stretched out, her eyes taking in the room around her. Life had indeed been tough these last few years. Now it was time to rebuild herself and become a stronger person. She wanted and needed to be better for her children; not a mother who regularly fell to pieces in front of them without warning. Things had to improve and she knew that more than anyone.

She sat up on the sofa and reached for the bottle of rosé on the coffee table, emptying the remainder into her glass. As she finished the wine, a loud thump against the window startled her. Elaine put down the glass, got to her feet, and paused to listen for a second or two before moving to draw back the curtain. She peered out, trying to see what had made the racket. Apart from it being dark outside, the grime-covered glass further impaired her vision.

Elaine went to the front door and switched on the porch light. She hesitated for a second or two before she opened the door and stepped outside to investigate. Nothing obvious showed, the lighting on the wall to the side of the door too inadequate; the bulb far too weak to be of any assistance. Cautiously, Elaine slid towards the living room window. She scoured the floor for whatever made the loud thumping sound but didn't see anything of note, no visible sign of something striking against the dirty glass.

A shoulder shuddering chill ran through her and it wasn't from the cold night air. Her nerves kicked and bit, as though a presence, someone's eyes upon her. Elaine stared out into the blackened grounds that encompassed the house. Was someone out there, peering back, watching her every move? They could be standing as little as twenty feet away and she wouldn't be able to see them. The thought gave her chills. Elaine waited a little longer for any sudden movement on the grass. She was sure the noise wasn't in her head. With one last glance around, she went back inside the house.

4

Friday, 10 August
5 Years Earlier

Chloé flicked through the TV channels while sitting on the sofa. She cut a frustrated figure in her Camden Town flat as she turned it off and tossed the remote control aside. Instead, she picked up the mobile phone next to her and checked it, impatient. A knock on the door launched her from her seat to answer.

'Oh, Robert, has there been any news?' she said, throwing her arms around him.

'No, nothing,' he groaned.

Robert placed his hands on her hips and moved her aside, wanting to get into the apartment. He looked unkempt and despondent as he brushed past her and plonked himself on the sofa. Chloé went straight over and dropped to her knees in front of him, grabbing hold of his hands.

'It'll be okay, I'm sure of it, the police will find him,' she said, offering words of comfort. In truth, she didn't believe the words coming from her mouth.

'What if they don't, Chloé, what if he's ...?' Robert couldn't say the word, dejected and almost in tears. 'This is all our fault,' he continued.

'Oh no no no, don't you dare put this on me as well,' she said, getting to her feet and walking away from him. 'I am not the man who took him.'

'But if you hadn't come to the fairground, Chloé—'

'How about if you hadn't chased me in the first place? If you hadn't wanted to cheat on your wife? I wouldn't have been at the stupid fair and none of this would ever have happened,' she snapped.

'You're right. This is all on me.' Robert sat up on the edge of the sofa, his head in his hands. A man defeated. 'I need to tell Elaine, tell her what happened. I can't live with it.'

'Are you also going to tell her you fucked me at your house while she was passed out on happy pills upstairs? Oh, and let's not forget to add that your children were in their rooms asleep. I don't think so.'

Robert raised his head to Chloé with a sorrowful expression as she continued.

'What about that you wanted me to leave my husband so you could have me all to yourself. I did that for you, Robert. I did that just for you. Why haven't you left her for me yet, huh? I haven't nagged you because I trust you'll do it when the timing is right, like you said. So no! You will not tell her about any of this. It is your dirty secret to own and own it you will.'

Tears ran down Robert's cheeks. Chloé joined him on the sofa and put her arm around him, held his hand, and spoke in a low, icy tone. 'We will not risk you losing your half of the business and your half of the money. We need to stay strong. I'm sorry about your son, Robert, I truly am, but I'm sure he will turn up. Who knows, all of this may send her even more crazy than she is and we will get everything. A blessing in disguise, no?'

Robert didn't raise an eyebrow to her comments. Had the same shameful thought crossed his mind? Surely not.

Chloé put her hands on his cheeks and turned his head towards her. She stared deep into his eyes and wiped his tears with her thumbs. 'Everything will be all right my darling, I promise.' She leaned in, placed her lips on his and then pulled back. 'I know this is difficult, but you will always have me here to hold you up.'

Their lips met again; her hand moved delicately along the inside of his thigh and rested on his groin. He placed his hand over her breast. She fondled him through his jeans as her tongue forced its way into his mouth. Robert held back, unwilling to kiss her. He put a stop to her hand rubbing him and pulled her arm away before pushing her back and jumping to his feet.

'I'm sorry, Chloé, I can't do this right now. I just can't. It – it feels so wrong. I mean, what the fuck am I doing? I should be out there, trying to find my son,' he said, running his hands through his thick hair.

'And where would you look?'

'I don't know – somewhere – anywhere. Shouldn't I be doing something?'

'Leave it to the police, Robert. There's nothing you can do.'

Robert slumped on the sofa and flung his head back, his eyes full of anguish. 'I feel so guilty, so ashamed,' he sighed.

Chloé pulled him into her. With his head resting on her chest, she wrapped her arms around him. 'It will pass, my baby. This is not your fault and it isn't mine. It's nobody's fault but the man who took him,' she said, trying to reassure him as her fingers caressed his head and face. 'Everything will be okay, I promise. I am here for you.'

Shattered in so many ways, Chloé's strength kept Robert going. She was the one helping him get through this. He had no idea what he'd do if he didn't have her. Running to his wife for compassion was not an option. Not only because the guilt would eat him up, but he knew she would never be able to help him; she wasn't nearly strong enough. Elaine had struggled for years. She was far too weak and he hated that about her – always had.

5

Tuesday, 1 August
Present Day

The digital clock on the bedside table showed 05.30 a.m. Elaine sighed. She'd been awake for most of the night, drifting off occasionally for mere minutes. Insomnia – another of her problems; tossing and turning, her head a merry-go-round of the tragedy that haunted her and the things she needed to do. Her sleep patterns in total disarray ever since the clown snatched Charlie. Horrendous nightmares and relentless thoughts about how her husband had lost sight of him in the first place. Everyone told her to let it go, that to keep re-examining that godawful night would drive her insane. Perhaps it had, but how could she simply dismiss his flimsy excuse of: "One second he was there, the next, he wasn't." She knew her boy and he wouldn't have walked away from either of his parents; he knew better than that. Something else happened.

Sixteen days from now would mark five years since that fateful morning when the police knocked on her door with the devastating news. A morning that not only broke her but, in time, her marriage to Robert too. The divorce had been coming for a long time. His persistent cheating throughout their marriage had set the wheels in motion long before.

A little while after the separation, Robert met Chloé, a gorgeous French woman in her late twenties. Every ex-wife's nightmare. Elaine suspected they'd been meeting in secret before they parted ways; after all, she did work for the accountants in their flourishing property development company, so it wasn't as if he'd only just met her. These days, Chloé worked with Robert daily, which wasn't something Elaine concerned herself with anymore.

For the last five years, she'd stepped back from the day-to-day running of the business, becoming more of a silent partner. Elaine's money got the company started and together, they'd worked hard to earn the rewards. As the majority shareholder, she regularly received a nice percentage of the profits for doing nothing, much to Chloé's annoyance.

Accepting Michael and Emily taking a shine to Chloé wasn't easy, but over time, she learned to live with it. Not that she had much choice. After struggles with her mental health, Elaine's primary concern was her children. Their happiness meant everything to her. The unremitting and compelling sadness would always linger around her. Her children now gave her the strength and courage to battle through her sorrow. Over the years, Michael and Emily both came to know something terrible had happened to their older brother but at the time, they were far too young to understand. Elaine and Robert made a concerted effort to shield them from as much as they could.

Moving the children to Yorkshire would be challenging for them at first. A change of location, school, and friends. At least Elaine had lived in Helmsley before. She knew the place well and hoped that would help make settling down a little easier for them. It wouldn't be easy but if they all pulled together, they could make it work. The devastating loss would forever be lurking, to jolt her back to the tragic wretchedness which was part of her life. Elaine was ready to fight on her terms and resist surrendering to her despair.

Dr Brown was only the second psychiatrist she'd ever seen, but there had been many different therapists and types of medication over the years. Until her son's death, things hadn't been too bad. Her husband cheated on her and as expected, she loathed it, but she'd almost come to accept it. As long as he helped build her up again, Elaine conditioned herself to live with it. If she'd found the spirit and strength sooner, she'd have taken the kids and left him a long time ago. At some point, without realising it, they used each other for different reasons. Robert used her wealth for his lavish lifestyle and she used his strength for support.

Chasing sleep was pointless, so Elaine threw back the duvet and sat up. Lying awake for hours on end, thinking, never helped. Her room at the front of the house was large, airy and underused, with plenty of cobwebs dancing in the draught. The white gloss had yellowed and, in a few places, she'd torn the floral wallpaper from the walls and bundled it into a corner.

Although still dark inside, it was light enough to see as she padded down the bare wooden stairs in her slippers, trying not to disturb anyone. The house had other ideas: the stairs shrieked

33

every step of the way. Decoration in the stairwell was much the same as her bedroom. The whole house had an aura of sadness. It would take more than a lick of paint to get the place anywhere near its best.

Ahead of her at the bottom of the stairs was the sizeable panelled front door. The aged and crusted white paint had flaked off in large parts to reveal the rotting wood underneath. As she stepped into the long hallway, a light filtered from the other end. The still form of her mother sat at the kitchen table. Elaine wasn't ready to face Margaret and her relentless sympathy, not this early in the morning, preferring to go outside for some fresh air.

After a tussle with the stiff bolt at the top of the door, she turned the rusty old key and pulled it open. Outside, with the door closed to behind her, she drew in a long, hard breath, filling her lungs with fresh, brisk air. She held it captive for a few seconds before parting her lips and letting it go. Daylight had almost broken through, chasing off the dark scattered patches, the night yielding to the new morning. The bitter cold loitered with no regard for the time of year; it had never played by the rules. A force of nature, it existed by its own design and today, it united with the early mist that hovered over the ground. Elaine's breath cut through the cold and collaborated with the vapour, masking a clear view of the grounds to the front.

She strolled over to the fragile-looking bench which was much sturdier than its appearance implied. Seated, Elaine tugged at her dressing gown, wrapping it tighter around herself, trapping warmth inside. Her eyes fixated on the swirling fog and unusual movement within. The ghostly outlines of men, women and children of all ages materialised, buoyantly drifting along. Was this her mind toying with her again? Such a surreal but magnificent spectacle. She imagined them to be lost souls searching for one last glimpse of their loved ones before departing for another plane.

Some of the figures smiled at her, conveying appreciation that she saw them. A look of tenderness blossomed on Elaine's face, connecting and wishing them well on their journey. Out in the mist with them, she spied a young boy. Her look of tenderness faded to disbelief. She leaned forward on the bench to study the misty apparition – Charlie! She no longer cared whether this was real or some dream-like state.

Charlie, like an angel, stared back at her. How she loved his cheeky grin. Had he come to see his mother one last time, willing her to let him move on so he could finally be at peace? Although bewildered by the delightful vision in front of her, Elaine observed it with pure emotion, full of the reassuring and unconditional love of a mother for her child. The angelic figure of her beloved boy returned a loving smile to his mum. He wanted her permission to move on but Elaine wasn't ready to let him go. He looked into the glowing light above him, all set to pass over to the other side. The spectre of her son ascending, a captivating image.

A smoky black haze swirled above the pure white mist beneath Charlie. Easing out of the inky smog, was an enormous deep red hand with long skeletal fingers that ended in sharp and pointed peaks. The demon of her subconscious always showed up to ruin and destroy any reflective or joyful moments in her life.

The ghostlike manifestations abruptly stood still and scowled at her. Elaine's countenance changed from devotion to apprehension as the unwelcome hand rose from the murkiness and wrapped its ugly bony fingers around the misty air of her son's apparition, preventing him from going any higher. Her son's eyes pleaded with her, conveying this was somehow her fault. The beast's crimson head loomed above the smoky pall into the pure white fog, his skin, cracked and full of crevices. His large repulsive bulging black eyes peered at her.

Leaping to her feet, Elaine leant on the wooden balustrade, gasping in the sharp air, terrified of this hellish incursion. This wasn't her first encounter with him. His bulbous lips widened to reveal loathsome dagger-like yellow teeth. The phantom figures of the fog men, women and children opened their mouths to expose their dark shadowy pointed teeth. The fiend grinned at her before he dragged Charlie's manifestation into the hovering gloom below. Her boy was gone, as were all the vaporous spectres.

Something touched her shoulder. She turned her head to see the huge slick red hand, its frightful fingers with elongated black claws resting there. Elaine awoke from her dream state with a scream and her body jolting on the bench. Beside her, Margaret had placed a comforting hand on her daughter's shoulder.

'Oh, Mum,' she gasped. 'You almost scared me to death.'

'You were dreaming again,' said Margaret.

Elaine, recovering from her emotional distress, glared out into the evaporating mist. Her mind frequently played tricks on her but she was grateful this was over, for now at least.

Quietness settled between mother and daughter until Margaret said, 'I'm worried about you, dear.'

'I'm fine, Mum.'

'I can't believe you're still having these terrible dreams. I thought they'd stopped. Are they about Charlie?'

Elaine paused, dipped her head and turned away to avoid her mother's eyes as she made the admission.

Margaret stretched an arm around her daughter and pulled her close. 'It will get better my dear, may take some time but it will, I promise.'

A sentence repeated to Elaine so many times by various people. Although she appreciated the sentiment, it had become tiresome to hear. They both sat for a while, watching the early morning mist clear before them.

6

Tuesday, 14 August
5 Years Earlier

Splayed across Charlie's *Harry Potter* bedspread, Elaine buried her head in his pillow. She'd spent almost every hour in this bedroom since his disappearance six days ago. His scent lingered in here which was as close as she could get to him right now. Elaine had barred everybody else from entering his room, her sanctum; the place where she could still feel the presence of her precious boy, untainted by the smell or touch of others. Before entering the room, Elaine took a shower, rinsing her body of any foreign matter using only water, with no contamination of scented soap or shampoo whatsoever. Clothes had been set aside after going through the same ritual. Unhealthy to some, but what anyone else thought at this point was of no consequence to her.

Matthew was Charlie's favourite teddy bear; it had been with him since the day he was born. There was a time it went everywhere with him but age and other things gradually took precedence. Its home was usually up on the shelf; however, there were mornings when Elaine found the bear in his bed when she went to make it. She'd smile to herself and place him back in position on the shelf and never mention it. Every time she came into this room, she'd take hold of Matthew, pressing her nose into the bear, drawing in her son's aroma.

Elaine often sat on the edge of the bed to stare through tearful eyes at every square inch of the room. She had an overpowering need to take in what Charlie could see when he was in here, from the posters that covered the walls to the view of the back garden from the window. She occupied all the spaces where he sat and slept in his bed. She touched the toys he played with and the books he loved to read. Apart from memories and photographs, these things were her only connection to him and she needed them. She clung to them with more tenacity than she'd managed to hang on to her ever-dwindling hope.

The loud doorbell echoed up the stairs and along the landing. Elaine didn't budge, all sound blocked out by the subdued noise in her head. It rang again a few moments later. She pulled her face from the pillow, gasping for breath. She had no reason or intention to bury her face, just an unexplainable urge to feel numb, to feel nothing but emptiness. An attempt to rid herself of all thought, all memory, all loss. Elaine sat up, her hair a mess and her face returning from strained red to chalk white, awash with the unknown. Her heavily stressed and overtired eyes were full of uncertainty and despair and lack of respite.

Dazed and wilted, Elaine wandered down the stairs and opened the front door. Her eyes barely took anything in, let alone who was on her doorstep.

'Afternoon, Mrs Davis,' said the suited heavyset man in a cockney tone. He flashed his identity card at Elaine who barely bothered to look.

'Is there any news?' she asked, without expectancy. Too many false dawns had come and gone.

'Er, no – I'm afraid not,' he replied.

'Well, you'd better come in,' she offered, turning her back on him and drifting into the darkness of the long hall, heading for the kitchen.

The man stepped inside, closed the door behind him and followed.

'Tea or coffee?'

'Tea, please, Mrs Davis.' The man loomed in the doorway of the large kitchen.

It was easy to see the room hadn't long been refurbished. Spotless glossy white units and gleaming black tiles. The worktops were a speckled black granite and every appliance looked just out of the packaging.

'Milk, sugar?' she asked, taking a glance over her shoulder. 'Take a seat.'

'Only a splash of milk for me, please, I like my tea strong. No sugar, I'm sweet enough,' Lenny said, walking over to the island breakfast bar to take a seat on one of the high stools.

'Haven't heard that one before,' she said with a subtle hint of sarcasm. 'You're new. DCI Hargreaves said there might be another detective joining the investigation.'

'Yeah, that's right – I'm Detective Inspector Grey. I have a couple of questions for you, Mrs Davis, if that's okay.' He ran a hand through his thick mop of greying hair.

'Just Elaine if you don't mind. I'm sick of being called Mrs Davis,' she said as she poured out the tea.

'I can understand that,' he responded as she carried the mugs over to join him.

'So why the questions, surely you've read through the case file to familiarise yourself?'

'Yes, indeed I have, but fresh eyes and all that. There are a few things I need to clarify for a new line of inquiry I'm working on.' DI Grey sipped his tea. 'Mmm, you make a lovely cuppa, Elaine,' he smiled.

Elaine wasn't too sure about this detective. He seemed too candid. She took an instant dislike to the way he said her name, emphasising the *E* at the beginning.

'So, ask away,' she said.

DI Grey pulled a notepad from inside his jacket and reached into his side pocket. 'I'm sure I have a pen in here somewhere,' he said, looking down. 'Here it is. Now, as I understand it, you were on the Ferris wheel when your son was taken. Your husband was in the hall of mirrors with Charlie when he disappeared. Is that correct?'

'Yes,' Elaine replied, tired of going over the same questions. She lifted her mug to her lips.

'And you saw your husband looking around for your son outside the attraction, yes?'

'That's right.'

'Then, seconds later, you saw Charlie over by the circus tent walking up to a clown before being led away?' DI Grey stared across the breakfast bar at her.

'Yes, but it was my other son, Michael, who spotted Charlie first and drew my attention to him.'

41

'Is it usual for your son to wander off?' DI Grey queried and took another swig of tea.

'He wouldn't do that. Not without good reason. He always knew to stay with us or whoever was looking after him.'

'And yet he must have walked off on this occasion?'

'I'm telling you he wouldn't have done that. He must have been taken from his father's side in the hall of mirrors,' she explained.

'Well, that simply cannot be the case.'

Elaine looked confused. 'What are you saying, that I'm lying?'

'Somebody is, Mrs Davis, because I've thoroughly examined the scene. There's no way your son could have travelled the distance from the hall of mirrors to the circus tent in the short space of time given in your statements. And you say you saw your son approach the clown before he was led away.'

'Look! My husband said he was right beside him. He turned away for a second and when he turned back – he was gone.'

Elaine was getting annoyed with the detective. Was he in some way accusing her husband of something – or even her? She knew what she saw, what Michael saw.

'Well, that's the other thing, you see. What I can't understand is how your husband lost him in the first place. I've been inside that hall of mirrors and for the life of me, I cannot work it out. Even if your son did come out of the exit before your husband, it would've been no more than a few seconds later that Robert came out behind him. There is no way Charlie could've got all the way to the circus tent where you saw him meet the clown in such a short space of time. Not unless your boy is the next Usain Bolt. So you see, Mrs Davis, I just can't see how it could've happened like you both say.'

Elaine sat in silence for a moment, processing everything the detective had said to her.

'Are you insinuating that my husband and I had something to do with our son's disappearance, Detective Grey?' she calmly asked him.

DI Grey put his notepad and pen away, looked Elaine in the eye and had another sip of his tea. 'I'm saying that one, or both of you must be lying.'

'So, this is what you do, is it?'

'What is it you think I do?' he grinned.

'Turn on the parents when you can't find their lost child.'

Detective Grey was so calm, never dropping eye contact with Elaine. 'All I can say is the facts don't add up. I've done some research on the two of you, Elaine. I know you have a history of mental health problems, to what extent I'm not sure. I also know your husband is a cheat.'

'Tell me something I don't know, detective,' she said as she downed some more tea and climbed off the stool. 'I think it's time for you to leave.'

'The thing about me, Mrs Davis, is I get these instincts about things – about people. I like to think of it as a sixth sense. I've been tailing your husband and I met him, albeit briefly. Not a very forthcoming bloke.'

Irritated with the detective and his ridiculous allegations, Elaine's grip tightened around the mug in her hand. 'I said, I think you should leave. Now!' The fury in her eyes suggested he should take notice of her. Nevertheless, Detective Grey didn't move.

'Your husband is secretive and he is a liar. He thinks more about the woman he's most likely pounding as we speak than his missing son. As for you, Mrs Davis, I see a darkness behind those eyes.'

She clenched her fist and launched the cup at the DI, watching as it just missed his head and smashed into the wall behind him. Splatters of tea trickled down the recently decorated walls.

DI Grey got to his feet. 'And there it is,' he said, 'that darkness.'

She turned her head away from him. How could this man accuse her of anything? She had done nothing wrong. If he could see into her heart, he would know of her desperate anguish.

Elaine faced the detective. 'So what's going to happen, are you going to arrest me?'

'Should I?' he challenged, hoping for a confession.

'Of course you shouldn't. You should be out there trying to find my boy instead of wasting your time in here asking ridiculous questions and making outrageous accusations,' said a tearful Elaine.

'Time will tell if these are, as you claim, outrageous accusations. But if there is any evidence to suggest something more sinister, believe me, if the police don't find it, I will – and it will make the front page of every newspaper in the country.'

'Get out!' she snapped, exhausted by this detective.

'Thanks for the tea, Mrs Davis. I can find my own way out.' DI Grey went to leave.

'Wait!' shouted Elaine. The detective paused and turned back to her. 'What did you mean, make the front page of every newspaper?'

He smiled at her, 'Oh, yeah. Well, I did show you my identity card at the door. You must have misread it or something. I'm Lenny Grey, Mrs Davis. I'm a journalist.' His smile widened.

'You fucker, you said you were a detective!'

'Did I, Mrs Davis – did I?'

'Get the *fuck* out of my house!' She raged and stormed towards him as he turned, pushing him to the front door and out of it.

Lenny Grey smiled all the way to the end of the drive and stopped to reach into his jacket pocket. His smile soon faded. He glanced back at the front door.

'You crafty cow,' he snarled and headed back towards the house.

The front door opened before he reached it and Elaine stepped out. 'Did you forget something, Mr Grey? Your mobile phone, perhaps?' She appeared so calm now, compared with a few moments back when she'd shoved him out of the house, removing the phone from his pocket as she did so.

'Give it back to me, please, Mrs Davis.'

'Sure, here you go.' Elaine drew back her arm and hurled the phone towards him.

Lenny stretched out and fumbled his catch, knocking it onto the paving. He reached down to grab it from the floor and gave her a derisive stare. He then stalked off down the drive.

'Oh, and by the way – you won't find any of your voice recordings on there. They must have somehow been deleted.'

Lenny Grey paused, looking like a defeated man as the door slammed shut behind him. He'd used the pen in the side pocket trick to turn on the voice recorder app on his phone. 'Bollocks,' he said.

Elaine marched into the kitchen and sat down. She'd been so stupid and was so angry with herself for not being more aware. It was only when he'd mentioned being a journalist that she'd cottoned on to his game. It was obvious he'd recorded their conversation. Not only that, the cheeky sod had even tried to get her to give him a confession.

7

Tuesday, 1 August
Present Day

Sitting on the swing bench, Michael's eyes were practically glued to his mobile phone, his fingers tapping away as he messaged his friends. With the temperature still escalating in the afternoon sun, Elaine took in the glorious blue sky, not a cloud in sight. She stepped through the doorway, pulled the door closed and made her way to the end of the porch. Emily was by the tree, fiddling with the swing, trying to re-attach the plank to the loose rope.

'Come on, Emily!' she yelled.

'You too, Michael, let's go,' she called as she passed him. She paused at the top of the steps, reached into her clutch bag for her keys and pressed the button to unlock the car.

Emily overtook her mum, dashing around the car to the front passenger side.

'The back, Emily!' Elaine called out in a way that suggested this was a regular occurrence. Emily obeyed with an unhappy gasp, as she usually did when she didn't get her way.

As she opened the driver's side door, Elaine clocked Michael coming down the steps, his eyes still glued to his phone and noted how grown up he looked. Inside the car, she checked to see if Emily had put on her seatbelt and fastened her own. A glance in the rear-view mirror showed Michael ambling over and the broken tree swing in the background, the reflection of which was briefly obstructed as Michael passed by the back of the car. When the swing reappeared, she saw the slimy dark red creature of her nightmares on the seat, leering at her. She twisted around in alarm; he wasn't there. Elaine turned back to the rear-view mirror. The swing seat dangled to the floor while the long rope hung unrestricted, just a subtle movement from the tapering breeze.

Elaine calmed herself, dismissing the image as Michael settled into the seat next to her. She started the car and drove down the uneven gravel. Her plans for the summer were to make some home improvements while also finding things for the kids to do and places she could take them. The first of those was Rievaulx Abbey, somewhere she'd visited on more than one occasion with her parents.

After wandering around the museum, they walked up the footpath, towards the impressive remains. Elaine, being a bit of a history buff, acted as a makeshift tour guide to her children. She picked up the odd stare or two from passers-by as she explained the history of the place from 1132 onwards. From how it expanded over the years, to how many monks it housed, and how in 1538 Henry VIII dissolved the monastery and ordered the buildings stripped of all valuables and rendered uninhabitable. She was a little mournful as she informed them how over the centuries, it fell into decay and in time, abandoned. To her, ancient ruins were exceptional; they had an indefinable beauty, a mystifying presence of history. She enjoyed seeing Michael and Emily showing an interest in things and laughing together.

The sunlight streamed over the ruins casting grand shadows across the ground from the giant arches and stone columns. Spectacular as it was now, you could imagine the splendour of once upon a time. Elaine sat down on what was once a wall to another room attached to the monastery. Other families ambled around chatting, pointing, taking it all in. Michael and Emily strolled beyond the arches into the presbytery and Elaine pulled out her phone to check for any messages. None: the story of her life at present, not much contact with anyone. She waited and people-watched for a while, longing to remember much more than she could about her past. She set off to see what the children were up to and failed to notice a woman taking repeated glances in her direction as she passed by with her child.

'Elaine?' A voice called out from behind her. 'Elaine, is that you?'

Who on earth could be calling her name? Nobody knew her here. A woman of similar age to Elaine, with her hair in a ponytail, held the hand of a small boy. Amazed and happy, Elaine recognised the familiar face of an old friend she hadn't seen for many years.

'Lila!' The name passed her lips almost as fast as it came into her head. 'Wow. I can't believe it, how are you?' she asked as the woman closed in for a hug.

Though delighted, Elaine held back. It was just her way. She found it hard to let emotions flow naturally.

Lila pulled away to take a better look at her old friend. 'You look incredible, Elaine. It's been such a long time,' she said, her accent distinguishing she was a Yorkshire lass.

'You look great too,' she replied, more out of kindness than anything because Lila didn't look at her best. To be fair, she wasn't wearing any make-up and had a couple of scars on her face: one of which was at least two inches in length on the side of her left temple. 'My God, it really has been years, hasn't it?' Elaine said.

Lila wrinkled her nose. 'Well, it's over twenty-five, that I do know.' It had, in fact, been twenty-eight years.

'I guess it must be. So, is this your son?' Elaine waved and smiled at the small boy who looked about nine or ten. He returned a bashful smile and squeezed his mother's hand before retreating behind her.

'Yes, this is Ryan, my youngest. What about you, you here with family?'

Elaine hesitated. 'I'm, I'm here with my two children,' she said.

'Oh, wow, where are they?' Lila scanned around for them.

Elaine pointed over to the presbytery. 'They're somewhere up there, probably hiding from me,' she said, laughing nervously.

'I wish I had more time to chat and meet them but I've got to get this little man to a friend's birthday party. We should catch up sometime soon.'

'Sure, that would be great,' agreed Elaine, doubting it would come to anything.

'How about tomorrow?'

Taken aback by Lila's prompt invitation, Elaine looked back to the haunting arches on the hill.

'Er, yes – sounds great,' she said, flustered and not doing a great job of hiding her reservations. 'Sorry, Lila, I really must go and find my two.'

'Of course.' Lila knew what Elaine had been through; after all, it had been all over the news. 'Around eight o'clock at The Royal Oak tomorrow then?'

'Yeah, sure,' Elaine said as she marched off. She may well have agreed but doubted she'd show up. She and Lila were best friends when they were children, but that was another lifetime.

Lila paused and watched her walk away.

'Who's that lady, Mum?' Ryan asked.

'Someone I knew many years ago. She was very dear to me,' she answered in a melancholic way, not taking her gaze from Elaine, both happy and sad for her friend, a friend she wished she'd never lost.

'Come on, let's get you to that party.' Lila turned away and headed back to the car park holding her son's hand.

Elaine walked through a big arch into the presbytery, now covered by a lush green lawn. She looked around for Michael and Emily but couldn't see them anywhere. Her heart rate increased and tension escalated, the fear of being alone consumed her. She hated being on her own, but at times like these, she never was. He was there, the fiendish beast who'd haunted her throughout her life, lurking around some corner waiting to pounce, ready to wreak havoc upon her.

'Michael, Emily!' she called out, her chest tightening, the back of her throat dry, unable to swallow. She heard rustling behind one of the columns, approached, and startled by a gentle tapping sound from somewhere behind her. Turning, she saw nothing. The knocking continued, only now it encircled her. Overcome, trepidation, whispering voices, the unrelenting tapping, columns and arches whizzed around her. Light-headed, she fell to her knees on the grass, her vision distorted as her eyes closed and she collapsed, her body flopping to the ground.

She woke to find herself stretched out across the stone-cold altar, her wrists and ankles shackled to the corners. Imposing shadows spread across the emerald lawn as the sun went down on the ruins of the Abbey. Nightfall accelerated around her. Unable to move, a tsunami of fear, confusion and panic surged through Elaine. Frantic, she struggled for breath, yanking her limbs, desperate to free herself from the chains.

'Help!' she yelled. 'Somebody, please,' she shouted, twisting her head from side to side. Elaine lay still, her heavy breathing easing, which made the deathly silence more noticeable. She had never known the night to fall so fast.

The light of the moon illuminated the formidable hollow ruins. The cold nocturnal air converted her exhalation to steam that lingered fleetingly before dissipating above her. A child's giggle from behind a column interrupted the quietness. She turned her head to see. The chuckle of a young boy resounded from every direction.

'Mummy!' A young voice whispered, close behind her.

She arched her neck, rolling her eyes to the top of her head to see Charlie's blue coat, the hood raised, a dark emptiness where his face should have been.

'Charlie, is that you?'

His arms rose to offer his small hands to hers. Elaine stretched out, straining her fingers to make contact with his. Their fingertips grazed. She wanted to see him. She wanted to hold her little boy and never let him go. Her eyes filled and overflowed. So close to what she'd wanted for so long, but still not close enough.

Their fingertips parted and his hands eased away. Elaine fought against the shackles, but all she could do was look on as Charlie's hands retracted into the outstretched sleeves to leave her demoralised and forsaken. The hope and dream of being reunited with her son snatched away.

Elaine detected movement within the empty shell of the jacket. Evil oozed into the void, crushing hope, terror realised. Creeping from the shadows of the coat sleeves, large red hands emerged. The beast had come. Petrified, she pulled at her restraints, despairing of escaping his grasp. His cold bony fingers drew nearer to hers. Elaine accepted whatever foul fate he had in store for her. His pointed fingertips brushed against hers. She screamed, but only a whimpering murmur escaped her lips. Tremors swept through her body as his long nails raked her skin, leaving a pale trail in their wake. A look of terror covered her face as his skeletal fingers caressed her veins, forcing them to protrude. So long, so thick, so blue.

'Please – no,' she begged. 'Don't do this.'

His razor-sharp claws deftly pierced through her skin, slicing along each vein in a time-perfected movement with surgical precision. Red rain erupted from the straight cuts. Elaine's screams bounced off the pillars and back at her. Warm blood seeped from the wounds as it pooled around her and trickled swiftly down the smooth sides of the altar.

*

Elaine sat up on the sofa to take in the familiar surroundings of the living room, somewhat thrown about how she got there. In the seconds that followed, the events of the day flooded back. Fainting at the ruins, being awoken and helped by security staff before setting off for home. She emitted a breath of relief and wiped the sweat from her forehead with the blanket that covered her. She laid her head back on the cushion, her eyes glazed and tearful, mirroring the flames of the fire.

Elaine hadn't always wanted to go on living but of late, something was different; she had a renewed desire to fight, as though she could sense a change coming. For a considerable time, she believed she was damaged, not knowing if it was to do with the loss of her child or from a time before. Her eyes shifted to her mother standing beside her.

'Hey, Mum, couldn't you sleep?' she asked, sitting upright.

'No, I'm too concerned about you,' said Margaret.

'I'm fine, Mum,' she said, curling her legs to make space for her mother on the sofa.

'You're not fine, if you were fine, you wouldn't have passed out at the Abbey.'

'I'll be okay, so please, stop with the concern. There is nothing to worry about, I promise.' Elaine rose to her feet. 'I'm going to make some coffee, do you want one?'

'No, not for me, thank you,' answered Margaret, and followed her daughter to the kitchen. 'So, tell me about the woman at the Abbey today.' She was more than a little curious to know who it could've been.

'Oh yes, I bumped into an old friend, Lila. I was surprised she still lives here. She used to say she couldn't wait to leave the place.'

Elaine poured milk into her cup while Margaret racked her brain.

'Lila – Lila.' Margaret pulled a chair out from under the table and sat down. 'Yes, wasn't she the pretty young thing who was here all the time? Had an unusual habit of purposely wearing odd socks, if I remember correctly.'

'That's her!' Elaine smiled at the memory. 'It was such a long time ago. I say she was an old friend. She was my best friend. We used to be so close. We'd tell each other everything. Anyway, she asked me to meet her for a drink.'

'Are you going?' Margaret asked, showing a keen interest.

Elaine paused from putting the second spoonful of sugar into the mug, still debating whether or not she would. 'I doubt it,' she said.

'You should go, dear. I don't think it would be such a bad thing. If you're going to settle back here, it may well do you some good,' Margaret stated, willing her daughter to take up Lila's offer.

'Maybe, we'll see.'

She poured out the hot water and stirred. Elaine thought it better to let her mother think it likely she'd meet her old friend, knowing she wouldn't hear the last of it if she'd said no right this minute. For Elaine, it was by no means a foregone conclusion. She would take her time to think it over.

8

Wednesday, 15 August
5 Years Earlier

With Robert and Elaine's stories not adding up, reporter Lenny Grey wanted to revisit the vintage fair. The trouble was, it had packed up and gone. He'd made some calls and found out the circus had travelled up north and the fair had moved to Lenny's old stomping ground: the East End of London. He wanted to speak with the man who worked at the hall of mirrors, which called for a trip to Victoria Park in Bow.

An old-school freelance journalist, to those who knew him, he was either Len, Lenny, or The Moth, a nickname he'd received from his colleagues at a major newspaper while investigating a crooked American property tycoon. Julius Grant was London's primary dealer in cocaine and laundered money through his dodgy property deals. He had some big names on his payroll, including top politicians, councillors, and high-ranking police officials, right down to the local bobby on the beat.

When Lenny got close to exposing everything, Grant had the building where he kept vital evidence, torched. Lenny Grey wouldn't give it up and ran into the burning building to retrieve the documents. He suffered third-degree burns on his back, shoulder, and leg in the process. He was a much younger man at the time, in his mid-thirties. Lenny received high acclaim and a book deal. Now in his early fifties, he still chased the big stories, especially when he felt something underhand was going on.

Blue skies and marvellous sunshine. Lenny had picked a lovely day for it as he entered the park through Gunmakers Gate, crossing over the Hertford Union Canal towards the funfair ahead. First, he had to navigate past the cyclists, joggers and youngsters kicking a football around.

As the ball came close to him, a kid wearing a Tottenham Hotspur football shirt, shouted for him to pass the ball. Lenny did a couple of kick-ups and turned, about to give it back.

'Just pass the ball, you fat git,' said the impatient boy.

'Fat git?' Lenny repeated with a grin. 'I'll tell you what, Tottenham, just for that—' Lenny picked up the ball and drop-kicked it in the opposite direction.

'Tosser!' yelled the kid.

'Fuck off, you little shit,' Lenny mumbled and continued on his way amongst the half-naked bodies lounging about, topping up their tans.

After some last-minute safety checks, the fair itself would soon be opening. Lenny took great pleasure in feasting his eyes upon some of the delightful vintage attractions. When he finally came across the hall of mirrors, a young man came out of the exit door carrying glass cleaner and cloths.

'All right, mate?' Lenny said, catching his attention.

'Hello,' the man answered in a not so friendly way as he carried on towards the kiosk.

'Is Stuart Hillier around?' asked Lenny.

'Who wants to know?'

The man seemed uninterested as he squirted liquid on the window and wiped. Lenny would have to put in a little effort if he wanted any information. One thing he had going for him was getting on the right side of people when he wanted something. A necessity in his line of work to make people think of him more as a friend than a reporter.

'Your accent, let me guess, you're from – Latvia?'

'Close, but not Latvia,' the man said, lowering his guard.

'I wanna say Poland but I'm gonna go with Lithuania.'

'Yes, very good,' the man smiled.

'I've always been good at accents. Anyway, I'm Lenny Grey, a journalist. I spoke with Stuart a few days ago.'

The man stopped wiping the glass and turned. 'Is this about the little boy who went missing?' he asked.

'Yes, it is. I have some questions I need to ask Stuart,' Lenny replied.

'I'm afraid he is not here, but he should be back soon.'

'I can wait.'

The man got back to cleaning the windows while Lenny lit a cigarette.

'I think it was wrong, the father leaving his boy alone like that,' the man said.

'What do you mean?' Lenny was curious.

'Well, I just think it was irresponsible to leave his ten-year-old son alone and disappear for a while.'

'Disappear? Did Stuart tell the police he saw the man leave the boy on his own?'

'Why would he? He never saw. Surely the father told them?'

This was new information. Lenny knew Robert hadn't told the police anything about leaving his son alone. 'What do you mean, Stuart never saw?'

'Stuart wasn't working when it happened.'

Lenny was surprised to hear this. His source at the police station had only given him Stuart Hillier's name, the owner of the ride, claiming he was the person who'd given a statement to the police. Someone either hadn't done their job properly or asked the right questions. 'As far as I know, Stuart told the police he was working that night,' Lenny said.

'Yes, he worked that night, but I mean he didn't tend this attraction at that time.'

'Didn't they ask him if he worked the hall of mirrors at the time the boy was taken?'

'No, they just asked if he saw anything suspicious. They asked us all if we saw anybody take the boy.' The man finished cleaning the windows of the booth.

'So, who tended the hall of mirrors at that particular time?' Lenny asked.

'Me. I was the attendant on the coconut shy, but I covered this attraction as well.'

'Useless pricks,' Lenny muttered, before walking closer to the man. 'Sorry, I didn't catch your name?' Lenny reached out to shake the man's hand.

'Romek Jakovskis,' he smiled, taking his hand.

'Do you remember the man and the boy?'

'Not so much the boy, but yes, I remember the man because he wanted me to go through the hall of mirrors searching for his son with him.'

'Did he mention how they became separated inside?'

'They didn't become separated in there.' Romek replied, pointing at the attraction.

Lenny was baffled, and not just by Romek's accent. 'I don't understand,' he said.

'The father never went inside the hall of mirrors with his son. He let him go in alone,' Romek explained.

'Where did the father go, did he wait out here?'

'Yes, but not at first. I see a beautiful young lady waiting for him down the side. The man paid for the boy to enter and he disappeared down the side with her. When he came back, we searched for his son together, but he was gone.'

'Jesus Christ. How long was the man away for?'

Robert shrugged, 'Maybe ten minutes.'

'And you never saw the boy come out?'

'The fair was busy, children coming and going.'

'But you're certain you didn't see anyone carrying or dragging a boy against his will?'

'I think that would be something I would remember. I'm sorry, I wish I could help more.'

'Oh, you've helped, Romek. Thank you.' Lenny shook his hand again and left.

9

Wednesday, 2 August
Present Day

Whether to meet her old friend this evening was the topic of debate through breakfast and well into the afternoon. Elaine's mother had badgered her to go through with it. In the end, she relented; after all, what did she have to lose? A dominant trait of her condition was social anxiety, a burden for her. The days after losing her son were, without a doubt, difficult beyond extreme. Unwilling to engage with almost everyone, she cut off what friends she had and retreated within herself. It had been a while since she'd done anything like this; another obstacle to overcome.

For as long as she could remember, everything had been a battle for her. There were times when every single decision was torture. Those simple choices, so natural to most, from getting out of bed to choosing tea or coffee. It was so severe that sometimes she didn't want to leave the house at all. One of her more complex decisions was going to bed; whether to lie there brooding all night or stay up until she fell asleep on the sofa. When she did stay up, it sometimes led to a few days without any sleep at all, but when she drifted off, she wanted never to wake up again. Her depression, her illness, cut deeper than any knife.

She stood in Market Place next to the large monument of William Duncombe, 2nd Baron Feversham. Ahead of her, The Royal Oak Pub and Hotel. The car park around her was almost full. It was a busy old town most of the time but during the summer holidays, even more so. People loved medieval towns and this area had plenty of history, with archaeological discoveries dating back to around 3000 BC.

Elaine still struggled with her decision to meet Lila and it made no sense to her why. The more she delayed walking into the pub, the worse her nerves became. A voice inside her head called her a coward, told her to go home and be on her own, but that wasn't going to happen. Not this time. She'd developed a stubborn side to her personality of late. It helped her not to listen to the bleak voices in her head that cast doubt on everything. She had a determination about her. Elaine was going inside the pub, no matter what. She checked herself over; skinny blue jeans, a long-sleeved white cold shoulder top and white slingback wedges on her feet. Her appearance was adequate for a casual drink with an old friend.

The charming old town embraced the gorgeous summer evening. The setting sun shaded the streets but still shone on the rooftops. There was a pleasant, invigorating freshness forming in the air after the hot day. Elaine heard Elbow's 'One Day Like This' playing inside the pub as she sauntered closer, one of her favourite songs. Plenty of people were drinking and smoking outside; some occupied the three bench tables, while others stood around them. Two young girls stumbled from a taxi: they'd clearly started their drinking earlier in the day. She glanced at her watch: 8.15 p.m. No more delaying the inevitable.

It was natural to feel jittery and awkward, but she knew this could be a good thing for her to do. She was in no hurry as she walked towards the door of the pub; anyone would have thought it was the first time she'd ever walked into a public house. She pushed open the door, the music louder, and stepped inside. Did the music stop? No! Did every head turn in her direction? Maybe a few, as happens when somebody enters a room. She spotted Lila immediately, which wasn't difficult as she sped towards her through the relatively crowded pub, waving her arms like an over-excited child. To be fair, the warm welcome by someone she knew eased the tension of entering a place full of strangers.

Lila wore a plain white vest top and a short denim skirt, a relief to Elaine that she hadn't overdressed for the occasion. A second glance at the shortness of Lila's skirt, perhaps she had. It wasn't a look Elaine had gone for in her younger days, let alone now. Always too self-conscious. To be fair though, it had been a roasting day outside and most people appeared to be making the best of their summer clothing, or lack of it.

It crossed her mind she may have been too quick to judge Lila's looks when she first saw her at the Abbey. Now, with her hair down and wearing some make-up, she was much prettier than she'd given her credit for. The small scars on her face at the ruins were less conspicuous now. The two-inch scar above her left temple, however, would take more than a bit of foundation and powder to obscure.

Lila grabbed hold of Elaine's hand. 'Come on, we're sitting over here!' She shouted over the music.

As Lila led her across the pub, Elaine glanced around for any familiar faces from the past. Nobody stood out until – ahead of her with his back against the bar, she caught sight of a handsome man staring at her. He was tall, her age, possibly younger and had the most amazing blue eyes she'd ever seen in her life.

There was something about the guy. Did she somehow know him? Their eyes remained locked as they passed each other. In her mind, everything slowed as she scrutinised him, working out where she'd seen him before. She couldn't be sure, but she imagined he was thinking the same thing. Could he have gone to her school all those years ago? She didn't think so. It was a strange but amiable few seconds that lingered, probably longer than either would have liked.

Arms linked, Lila led her across the pub. Elaine glanced back in the man's direction; he was no longer standing there. Lila drew her attention to two women sitting at a table, smiling. Also at the table were two men, talking and laughing. Elaine couldn't tell if they were part of the group or not. The ladies stood to greet her as Lila made the introductions.

'This is Nicole and Georgia,' said Lila, pointing respectively. 'And this is my old friend I've been telling you about, Elaine.'

Elaine locked on to Nicole's beautiful reddish-brown hair that contrasted with her exceptionally pale skin. Georgia was a lot younger, tall with broad shoulders. Elaine found out later she played rugby for Harrogate. Georgia knocked the table as she leant forward to shake her hand and sent the guys' pints of beer swirling to the top and plopping back into the glasses. The men raised their eyebrows at almost losing their drinks and resumed their conversation.

'Oh, don't worry about them,' said Lila. 'That's just Steve, Nicole's other half. And the scruffy one on the end is Ashton,' Lila raised her eyes in jest, 'My husband.'

The men broke from their no doubt, scintillating discussion and gave Elaine a contrived grin. Ashton gave her more of a prolonged leer, which she ignored as she waved across the table to them.

Ashton was a burly man with messy hair that could've done with a good brush and, well, a trim wouldn't hurt. His facial hair was beyond the stubble stage and well on its way into beard territory. Not much older than Lila, his unkempt exterior didn't do him any favours. Steve was somewhere between tubby and stocky, well groomed and smartly dressed.

'Right, introductions over, let's get some drinks in,' said Lila.

Smiles were plentiful as the ladies made their way to the bar. They had a head start on Elaine with the alcohol, reflected by their over the top behaviour. Elaine did her best to join in but she certainly wasn't ready to partake in any screaming "*Woo Hoos.*" For most of her adult life, she'd shied away from social occasions, preferring to remain inconspicuous in the background.

The night went on and the drinks kept coming. Tequila shots downed, they danced to songs selected on the jukebox, Elaine grudgingly pulled up to join them. The one thing she never expected from this evening was to have fun. *Fun*! Something that was a distant memory. Dancing, she made contact with those dazzling blue eyes again. He stood at the bar behind Ashton and Steve, who were busy checking out other women about the place.

She'd kept an eye out for the handsome stranger throughout the evening and assumed he'd left. She found it difficult to contain her delight to see him still there. He raised a flattering smile towards her and she managed one back. Not even the copious amount of alcohol she'd consumed prevented her knees from weakening. Elaine failed to notice Ashton launch a smile in her direction at the same time.

Hot and flustered on the dance floor, Elaine waved to Lila in an unsuccessful attempt to grab her attention. In the end, she had to go and tell her she needed some air. Elaine paused before exiting the pub to take another look over at the bar. She wanted to let the man see her go outside, hoping he'd follow, but again, he'd performed another vanishing act. Steve and Ashton were still there, the latter with a lascivious expression on his face. He winked at her. Not impressed with his unseemly behaviour, Elaine smiled politely before going through the door.

Outside, it was dark and a lot cooler. The floodlights high up illuminated the walls with a yellow radiance, highlighting the beautiful stonework of the seventeenth-century pub. Plenty of people still lurked outside, smoking, drinking, and talking loudly. Listening to their voices reminded her of how she loved the Yorkshire accent when she was a child.

The night had been a pleasant surprise. To have taken such an unexpected step into what for her was the unknown, made her both pleased and proud of herself. This was a gigantic leap. Throwing back her head, exhilarated, she took in the crisp evening air, impressed by how clear the night sky was in the countryside. So many stars visible, unlike those over illuminated and overpopulated cities emitting a pollution of light, blocking the beauty beyond for miles around. She thought back to living here as a child; the first time she'd ever noticed the sky with a deep sense of reverence. Sometimes, sitting on the porch in the evenings with her … a blank space in her memory. Who was it she used to sit next to? Her mother a few times, but there was someone else – Lila?

'*Boo*!' Lila had sneaked up behind her. A stunned Elaine jerked, raised a hand to her chest and laughed, taking it in her stride. Lila grabbed hold of her hand and held it as they stood side by side, both of them overflowing with sentiment and warmth. It must have pleased them to find the flame of their rekindled friendship had never burned out.

'Thank you for inviting me tonight,' said Elaine.

'I'm so happy I bumped into you again. I never stopped thinking about you. We haven't had much of a chance to speak properly tonight, have we?' said Lila.

Elaine smiled, 'It's okay, I'm sure there'll be another time.'

'That's reassuring to know.'

Side by side, shoulders touching and still holding hands, an awkwardness surfaced in Lila.

'I know about your son, Elaine. I mean, I know what happened.' There would never be a right or correct way to approach such a delicate matter.

Elaine peeped in her direction before turning away. She wasn't sure anyone here would even know about what happened.

'When I saw it on the news, I was heartbroken for you,' Lila's sympathy was sincere, her tone soft. 'I saw you on TV and wished I could have been there for you.'

'It's all right, Lila.' Elaine wasn't sure how to react but tried her hardest not to let her emotions take over.

'After everything you—'

Elaine politely cut her off mid-sentence, 'Honestly, Lila, it's fine, I'm fine. Shall we go back in?'

Lila grinned, accepting she didn't want to talk about it. 'Yeah, come on.'

As they were about to head back inside the pub, Elaine paused. There he was again, leaning against the wall outside. She caught him staring at her with his charismatic boyish smile before he turned away. On this occasion, it occurred to her that not once during the evening had she seen him drinking or smoking. Nor had he been in the company of anyone else all night, which struck her as odd. She supposed he could be from out of town. As unusual as it seemed, she was still flattered to be on the receiving end of his attention. What she couldn't work out was why he kept making blatant eye contact without making an effort to talk to her.

'You coming?' Lila asked.

'You go on. I'll just be a minute.'

Lila tracked Elaine's gaze and caught the gentleman steal a glance. 'Ah, I see,' she said with a cheeky grin.

A little embarrassed, Elaine nudged Lila away with her hip. She watched her go back inside and from somewhere, discovered courage. It wasn't something she'd been familiar with throughout her life. She was about to take the initiative and approach him when Nicole stepped into her path.

'Hey, Elaine, stay with me for a minute while I smoke.'

She linked arms with Elaine and led her away from the door, and away from the man.

'So how long have you known Lila?' Elaine asked.

Nicole pulled a pack of cigarettes from somewhere on her person, and for the life of her, Elaine had no idea where.

'Must be about seven years now,' Nicole answered, and placed a cigarette in her mouth. She lit up, took a long, deep puff and blew smoke upwards. 'Sorry, want one?'

Elaine shook her head.

'She hasn't stopped talking about you since she ran into you the other day,' said Nicole.

'Honestly?' Elaine responded, happy and surprised.

'God, you're all she's gone on about. Talking about how you were the greatest of friends as children and how she missed you when you left.' With another long puff of her cigarette, smoke signals punctuated her words, 'I don't think she took losing your friendship well at all.'

Elaine was at a loss. She'd always put it down to moving away, but why hadn't they kept in touch? Perhaps Nicole knew. 'How did—'

'Ashton!'

'Excuse me?'

'The scar on her head, I thought that's what you were going to ask about.'

It wasn't. 'Well, I did wonder,' said Elaine.

Throwing her head back after another puff, Nicole dispelled the smoke. 'They were arguing and Ashton pushed her through a glass door in the kitchen.'

'Oh, my God.' Elaine was shocked Nicole was so blasé about something so serious, which suggested either it was an accident or violence was a regular occurrence in their relationship. 'He didn't mean to do that, surely?'

'Well, I'm sure he didn't mean to mark her face, but he certainly meant to push her through the glass door.'

Nicole registered the astonishment on Elaine's face. 'They fight all the time, it's pretty normal behaviour for them,' she said.

Nicole took one last drag on her cigarette and walked over to a table. She excused herself to the people seated there and stubbed out what was left in the ashtray. 'Coming back inside?' she asked.

Digesting the information and miffed by the lack of empathy and concern in Nicole's attitude, Elaine thought better of taking it any further. The stranger no longer stood by the wall.

'Sure,' she said, with half a smile and pang of disappointment.

When they re-entered the pub, it didn't appear he'd come back inside. She presumed he'd gone and it was an opportunity missed for the both of them. They drank some more and danced until last orders. Elaine was ready to leave and Lila called for a couple of taxis. After saying her goodbyes to the girls and a quick wave to Ashton and Steve in the pub, Elaine received a massive hug from Lila before getting into the cab. There was a visible connection between them, a special bond that had lain dormant for so long, finally re-awakened.

10

In the back of the taxi, Elaine contemplated how she'd enjoyed the night better than she'd expected; however, confusion remained about the man in the pub: his familiarity and why he didn't approach her when it was clear he had some form of interest.

The taxi made its way along the dark gravel drive up to the house. Elaine gazed out through the car window across the grounds irradiated by the moonlight. She thought about Lila and their childhood friendship, the joyful times together. Memories she'd long forgotten filtered through. Viewing the oak tree with the rope swing brought a pleasant smile to her face. She visualised the pair of them playing on the swing and how high they went. She recalled the time Lila fell off and hurt her ankle and observed the dangling seat and loose rope. She'd fix it for Emily, who would no doubt make friends and create her own fond memories here.

Her eyes were then drawn to the towering tumbledown barn further behind the house. It was easy to see under the bright moon how battered and decrepit it looked, its roof partially collapsed and slats missing. Her alcohol-induced reminiscing faded as she shuddered with dread. A disconcerting chill crept up her spine from the small of her back and eased its way to the top of her neck. The horrific sensation of crawling beneath her skin, entwined itself around her bones like brambles. She rolled up her sleeve to look at the top of her forearm. The torchlight moon flashed its beam over the enlarged goosebumps as each hair on her arm rose to a point.

'All right, my love, here we are.' The taxi driver interrupted with his broad Yorkshire accent.

'Uh, oh – of course,' she stuttered, caught off guard. She tugged down her sleeve and delved into her handbag for her purse to pay.

A sluggish Elaine held onto the handrail as she climbed the three steps to the porch. She regarded the light on the porch and its utter uselessness; she'd had candles burn brighter. Another item to add to the ever-growing list of jobs to do. She watched on as the cab pulled away from the house, red tailgate lights glowing and the taxi roof light switched off. She must have been his last fare of the night.

What happened in the car left her a little perplexed. Why *had* she become so spooked? She was troubled. Unlike the nightmares that scared the living daylights out of her, this was new, and anything new or unfamiliar did not sit well with her. It had been a long time since she'd been out like this and even longer since she'd consumed booze to this extent. *Wait*! Maybe that's it, yes – of course, it is, you silly woman. She convinced herself alcohol was the reason for her current state of mind.

The kitchen looked untended. A yellowing brown stained the grubby white wall tiles that once gleamed. She'd made a lacklustre attempt to clean the kitchen units where most of the doors and drawers were askew. As dark as it was outside, the grime on the windows added to the cheerless room. Elaine made a cup of tea and sat at the table. Footsteps coming down the groaning stairs distracted her. Who was awake at this late hour? Eventually, her mother came into view, tottering along the hall.

'Hey, Mum. Tea?' Elaine stood, pre-empting her mother's reply.

'Not for me, although I wouldn't say no to a glass of water,' Margaret replied as she entered the room and took a seat at the table.

At the tatty butler's sink, Elaine filled a glass tumbler and placed it in front of her mother. 'Couldn't you sleep?' she asked, before sitting across from her.

'I never sleep well any more. It's an age thing. I forgot to take some water up with me and you know how I like to keep a glass on the bedside table. Well, how was your night on the town?' Margaret questioned with a yawn.

Elaine caught the yawn, sipped her tea and placed it back on the table.

'Yeah, it was okay, good.'

'Well, which was it, okay or good?'

'Good, Mum. It was good,' Elaine smiled. 'I saw this guy there.'

'Oh, do tell.' Margaret's ears pricked up as she leaned forward in anticipation.

'Nothing like that, Mother. He was – I don't know, familiar to me in some way.'

Margaret took a mouthful of water from the glass. 'You probably knew him when you were younger.'

'Yeah, I guess so. It felt like there was more to it than that. Certainly a looker though,' Elaine grinned.

Margaret laughed and took another sip of water.

'There was something else tonight, Mum,' she said, becoming a little more earnest.

'Oh, and what was that, dear?'

'The barn!'

'The barn?'

'Yes, the barn. I got a weird feeling coming up the drive when I saw it. It's difficult to explain.'

'Why on earth would you be thinking about that old thing? I can't even believe it's still standing.'

'I don't know, it was odd. I felt so cold and – scared.'

'My poor girl, I'm sure it was nothing. Probably the alcohol having a strange effect on you. It's been a long time since you had a drink.'

'Yeah, I did think that myself.'

'Well, there you go, all sorted.' Margaret drank some more water, placed the glass on the table and got to her feet. 'Right, I'm getting myself back to bed. Where you should probably take yourself off to as well, young lady.'

She walked around the table and kissed her daughter on the forehead, gently rubbing her shoulder before walking off along the hallway.

'Mum!'

'Yes, dear?' She glanced back.

'Did the kids behave for you tonight?'

'Of course. They always do,' she smiled.

Margaret set off again and without stopping said, 'Oh, they did mention they were excited about their father coming to see them on Saturday.'

'Shit!' Elaine placed her head in her hands.

It wasn't that she'd forgotten Robert was coming, but what with one thing or another, it had slipped her mind. She had so much she wanted to do around the house before he arrived. With a final mouthful, Elaine finished her tea and stood from the table. With her mug in one hand, she reached across the table to grab her mother's glass. Why hadn't she taken her water to bed with her? And she'd hardly touched it. Her mother did baffle her sometimes.

'Thought you were thirsty, Mum,' she mumbled, shaking her head as she took the cups to the sink.

11

Friday, 17 August
5 Years Earlier

The vibration of his phone on the bedside table woke Lenny. The luminous green digits of his clock radio read 1.57 a.m. He let out a growl as he answered. The call was from his source and old friend at the police station. A young boy's body had been found in an area called Tumbling Bay on Rammey Marsh in Enfield, North London. Early indications suggested it might be the body of Charlie Davis.

The call ended. Lenny moved to the edge of his bed and sighed, rubbing his hands over his weary and unshaven face. He switched on the bedside lamp, grabbed his cigarettes and lighter, and shuffled over to the window to look down from his twelfth floor flat at the illuminated streets below. He took a cigarette and tossed the pack on the table before lighting up. He cut a sad and lonely figure as he stood there. Throughout his career, Lenny had seen the worst aspects of humans and what they were capable of. Regardless of what he'd tell people, it had cost him more than the burns down the left side of his body, the scarring clearly visible. The scars had healed over time but still looked tender after all these years.

Within an hour of the call, Lenny arrived on the scene and squeezed into the last available space in the small car park off Smeaton Road. The emergency access gate to the marsh was open for police vehicles and the forensic pathologist to park on the site. It was dark, wet and windy. Lenny hastened along the grass path towards the flashing blue lights and the crime scene. Off to his right, the River Lea and a few moored houseboats.

Emergency lighting picked out three people wearing protective white suits stood by the body. One of them was Detective Chief Inspector Colin Hargreaves, who turned and didn't appear happy to see Lenny standing behind the cordon.

'You shouldn't be here, Len,' he said, walking towards him.

'You shouldn't have bloody called me then,' Lenny retorted. 'Is it Charlie?'

'Looks like it. The boy's about the same age and wearing the clothing described when Charlie was abducted. It looks like his body may have been dumped here around midnight. The call came not long after that. The body was only partially hidden, which suggests whoever brought him here was disturbed, possibly by the youngsters who found him.' DCI Hargreaves looked crestfallen.

Lenny glanced over to the body on the edge of the path. The boy lay on the wet grass, his hair dark, damp, and matted; a smear of dirt across the cheek of his pale-skinned face added to the wretched scene.

'It ain't fair,' said Lenny.

'I know it's not.'

Both men looked despondent. An abysmal night in every way.

'Who'd you say found the body?'

'A couple of young dope heads. Junkies come in here all the time to shoot up, smoke, and get pissed. I'm surprised they even called it in.'

'Has he been dead long and has he … you know?' Lenny couldn't bring himself to complete the sentence.

'Early assessment is he may have been strangled between two to four hours before we got the call. We won't know anything else until the autopsy.'

'That means he was alive all that time. Christ, the poor kid must have been terrified,' Lenny huffed. 'What about Robert Davis?'

'He and the wife have been indoors all evening. The car hasn't moved.'

'Could be they got someone else to bring him out here,' said Lenny.

The DCI shook his head in disbelief. 'For the umpteenth time, Lenny, they had nothing to do with this. I can't understand why you think otherwise.'

'The father lied, Colin.'

'Yes, but only because he was getting his end away at the time. Besides, none of that matters any more.'

'Why not?'

'We have a new witness who saw a clown with a boy in the car park. She caught the news for the first time yesterday and only recalled the incident because the kid seemed distressed when his balloon got away from him.'

Lenny looked dismissive of this new information. He didn't like to be wrong and most of the time, he wasn't. 'No, I'm not having it. There's something about Elaine Davis,' he said as a gust of wind ruffled his hair.

'For God's sake, Lenny, the woman is upset and in shock. Her boy taken, her husband shagging about, which she probably suspects. And when DI Harris gets here, we have to go and inform them the body is likely their son.'

Lenny wouldn't have it. 'No, it's something else. It's her eyes, Col. I've seen it before, there's a darkness in there.'

'Well, they've made a complaint against you, so you need to stay away from them.'

'I can't just leave it.'

'Let it go, Len. Your instincts were wrong on this one. Now get out of here,' Colin said.

Lenny scowled at the DCI before turning and stepping in a pile of dog shit. Swearing to himself, he tried to wipe his shoe clean on the grass. Hargreaves shook his head and went back towards the body.

Perched on a high stool in the middle of the kitchen, Elaine slumped over the breakfast bar. She held her head in her rough hands, hypnotised by the steam swirling up from her large, white mug of coffee. The last nine days had been horrific for her and Robert. Time and again, she'd thought about what happened, wondering if she could have done something different and blamed herself for agreeing to take the children on the Ferris wheel. If only she'd refused.

The rain slapped against the double-glazed window as the wind forced it fast and hard. Reluctantly, Elaine wiped her long, curly morning hair from her face to look at the dismal weather outside. The splatters of water on the glass reflected in her watery eyes.

Elaine cut a forlorn figure in her wrinkly white pyjamas, an old blue dressing gown, and a pair of well-worn slippers that had seen better days. Her pale face, a despairing wasteland, sat well with the weather conditions befalling the North London suburb. Elaine bore the appearance of several sleepless nights but right now it didn't matter how she looked. She didn't care, something that wasn't always the case. Now was not the time to care about material things such as make-up.

She'd slept a little in the early hours, albeit interrupted. Beyond any sleep she did get, followed extreme guilt. Far too many emotions clashed in her body; the unbearable not knowing about Charlie made rest or sleep a forgotten country. Nightmares invariably accompanied the infrequent naps when her body succeeded in shutting down. She accepted those as part of her life, plagued for years as she was by night terrors. The last nine days were even worse and she saw no end to the agonising, heart-wrenching pain.

Two dinner plates from the previous night sat on the worktop, overlooked by the tea stain on the wall where she'd thrown the cup at Lenny Grey. Below the work surface, two wine glasses lay on the rack of the open dishwasher. Michael and Emily were staying with their grandparents because of the tension between their mother and father.

As she sipped her steaming coffee, Robert entered the kitchen wearing black boxer shorts, a white T-shirt, and a sombre expression. Although not much older than Elaine, he had one of those mature faces that exuded a friendly, confident charm. After a glance in each other's direction, Robert went straight over to the wall unit and fetched himself a mug. Much like Elaine, every single movement he made described distress. She continued to stare at the window and the driving rain beyond, her eyes doleful and tired.

Robert flicked the switch on the kettle and spooned coffee and sugar into his mug. He poured in the milk Elaine had left out and put the plastic bottle back in the refrigerator. When he closed the fridge, his attention focused on the children's drawings attached to the door. Among them, a photograph of Robert and Elaine with the children on The London Eye, an amazing view of the city in the background. Stuck in a moment, he observed the photo taken less than a month ago. Sadness and guilt engulfed him as he gazed at his eldest boy. His insides torn apart because Charlie would still be here if he hadn't sneaked off to have sex with Chloé. It had been an impetuous moment of madness.

The kettle clicked, his thoughts interrupted. The clock above him on the wall showed it had just gone seven. He carried his coffee leaden-footed to the window by the sink. He stood watching the rain as it lashed heavy drops against the glass, without realising he'd obscured Elaine's view.

Robert narrowed his eyes to see beyond the rain. He leaned forward and stared at the impenetrable murky clouds that enshrouded London. A police car had been parked outside the house for the last few days. To keep the press from the door, they said, though Robert wondered at times if they were watching him, believing him to be a suspect. He blew his coffee to cool it before taking a sip, enjoying insignificant relief as it trickled down his throat. Turning, he contemplated his wife and the intense hostility between them. The irritated expression on her face revealed far more than words as she went back to her coffee.

Robert ambled over to the stool opposite her. A few days without shaving had left a shadowy stubble covering his face. Elaine's head rested on her hand. They glared into each other's eyes but still no words passed between them. Countless conversations had been and gone and there was nothing left to say, words obsolete, the pair of them demoralised. Sitting around, waiting for something to happen, for what they didn't know, had been nine days of complete hell, every single one dragging into the next. At times it felt like only a day had passed since somebody took their son. One never-ending miserable day.

A flat toned doorbell echoed through the hallway and around the kitchen, interrupting the uncomfortable silence. Unsettled, neither moved. Robert placed his mug on the work surface, the look on his face ominous. Slow and demanding, he rose from his stool, his body heavy, disinclined to budge.

Elaine's eyes followed Robert as he left the kitchen, his legs quaking, struggling to carry him. Even if she'd wanted to go with him, her body wouldn't have let her. Tears threatened in anticipation of the expected and heart-breaking news. The dry, pale skin on her face flushed as she trembled – bad news was coming, and her whole body knew it.

A cry so profound and hollow roared through the hallway. Elaine's tired and reddened eyes mimicked the hefty droplets sliding down the windowpane as they surged down her scrunched-up face as she crumpled to the floor. Her fists clenched, the veins in her neck bulged and she strained to summon a scream. Nothing. Unbearable torment ruptured every fibre of her being. She cowered on the floor, in despair.

Pictures of lonely uninhabited lighthouses encircled by rough seas scattered the long, narrow and dark hall walls, no doubt hung in haste to cover the bareness. A small, off-white shabby chic console table housed an old-fashioned black dial telephone, a retro replica of a 70s classic. The only light emanating into the hall was from the open front door and the small skylight window above it.

The silhouettes of two authoritative figures stood in the doorway. Robert staggered back until he was pressed against the wall and his head thumped against the plaster. He slid down the wall to the floor. DI Mel Harris advanced into the hallway. Her long straight hair dangled as she leaned forward on bended knees to comfort Robert. The other silhouette lingering inside the doorway was that of DCI Hargreaves.

Robert's lamentation mirrored the bleakness of the wet London morning. His back against the wall, his head straining upwards, his skin taut around the prominent lump of his Adam's apple. Robert's arms flopped down by his sides, hands open, numb fingers curled up. A sudden lull in the wind and rain, silence fell …

A prolonged, piercing cry came bawling from the kitchen. The sound spurred DCI Hargreaves into action. He rushed past

DI Harris kneeling in front of Robert. Elaine's screaming stopped. Quietude and emptiness … oblivion. The DCI called out her name repeatedly, in her moment of non-being.

Her re-emergence to reality confirmed that the harrowing nine days of not knowing had come to a cruel and heinous conclusion: the news they'd both feared, the kind they could never have prepared themselves to receive. Charlie, their sweet and innocent ten-year-old son, was dead.

12

Saturday, 5 August
Present Day

Over a week had passed since the big move and Elaine had made some improvements in the house. The children's father was due to arrive any time now. Elaine was busy in the kitchen cleaning the work surfaces and units. For the past two days, she'd been unrelenting in her efforts to get the house cleaned up. She'd steam cleaned the tiles and scrubbed them to almost white. She'd taken a screwdriver to straighten the uneven unit doors and drawers. The chessboard-tiled floor gleamed. The windows in the kitchen above the sink and on the back door were grime free. Among other jobs, she'd found time to fix the tree swing for Emily.

Margaret materialised behind Elaine in the kitchen. 'You've managed to do so much around the house this week, Elaine. I do appreciate everything you've done,' she said.

'I know you do,' she replied, bent over wiping a base unit door with a damp cloth. 'It must've been hard for you all alone in this big house these past years,' Elaine added as she finished cleaning. 'I don't know why you didn't sell up a long time ago.'

'And go where?'

Elaine stood up straight, light-headed and shaky, her legs threatening to give way. Faint and unstable, she used the work surface to steady herself.

'Good heavens, child, are you all right?'

'Yeah, I must have got up too fast, I just need a minute.' She manoeuvred with care over to a chair at the table.

'You take your time. You must be exhausted.'

'I'm okay, Mum. As I said, I probably got up too fast. It'll pass,' she responded.

Angry with herself, Elaine believed she should have made a start on the work sooner. She felt guilty about going to the pub on Wednesday, as if *not* going would have made a difference.

Margaret took a seat. 'When is Robert getting here?' she asked, changing the subject.

'Going by his earlier text, any time now.'

'I bet the children are excited.'

'I hope so, Mum. I truly do,' she said, with a touch of despondency in her voice.

The sound of a horn signalled Robert's car coming up the drive.

'Say the devil's name and he shall appear,' said Margaret.

Elaine gave in to a weary smile and took a few seconds before rising to her feet. Hesitant, she traipsed along the sun-drenched hallway and saw Emily, followed by Michael come out of the living room and disappear through the blazing light of the open front door to greet their father. Time to put on a different face. Elaine stepped through the open door and out into the scorching sun, the tiredness and self-doubt replaced with a confident beaming smile. A strange, swift turnaround.

Elaine gazed at Robert in his flashy black Mercedes convertible. The top was down, as it should be on such a glorious day. Her chest tightened and her stomach churned. Did she detest the sight of her ex-husband that much? You bet she did. Elaine watched the children with their father and understood Emily's excitement. Michael though, looked annoyed down by the car. Perhaps he disliked his father as much as she did.

He stamped up the steps to the porch. Surprised by his moodiness, she enquired, 'Michael, what's wrong?'

'Just Dad, being a dick, as usual,' he said, and breezed past her, straight into the house. She'd hoped Michael would be more enthusiastic, seeing as his father would only be here for a few hours.

'Mummy! Mummy!' Emily shouted as she ran up the three steps and grabbed onto her mother's leg, wrapping her arms around it. 'Daddy's here.'

'I know, sweetheart. I know,' she said, watching Robert approach the house.

'Can I go and play on the tree swing, Mummy?' Emily asked.

Elaine knelt down to her. 'Don't you want to see Daddy?'

'I've seen him, silly,' she giggled.

'Go on then.' Refusing her cute little face was impossible.

As Emily ran off for the swing, Robert had to step aside to avoid her running into him.

Elaine smiled at Robert and said, 'She's going to love the swing now it's fixed.'

'I'm sure she will,' he said, watching Emily as he climbed the steps. 'How are you, El?'

'I'm good. You?'

'Yeah, I can't complain.'

The uneasiness between the couple was nothing out of the ordinary. Robert looked well, aided by his impressive tan. He was rarely without a healthy skin colour these days, especially as he and Chloé flew to one of their homes abroad whenever possible. For the first time, she noticed his greying hair, realising she hadn't paid much attention to his looks of late. No doubt he'd been dyeing it for a while. He looked a tad more portly, too; nevertheless, he was still a fine-looking man. For a long time, she'd been of the opinion he was a bit of a show-off. His confidence drew her to him early on, but over the years, she'd watched it turn to arrogance. When they separated, she appreciated how he'd been up his own arse from the very beginning. Of late, though, they'd managed to get along better for the sake of the children.

'Well, you'd better come in,' she said. 'Would you like tea, coffee, or a cold one?'

'Coffee, please, if it's no trouble,' he replied, and followed her into the house.

As they passed the living room, Elaine glanced in at Michael on the sofa, watching television while busy on his phone. He was definitely in a strop about something or other.

Elaine made the coffee while she and Robert exchanged the odd, strained word. They took their drinks outside to make the most of the fantastic weather. Seated on the swing bench, they made a gentle swaying motion with their feet, taking occasional sips of their coffee. There wasn't much for the pair to talk about, but Emily's antics on the tree swing entertained them.

Elaine broke the silence. 'I was sorry to hear about your Uncle Charlie. I know how close you were to him.'

'Thanks, that's kind of you,' Robert said.

Elaine smiled, 'He was a lovely man, very funny. Do you remember that awful gold pocket watch he used to carry about with him?'

'Yeah,' Robert sniggered. 'It's funny you should mention that.'

'Oh, why?'

Removing his hand from his pocket, Robert pulled out something to show her.

'Because he left that awful gold pocket watch to me.' They both laughed, which helped thaw the frost between them. He flipped open the watch; it played a quaint musical tune. 'It reminds me of him every time I hear it. He actually left it for my dad, but Dad said I should have it and one day pass it on to Michael.'

'That's nice. I've always loved your father.'

Robert tucked the watch back into his pocket. 'Yeah, and he's always loved you, more than he loves me,' he said.

'Don't be silly,' Elaine laughed. 'Well, maybe a bit,' she said, gesturing her index finger and thumb about an inch apart and steadily widening the gap. They both smiled again.

After another lull in the conversation, Robert said, 'I see you've been doing some repairs and having a good tidy.'

'I have. It'll take time but I'll get there. I'm hoping to make a start on the painting soon.'

'It's a lot of work to take on, El. Why don't you let me send some of our guys over to do it for you?'

Elaine faced him. 'Robert, we refurbished properties in a much worst state than this on our own when we first started out. Besides, it's personal to me, something I need to do.'

'I can understand that. Have you decided on staying here for the foreseeable future?'

'Yeah, I think so. I don't know what it is, but something inside tells me this is where I need to be right now.'

'Well, it'll keep you busy for a while, that's for sure. At least when you feel it's time to move on, the house will be in better shape to sell, not that you need the money,' he said, and sipped his coffee.

A prickly silence lingered. 'Do you still have the nightmares, El?'

She hesitated as she thought how best to answer. 'Not as much,' she said.

'What about the other matter?'

She could tell he was doing his best to tread carefully, not wanting to upset her. It wasn't working. 'Other matter?' Confused and becoming restless, she kept a lid on her escalating annoyance. He was pushing his luck.

'The issue with your mother and stuff?'

Another pause followed. 'Oh, yes, that's all good now. Much better,' Elaine said with confidence and a nod of her head.

Robert smiled, relieved. He mistakenly believed she felt okay about opening up to him. 'Good, good. What about the new doctor and the medication?'

Elaine plonked her mug of coffee on the floor, stood from the bench and wandered to the edge of the porch. With silent restraint, she squeezed hard on the rail, incensed by Robert's barrage of questions. This man! Who did he think he was? He wasn't her husband anymore and had no right to quiz her. She needed to keep it together and calm down. Watching Emily on the swing helped. Her anger receded and her grip eased.

She turned to him, relaxed, as she leaned back against the rail. 'Everything is fine. I'm feeling good about myself,' she said calmly, confident she'd concealed her deceptive self-assurance.

'I'm glad, El, I truly am.' He eased himself up from the bench. 'Right, I'm going to have a chat with Michael,' he said.

'Good luck with that. Don't be too hard on him, though, it's a difficult and confusing time,' she said, her phoney smile in place until he'd gone inside.

She let out a fuming burst of air, glad his interrogation was over. She should have put a stop to it as soon as it began. It wasn't inconceivable that he wanted to make sure she was okay, after all, he'd loved her once and together they'd been through so much heartache.

She returned to the bench, exhaling to bring her silent rage towards Robert to an acceptable level. He had an insufferable way of getting her riled up.

'Mummy!' Emily shouted, tugging at her shirt. Elaine hadn't realised her daughter had come to sit beside her.

'Yes, sweetheart?'

'I'm hungry.'

'Well, we'd better go and find you something to eat then, hadn't we, my little girl?' Elaine smiled, reached down, and lifted Emily playfully into the air.

The day pressed on and it was almost time for Robert to leave. He'd taken Emily to the large secluded pond at the rear of the house beyond the line of trees, trudging through long grass to get to it. The pond was covered with leaves, water grass, and enclosed by large bushes and low covering trees. If you didn't happen to walk the extra twenty feet or so past the line of trees, you wouldn't know it existed. Elaine had only found it by luck when she was a little girl. She and Lila used to come here and feed the ducks together, the same reason Robert took Emily. Elaine would never allow Emily to play here alone: it was far too dangerous and overgrown. When she and Lila first discovered the pond all those years ago, it had been abandoned, and all these years later, that was still the case.

Emily and her dad tossed oats and defrosted peas into the pond where the ducks waited in anticipation. Before they ventured out, Elaine handed them a loaf to take but Emily protested. Mrs Maudsley, Emily's beloved teacher, had told them not to feed bread to the ducks as it upset their tummies and wasn't good for the water. Both parents were impressed as their daughter reeled off the list of things they could safely eat.

'Daddy?'

'Yes, sweetheart.'

'Is it because of Chloé we don't all live together anymore?' queried Emily.

'We haven't lived together for ages, what makes you ask now?'

'Hannah in my class asked. Her mum chucked her dad out of the house because he kissed another lady. Her mum called her a slut.'

'I see.'

'Does that mean Chloé is a slut?'

These awkward questions always caught Robert off guard. 'No, Emily, it doesn't. It's a naughty word and not a kind word to ever use.' He knew there'd be many more questions like it from Emily. 'Anyway, I thought you loved Chloé?'

'Well, I do, but I love Mummy more.'

'And so you should, but it isn't Chloé's fault we no longer live together. It's sometimes how it is. Not all parents live together.'

'Why?' she asked, with sad, quizzical eyes.

'Many reasons. You know how sometimes you don't get along with your brother?'

'Yes, like – all the time.'

'Well, sometimes it's the same with mummies and daddies.'

'Does that mean Michael will have to move out if I don't get along with him?' she asked.

Robert smiled to himself; he guessed that a plan was being hatched in Emily's mind to get rid of her annoying brother. It was all so black and white with young children.

'No, Emily. It doesn't quite work like that,' he said.

With the knowledge she wasn't going to get rid of her brother any time soon, Emily went back to chucking the remaining oats and peas to the ducks, a disappointed look on her face.

'Daddy?'

Robert hesitated, wondering what might come out of her mouth next. 'Yes?'

'What is a slut?'

'Right, come on, we'd better get back.'

Other than Elaine's discomfort early on, the visit had gone pretty well. They'd spent time together with the children, talked, mostly about the kids, and her plans for the house. Even Michael had cheered up as the afternoon progressed, no mean feat for a teenager. On the swing bench with Michael, Elaine supposed Robert would be on his way back from the pond with Emily.

'Mum, I'm sorry about earlier. I know you've both tried to explain things to me. It's just so hard,' Michael said, sincere in his apology for his sulky behaviour.

Elaine put an arm around him, 'It's okay. I know it's not easy to understand but everything will work out, don't worry.'

Robert and Emily came around the corner of the house. Emily toddled up the steps and straight into her mum's lap.

'Here's my little treasure,' Elaine said with a huge grin, grabbing hold of her tight and holding her close. Emily had the most endearing giggle.

'Right,' Robert said, standing at the bottom of the steps. 'Better be heading off.'

She lifted Emily from her lap and onto the porch. Emily carefully negotiated the steps and ran over to the tree swing. Elaine called after her but there was no stopping her now.

She gave Michael a meaningful look as she stood from the bench for him to go and fetch his sister. 'I'm going,' he groaned with a slight smile and went after her.

'Thank you, El, for a pleasant day and lunch,' said Robert.

'It's been nice.'

Robert went onto the porch and moved in close. He embraced her for a second or two before he stepped back, leaving his hands on her shoulders. 'You take care. You need anything, call me. I'm only a couple of hours or so away,' he said, referring to his house in Solihull. He walked over to the car.

'Come and say goodbye, you two. Your father wants to get going!' she shouted.

Elaine watched on, tears forming, as Robert's Mercedes veered off the drive onto the road. Margaret joined her.

'Don't spend any more tears on that man, Elaine. All he ever did was cheat on you and when you needed him most, he walked out and left you,' Margaret stated.

Elaine knew her mother was right. She wiped away a lone tear and in a nanosecond, her manner shifted from sad and fragile to an unwavering, almost angry disposition. Standing straight with an icy glare in her eyes, she disappeared with Margaret into the shadow of the open front door.

13

Wednesday, 22 August
5 Years Earlier

Since Friday, Elaine had left the house only to identify Charlie's body with Robert. For the most part, she'd kept herself away from everyone. On the rare occasions that she did leave Charlie's bedroom, it was to use the bathroom or to fetch a drink. Her skin turned a shade lighter, her body thinner with each passing day as she surrendered to her fragility.

For Robert, he overcompensated by keeping himself as busy as possible. It was the only way to keep his shame and guilt at bay. Every single day, he'd visit Michael and Emily who were still at their grandparent's house. He also made the funeral arrangements and popped into work on a regular basis to keep things ticking over. Robert had tried to stay away from Chloé, even to the extent of ending their relationship. She pleaded with him to change his mind, calling and showing up wherever he was. Robert missed her. He loved her, but his horrendous remorse ate great chunks of him. Not seeing her was an attempt to punish himself in some way.

As he entered Charlie's bedroom, he was struck by the darkness, the curtains drawn to block out the daylight. Elaine was curled up on the floor in the corner of the room. Close to her chest was her son's most prized possession, his teddy bear, Matthew. Robert went straight to the window and pulled the curtains wide open, which forced Elaine to close her eyes and turn her head away from the streaming morning sun. He stood over her, staring down, contemplating what he could possibly say when there weren't any right words. How could there be?

'Elaine?'

She didn't answer. Deflated, Robert's shoulders slumped. He released a sigh and tried again. 'Elaine, you can't go on like this.'

She continued to stare at the wall, a blank expression on her face.

Robert's voice went up a notch, 'Do you think you're the only one suffering here?'

Still, she didn't acknowledge him.

Angered, he dropped down in front of her. 'Elaine!' he shouted in her face, gripping her shoulders and shaking her, a broken woman. She turned to him, her dehydrated face so desolate, so abstracted. Her eyes inflamed and tired, her aching agony hiding in plain sight.

'Michael and Emily keep asking about you. They need you, they need their mother now more than ever, Elaine,' he said, his voice breaking as his emotions rose to the surface.

'They miss you and don't understand what's going on. I can't seem to find the right words, El. I don't even know what to say to our kids,' he sobbed. 'They are our children, we had three, not one, and they need their mum.'

Tears tumbled down her face. Robert had found a way through. There was so much pain, she needed to let it out; it had to come out; nobody should have so much suffering locked inside.

'I can't stop the hurt,' she cried out. 'I want it to stop, but it won't leave me, and I'm dying – I'm dying inside.' Her cries now muffled screams as she buried her face in his chest.

Robert pulled her into him. 'Come here.' He wrapped his arms around her as her tortured soul broke free. Her agonised wails broke his heart.

'I just want my boy back. I need him, Robert. Please, make him come back,' she sobbed.

For long minutes they stayed entwined in shared unbearable sorrow as Robert rocked her, taking the comfort they needed from one another, a respite from the grief they would forever carry. Elaine pulled back from him and looked into his red eyes and tear covered face.

'Let's fetch our children,' she whispered, a faint but tender smile shining through the gloom.

14

Sunday, 6 August
Present Day

Late evening and content, Elaine stretched out on the sofa to read. Reading was one of the few things that helped her to relax and kept unwanted thoughts at bay. Seeing Robert yesterday had been difficult for her. Today she'd done some more cleaning followed by some shopping for plants and other knick-knacks for the house.

Every so often, her eyes drifted from the book to her mobile phone on the coffee table in the hope it would ring, or at least do something. She thought about calling Lila but didn't want to come across as overly keen.

When she came close to making the call, an inner voice whispered, "Lila doesn't want to hear from you, nobody does." Then she'd return to her book to block out the pessimist within, denying herself something positive.

At a loud crash outside, Elaine jumped up from the sofa and scurried to the window. She pulled the curtains apart but it was a challenge to see anything obvious. However, it was a reminder to change the bulb in the outside light. She went to the front door and stepped outside to see one side of the swing bench had collapsed to the floor. On closer inspection, one of the holding hooks for the support chain had broken away leaving a small hole in the ceiling. Nothing she couldn't fix.

Turning to go back in the house, she gasped, staggered to see a tall, dark figure a few feet away from her on the porch. Her heart pounded, her legs leaden, anchoring her to the spot. The glow of the moon behind him and the ineffective porch lighting made it impossible to see a face. Elaine didn't have a clue what to do next. She wished she could see the face of the intimidating stranger. Running for the front door wasn't an option, he was closer to it.

'Hello! Can I help you?' she faltered.

The unnerving silence escalated her apprehension. She was too afraid to move, fearful of making the situation worse. The seconds ran into minutes and the minutes felt like hours. In one swift move, the shadowy figure made a dash for the front door, scurried into the house and shut her out.

'No, no, no!' she shouted in astonishment as she ran towards it. Elaine tried the handle but it was locked. Her clenched fists thumped against the door.

'Let me in!' she screamed, kicking the bottom of the door with her barefoot, desperate to get back inside the house.

'The kitchen,' she said, and raced to the back, hoping she'd left the door unlocked.

Light flooded through the open kitchen door and cast a beam across the grass. Her eyes followed the well-lit trail to a shadow at the edge of the light, where the intruder watched from a distance. Elaine rushed into the kitchen, closed, and locked the door. Peeking through the glass, she saw the man walking away, fading into the anonymity of the night. He must have run straight through the house. Why would anyone do something like that? Disturbed and upset, Elaine hurried to fetch her phone from the living room and called the police. Although convinced he wouldn't have had enough time to go upstairs, she still checked the children's bedrooms and every other room in the house.

Thirty minutes later, the police came up the drive, blue lights flashing but no siren. Elaine was already out on the porch, having chosen an odd time to replace the outside bulb for a more powerful one. She finished screwing the cover back in place and switched it on. Two officers emerged from the car and she went to the top of the porch steps to greet them. Both men had on identical clothing, peaked caps, black trousers, and stab vests over their short-sleeved white shirts. The blue lights on the roof of the car strobed behind them. One of the officers was tall, mature, possibly in his early fifties, rugged and handsome with a trimmed grey beard.

For a second or two, the older officer seemed taken aback, almost as though he recognised Elaine. 'Mrs Davis?' he said.

'Yes, thank God you're here.'

'I'm Sergeant Burgess,' he informed her with his booming Yorkshire accent. 'And this is Police Constable James,' he gestured to the younger man who looked to be in his mid-twenties. 'You called about an intruder.'

She explained everything to them and how she'd been through every room in the house. As far as she could see, nothing had been disturbed or stolen.

*

The sergeant and constable headed off with their torches to search the grounds. Sgt Burgess asked PC James to go on ahead and check out the barn, while he went to search the shed. The young PC entered the dilapidated barn unable to see much, his torch not illuminating anything of significance. He skimmed the scant light over some old furniture, a kitchen table, chairs, an old bed frame, and a thick support post that rose up to a cross beam. Through the massive hole in the roof, he could see the clear night sky and plenty of stars. As he turned to leave, his foot sent something clattering along the ground. He shone the torch over an empty baked bean can next to a couple of blankets and other discarded food packaging. He reached down and picked up a plastic milk carton with barely a drop left inside. It was still in date. He tossed it back on the floor and went to find Sgt Burgess.

Their search completed, they returned to the house and knocked on the door.

'We've had a good look around out there, Mrs Davis. Whoever it was, seems to be long gone now,' Sergeant Burgess reassured her. 'It was likely some young lad messing about with his friends as a dare or something. They get bored out here and boys, well, they will be boys,' he added.

'Maybe, but I'm sure it was a man and not a boy,' she said, unconvinced by the sergeant's young prankster theory.

'There are plenty of youngsters around here who are pretty well built for their age.' Sergeant Burgess recognised the look of uncertainty on her face. 'If you'd like, I could get forensics out here to dust for fingerprints.'

She took her time before making a decision. 'No, it's fine. As you said, probably just boys.' It was more hassle than it was worth.

The younger policeman stepped forward until he was right under the now much brighter light. A sparkle caught Elaine's eye from the silver-plated digits on the epaulette of PC James.

'Do you know if anyone has been using your barn, Mrs Davis?' he asked. From his accent, the young PC was from somewhere further south. London would be her first guess.

'No, not at all, or at least there shouldn't be. It's dangerous and falling apart,' Elaine said, puzzled as to why he'd asked.

'Yeah, you're right there. It is a bit of a state, but it's clear that someone has been sleeping in there recently. It was very dark inside. If you want, I can pop back tomorrow and check it out for you. Probably teenagers using it as a camp, but it's best to make sure.'

'That would be kind, thank you.'

'Not a problem, I'll come by some time in the morning before my shift ends,' he smiled.

'Do you need me to be here? Because I have to go to York in the morning.'

'No, it's fine, I won't need to trouble you at all. I'll be in and out.'

'Right, Mrs Davis,' said Sergeant Burgess. 'We'll be going then. Don't hesitate to call us if you have any more bother. *And please*,' he stressed. 'Do lock all your windows and doors.'

As the car pulled away she took one last look at the surrounding darkness. Elaine pulled her dressing gown tighter together, unsure whether the bitterness outside made her shiver or she was simply scared. She went back inside the house and secured the door.

In the living room, perched on the edge of the sofa, Elaine studied her phone. Should she call Robert? She didn't want to but was more than a little shaken by the incident. It wasn't as if she had anyone else to call or talk to, and it wasn't every day a strange man ran through your house. Elaine buried her head in her hands, agitated by not knowing what to do.

'The children are all settled now.' She looked up to see Margaret, who'd come from nowhere and was now seated next to her.

'Thanks, Mum.'

'I'll check on them again when I go back up in a minute,' said Margaret.

Elaine's tension eased but she doubted she'd get any sleep; nevertheless, she still fancied making herself comfortable in bed and reading for a while.

The police radio was quiet as the two officers drove back to the station along the dark country lanes, the silence between them amiable. Without looking, Sgt Burgess hadn't failed to detect PC James shifting around in the driver's seat as though he wanted to say something.

'Spit it out, James,' demanded Sgt Burgess in the end.

PC James smiled. 'Well, I was wondering about Mrs Davis.'

'What about her?'

'Didn't seem to be a husband in the picture, I thought maybe—'

'Don't even think about it, lad,' the sergeant interrupted.

'She's a bit of a sort. I've always had a thing for the more mature woman.'

'Not this one you don't. Mrs Davis has been through enough,' he said with an air of regretful familiarity.

'What do you mean?' PC James was intrigued.

'I know her. Well, I know of her,' he said.

'How come?'

'It was such a long time ago now. A case my father worked on when he was a DCI. I'd not long become a constable.'

'And?' PC James was eager to learn more.

'Sad story. A terribly sad story,' he said, downcast, not wanting to add further comment.

'What happened to her?'

'About five years ago, she lost a child. It was all over the news and in the papers. Her son was abducted and murdered. Not good, not good at all.'

'Christ, that's awful.' Stunned, PC James paused before continuing. 'What about before? You made it sound like there was something before, with your father's case?'

'Leave it, James. Let it go.' Sergeant Burgess closed up, his eyes glistening. He gazed out of the window into the darkness as they drove.

PC James had never seen his sergeant like this. He hadn't known him for too long; however, he knew when to keep quiet. They drove on for a short spell.

Breaking the silence, the sergeant mumbled, 'I'm just astounded she came back here, to this place – to that house.'

15

Wednesday, 22 August
5 Years Earlier

A hand reached over the top of the garden gate and slid the bolt across. Lenny Grey stood in the opening. He had a look around before walking into the garden and closing the gate behind him. He skulked along the path towards the back door. Lenny had been watching the house for three days, so he knew they were out. As much as he would've liked to have entered earlier, he'd waited for the cover of night. He kept his eyes peeled for any curtain twitchers peering through windows.

Brought up on a council estate in Hackney, most of Lenny's friends weren't the sort of boys his mum wanted him to hang around with. His dad, on the other hand, a right proper old East Ender had a different perspective. He'd wanted his boy to get up to mischief and prepare himself for the harsh reality of life. Of course, his father had been in prison on several occasions. At least he hadn't followed his father's example. There was no question he'd been a bit of a boy back in the day and picked up one or two tricks in his youth that had come in useful. Learning how to pick locks, for instance.

He was a bit rusty, but it wasn't long before he worked his magic and let himself inside the house. Lenny had staked the place out long enough to know they rarely used their house alarm, and luckily for him, this was one of those times. He closed the uPVC door behind him and used the torch app on his phone. He crept through the dining room and into the hall. He'd been inside the house once before when he'd managed to lie his way in.

He searched room by room until he located the office upstairs. The laptop was on the desk. Lenny made himself comfortable in the leather chair and turned on the computer. He had no idea how much time he had before they returned home. When the screen came alive, it demanded a password.

'Shit,' he muttered. It hadn't crossed his mind he might need to enter a password. He rummaged through the desk drawers beside him, looking for a notebook or anything where it might be written down. With passwords required for everything these days, most people made a note of them.

There was nothing noticeable in the drawers. He examined under the mouse mat and the keyboard. He checked around the desk and shone his phone torch around the office to see if anything stood out. It didn't. Relaxing into the chair, thinking, his eyes rested on the monitor and a cartoon sticker of Wyle E. Coyote on the side of the screen.

He smiled, 'No, it couldn't be that easy, could it?' Lenny typed the cartoon character's name. He was in.

Lenny knew it was a long shot but he was desperate to find something, anything that would prove his suspicions correct. Browsing through the computer revealed nothing out of the ordinary. The headlights of a car pulling into the drive set the room aglow. He looked out of the window.

'Bollocks,' he blasted, turned off the computer and snapped it shut. At the top of the stairs, he heard them coming through the front door. He slinked along the landing and squeezed into the linen cupboard to wait it out until an opportune moment to leave the property came. He hoped to God they weren't night owls who watched TV until the early hours.

Twenty minutes passed, and Lenny's muscles ached. Standing up straight in an enclosed space wasn't doing his back any favours. Relief coursed through him a few seconds later when he heard them coming up the stairs to put the kids to bed.

'Can I have a story please, Mummy?' he heard one of the children ask.

'I want one, too,' said the other.

'You can both have a story,' Elaine told them. 'Michael, you get ready for bed and I'll come to you after I've read to Emily.'

'I'll get Michael settled, sweetheart, then I'm going to take a shower,' he heard the man say.

Lenny played the waiting game a little longer. It had gone quiet, time to make his escape. As he reached the top of the stairs, Robert emerged from the bedroom. The men locked eyes in shock, a look of disbelief covering their faces.

Robert recognised the reporter, outraged at the audacity of the man. How dare he invade his family home in such an arrogant fashion? Lenny looked like a boy caught with his hand in the cookie jar and dashed down the stairs, until he stumbled and fell part of the way, thumping onto the hallway floor. Robert landed on top of him, punching him anywhere he could connect.

Flying down the stairs behind them, Elaine yelled for the pair to stop. Lenny pushed Robert off and scrambled to his feet. He stared up at Elaine. She didn't look surprised he'd gone so far as to break into their house.

Robert punched Lenny in the face. 'Get the fuck out of our house!' he raged, about to strike him again, but Elaine intervened.

'Stop!' she shouted, 'That's enough!'

Lenny touched his bleeding lip and gazed at his fingers. 'I'll give you that one,' he said, riling Robert again.

'Robert! Go upstairs. Now!' Elaine was in total command, so unlike her.

He glared at Lenny as he turned to go up. At the top of the stairs, the children, with expressions of fright and disgust. The three adults looked ashamed and embarrassed. Robert continued up the stairs, passing Elaine halfway, and led Michael and Emily into one of the bedrooms, closing the door.

Elaine calmly sat on a step close to the bottom. 'What were you thinking, Mr Grey? Why do you believe we had anything to do with what happened to our son?'

'Because something ain't right here,' he said.

'You're right. Something is wrong here, but it's not what you think it is.'

'Then what is it?'

'You're the investigative journalist, Mr Grey. I shouldn't have to do your job for you. But if you'd ever had some form of a relationship or family, you'd understand things aren't always as they appear,' she said.

'How do you know I don't have a wife or family?'

'It's not difficult to find information on a jaded reporter

whose best years are behind him. A sad old man who's always been alone and in all likelihood always will be. Do you think I didn't know you've been parked outside the house for the past three days? I may be grieving but I'm not blind. If you wanted to come in and look around, all you had to do was ask. I had a feeling you'd sneak into the house for a snoop. When we returned home and I saw you weren't in your car, I guessed you'd made your move. I just didn't expect such a shambolic effort.'

'Why don't you care about me breaking into your house?'

'Because we didn't have anything to do with our son's death. In which case, there is nothing for us to hide and nothing for you to find. I never said I didn't care about you breaking into our home, though, in fact, I wanted you to.'

'And why would you want that?' She'd piqued Lenny's curiosity.

'So I could call the police, have you arrested, and charged. I'll also take out an injunction against you. You will never be allowed near my family or me again, Mr Grey. Not for a long time. I'm certain it won't look good for you to be caught stalking a family that has lost their child in such a cruel way.'

'I'll be gone by the time the police get here.'

'I don't think so. It looks as though your ride has already arrived,' she said, her face devoid of emotion.

Lenny looked around at the front door. Blue lights flashed through the frosted glass and two figures walked up the path.

'Accept the injunction for harassing us, Lenny, and I won't press charges against you for breaking in and assaulting my husband.'

Lenny smiled; nobody would buy his word over hers. He'd been bested by Elaine once again.

'When did you call them?'

'Before we came upstairs. You left the back door unlocked and I knew I'd locked it before we went out. It wasn't hard to put two and two together.'

Lenny opened the door to see a second police car pull up. He looked back at Elaine, grinning. 'You win. I'll take the injunction,' he said, and walked outside. One of the officers recognised Lenny and marched him to the car, while the other went inside to take Elaine's statement.

16

Monday, 7 August
Present Day

Staring at the empty red leather seat opposite her, Elaine had no clue how she came to be alone in an open-air carriage on an old-fashioned Ferris wheel. She glanced over the side to see she was high up and staring down over a vintage travelling funfair, enthralled by the beautiful multicoloured lights that gleamed into the black night sky above. Contentment replaced her previous confusion. She tilted her head back and inhaled the freshness of the night air.

In the distance, Elaine picked out the red and white stripes of the circus tent where an eclectic mix of clowns stood, enticing people inside for the next performance. She spotted a young boy in a blue hooded coat. Charlie. She watched on as he approached a clown who beckoned him closer. The clown held the strings of two balloons, one red and the other yellow. They floated above his white bald head, sporting tufts of fluffy yellow hair either side. There was nothing unusual about the clown that made him stand out from any other, but something was wrong. An uneasiness engulfed her and her breathing accelerated, more agitated with every passing second.

'Charlie!' she shouted, barely audible over the organ music and the joyful screams of pleasure that could be heard all around.

Elaine lurched forward, taking a risk as the carriage tilted. She called his name again, louder this time, but to no avail. The clown handed the yellow balloon to her child. Alarmed, she instinctively reached out to her son.

In menacing fashion, the clown glared up to where she stood, his thick-coated cherry-red smile hard to miss. An unnerving, mischievous grin, mocked her helplessness. He leaned forward, his words for the innocent young boy's ear only. The clown's bright red lips moved, his icy gaze – fixed on Elaine.

He held out his large, white-gloved hand for the boy to take. Elaine was horrified as Charlie accepted, placing his small, trusting hand into the creepy clowns. With one last triumphant grin up to Elaine, he led her son away. She screamed out his name again, begging him not to go, her cries unheard. Without a care in the world, the clown walked her little boy down the shaded side of the big top, the balloons noticeable as they hovered above their heads until they vanished into the shadows.

The Ferris wheel started to turn and passed the exit point. The carriage rocked as Elaine shifted about in sheer panic, willing it to stop so she could leave the ride and give chase. The yellow balloon her son had been holding drifted in her direction from beyond the circus tent. Leisurely, it traversed the sky, taunting her as it passed overhead. The dangling string grazed the tip of her forefinger before it floated into the dead night sky.

As the Ferris wheel came to ground level, she leapt off, tripped, and stumbled onto the patchy grass below. Elaine raised herself to see that everyone had vanished. Not a single person in sight. The rides twisted and turned while the haunting organ music continued to play, the multi-coloured lights relentless, as they dazzled around her. An uncanny emptiness fell over the fairground. She rose to her feet, perplexed and fearful of what was to come. This wasn't her first time. Elaine had been here before, many times, and it never ended well. She faltered her way to the circus tent.

Elaine arrived at the exact spot where Charlie had disappeared with the clown. Hesitant, she looked down the shaded side of the circus tent. As she edged forward, about to set off into the unknown, the organ music stopped. A disconcerting echo faded into complete silence. Elaine turned to investigate, her eyes wide and filled with dread. All the rides had ceased operating. How daunting to see all the lights flickering and moving in sequence with the absence of sound or the presence of people.

In a heartbeat, the colourful illuminations of the fair plummeted into total darkness, blindfolding her with the cloak of night. For a moment, she stood alone, deprived of her sight and blinded by terror. Fear pervaded every part of her being. Her eyes made a gradual adjustment to the gloom. The moon was her only friend now, bestowing a luminous glow of welcome light on her current surroundings. Looking across the pitch-black, deserted fairground, Elaine's skin crawled and chilled, the hairs on her arms and the back of her neck forced upright. Silence seized the night.

Somewhere in the distance, faint organ music commenced, coming from the vicinity of the Ferris wheel. Oh, how she loathed that now familiar sound. She stepped forward to locate its source. In the blackness beyond, a yellow oasis of light appeared.

The carousel had burst into life. Her pace quickened as she approached. The carousel turned at an unprecedented speed.

She stopped when she reached it, fixated by the horses rising and falling on their poles. The ride looked deserted until a boy wearing a familiar blue coat came into view. The raised hood made it impossible to see his face as he whizzed past her, seated on a horse on the inside row. She knew it was Charlie; it had to be. Elaine knew she'd have to board the carousel, a feat not only challenging but considering its high speed – foolhardy.

Elaine kicked off her shoes and observed the ride. She'd have to time her leap with precision. Running barefoot alongside the carousel, her eyes focused on the curved poles she'd need to grab to pull herself aboard. Elaine leapt into the air, simultaneously placing her right foot on the low step while her right hand grasped a pole. The centrifugal force worked against her, trying to stop her from boarding. Her foot slipped and she fell, banging her knee on the edge of the lower step. She cried out in pain and yet still managed to hang on. Her left arm and leg dangled from the ride, the surge pushing against her, preventing her attempts to bring them around for more stability.

Mustering all her strength, Elaine heaved herself up, swinging her other arm inward. She gripped the pole with both hands and hauled her body onto the central platform. The ride slowed down. She took a moment to recover and climbed to her feet. Exhausted from her efforts, Elaine staggered through the carousel, closing in on her precious boy.

As Elaine placed a tentative hand on his shoulder, he turned to her, at the same time removing his hood. Scowling back at her in the guise of Charlie was the evil beast from her nightmares. Any trace of a smile vanished from her face. Cold shivers penetrated her skin and coiled around her backbone. His big black eyes of emptiness pierced her, the dark crevices in his slimy red skin alive with writhing worms. His ghoulish red lips parted to reveal long, sharp yellow teeth.

A stunned Elaine backed away, only to be confronted by an even more distressing sight. All the exquisitely decorated horses morphed into rotting dead carcasses, flesh sliding from their bones. A sickening spectacle played out before her as they soared and plummeted on the poles that impaled them. Blood of the darkest colour cascaded down the twisting grooves of the curved poles onto the platform. The centrifugal force increased as the carousel rotated at speed, causing an outward surge of the semi-gelatinous liquid spewing across the ride. Elaine sought to avoid the sticky goo as it gushed towards her bare feet.

An unsettling grinding and snapping sound encircled her, compelling her to look up at the drooping heads of the horses as they came to life. Their eyelids slowly lifted to reveal glowing balls of white. Jawbones clacked as their mouths eased open, exposing sharp, jagged teeth. Transfixed, Elaine was unaware of the thick maroon fluid that covered her feet. Each of the undead horses crooked their necks to glare at her. Dark bloodied drool hung from their mouths. Long black lizard-like tongues emerged from the backs of their throats, flapping and sliding across their revolting sharp teeth in anticipation of tasting her flesh.

Her eyes drifted to the crimson creature. A ghastly growl emanated from his vile mouth as his thick black tongue unrolled towards her. Elaine jerked backwards and slipped, falling hard onto the blood-soaked platform. As she slid, she reached out to grab hold of anything that could prevent her from being thrown from the accelerating carousel. She latched onto the tail of a horse, its neck winding around, eyes glowering at her. The dripping dark red on her face did not mask her unmistakable fear.

The steed whose tail she held rose with the pole. The beastly horse behind would soon be within reach as it moved downward, champing at the bit, eager to strike. Elaine would have to let go of the carousel but the speed with which it turned prevented her. Its long tongue lashed at her and retracted into the slobbery black hole. Its teeth snapped together as it closed in on her. She released her grip and her body slid fast across the platform smashing her head against the outer pole. Unconscious, she was tossed from the carousel like a ragdoll.

The falling sensation forced Elaine to wake, overwhelming angst permeating her body. She struggled for breath and grabbed a small white paper bag from the bedside table, put it over her mouth and blew. The bag was her first aid in the aftermath of these night terrors. Tiny beads of sweat covered her face and neck, her shoulder-length hair damp and clinging to her skin, the pillow and bed sheets saturated with perspiration. Not long back in her childhood home and the nightmares were well and truly underway.

17

Monday, 7 August

As usual, Elaine was up early. She'd driven to York for her second appointment with Dr Brown. Her nerves on display, she jiggled her foot in the same comfortable leather chair as the week before. Wearing a white long-sleeved blouse, a dark grey skirt, black tights, and black high heel shoes, she looked like a woman attending a job interview. Although dressed for confidence, she had trouble letting that characteristic show through.

At the first meeting, she was happy he had a gentle and soothing way about him. It would take more than a couple of sessions to find out if he was the right therapist for her. Trust, a vital factor between a patient and psychiatrist, and building trust could take some time. She remembered taking in the surroundings of the room last time. Elaine stared upwards, awestruck by the ornate ceiling all over again. Dr Brown settled into his comfortable chair, notepad in hand.

'Right, Ms Bennett,' he said. 'This is our second time together. The first session went well and I learnt a little about you. You did get a little upset when we talked about your son and that's completely understandable. How have you been this past week?'

'All in all, things have been a little better.' She failed to conceal her nervousness and continued to lie. Should she tell him about the terrifying nightmare that morning? What about the intruder?

'Thinking back to our last session and going over the notes, without meaning to sound rude or offensive, I was surprised you said you'd never seen a mental health therapist in the past.'

A sudden lull swept through the room. Something altered in her body language. One second she was on edge, the next, she looked windswept with self-confidence. She crossed her legs and relaxed into her chair.

'I had thought about it, believe me – but in the end, I managed to muddle through,' she said.

'Okay. We also talked about the break-up of your marriage and moving back to Helmsley. You didn't seem comfortable talking about your childhood. How would you feel about visiting that part of your life in this session?'

'I wouldn't. It isn't necessary. My childhood was as normal as could be. I don't think it has any relevance to why I'm here now,' Elaine fired back.

Dr Brown looked at the previous notes on his pad, about her holding back, hiding something, or that her troubles went much deeper than the loss of her son. He suspected her problems related to something else in her past and that she'd lied about not having therapy before. Underneath, he added how her personality altered when asked about her childhood. Taking everything into account, he knew engaging with her would be tricky. It wasn't easy to help those who knew they needed help but their subconscious wouldn't allow them to accept it.

'Why have you come here, Ms Bennett?' he enquired, evermore curious. 'Why do you feel you need my help? Something must be telling you that you need to be here.' His soft and gentle approach projected a calm but firm manner.

He locked eyes with her, each waiting for the other to turn away. Dr Brown's remained steady, while Elaine showed signs of wavering as she fidgeted in her chair. The air in the room was thick with tension. Increasingly uneasy, her eyes threatened tears.

'I'm here to help you, Elaine. I want to help you, but you need to drop the barricade.'

Another turnaround took place in front of Dr Brown as Elaine reverted to the nervous woman who'd earlier entered his room. All the confidence she'd shown in the last couple of minutes, evaporated. Dr Brown made more notes before placing his pad upside down on the floor. He passed a box of tissues to her.

'Thank you,' she said, and removed a single tissue to wipe her eyes, attempting not to smudge her mascara.

Dr Brown assumed he'd made a significant breakthrough but for the remainder of the session not much talking went on. Elaine revealed more about the night of her son's abduction and how it felt like her heart had been ripped out. She also went on to explain about an intruder. It was a slow process, one small step at a time.

Dr Brown showed her out and closed the door. He paused in thought, a concerned man. Back into his chair, he contemplated his time with Elaine, reached for his pad and added something to the previous notes: *Research patient's mental health history.*

Reaching home in the early afternoon, Elaine was hot and clammy. The air conditioning in the car had packed up on the journey. Up ahead, was a parked police car. She assumed it to be Constable James, there to check out the barn. She parked next to the empty police car and supposed he must be out the back. Elaine fetched two grocery bags from the boot and went into the house. She put the bags down for a second, removed her shoes and kicked them next to her trainers.

As soon as she entered the kitchen, Elaine switched on the kettle and put away the groceries. A cup of tea would restore her after the long drive and the harrowing appointment with Dr Brown. And it would be polite to offer Constable James a cup when he returned from the barn.

Twenty minutes went by and there was still no sign of PC James. Elaine checked whether his police car was still there. It was strange he wasn't back yet. She slipped on her trainers and headed out of the back door. Her Converse shoes, although not a good look with black tights and a skirt, were ideal for walking across the uneven ground.

Back at the house for almost two weeks but she hadn't yet ventured out to the barn. She approached, her chest heavy, constricted. An intensifying panic. Was it the boiling heat and the hectic morning she'd had? No! That wasn't it. It was something else and whatever it was – it wasn't good. Even in the current humidity, cold fingers caressed her, spreading like icy ivy.

She'd had the same reaction in the back of the taxi after her night out at The Royal Oak pub, but no way as intense as now. Queasy and troubled, she struggled to breathe in the stifling heat. Fifteen feet from the barn, her legs refused to carry her any further forward. What held her back? Fears and dark thoughts sparked anxiety in her mind and body.

'Constable James!' she cried out, exhausted and gasping for air.

Hands to knees, she leaned forward, nauseated under the raging sun. Elaine lifted her head.

'Constable James!' she shouted again, throwing every ounce of energy she had into her voice.

Weak and wheezing, her vision faded to a blur as the barn door flew open. A figure in black and white approached. Her eyes demanded to close. She fought back, straining to keep them open, her energy sapped as she fell to the ground.

Flustered when she came to, she was back at the house on the living room sofa. Elaine looked at the clock on the mantle over the fireplace; it had been over two hours since she'd arrived home from York. She remembered being out near the barn trying to find PC James but – what happened?

Rising from the sofa, she noticed she wasn't wearing anything on her feet. In the hall, her Converse trainers were next to her black shoes. She opened the front door: the police car was no longer there. Was it on the drive to begin with?

'You're starting to lose it, girl,' she said aloud.

A little later, having changed into a pair of old work jeans covered in paint, a check shirt and white undershirt, Elaine sat at the kitchen table eating a sandwich. She'd done some more work around the house to keep busy and earned a break.

'Hmm, correct me if I'm wrong, but that smells like – peanut butter and banana, *again*,' her mother said disapprovingly as she appeared in the kitchen.

'You're right, Mum. You caught me. That's exactly what it is.' Elaine took a bite. 'Did you have a good day with Michael and Emily?' she continued, chomping away.

'How many times have I told you about speaking with your mouth full?'

'Loads,' Elaine smiled, covering her mouth.

'We had a lovely time,' Margaret stated, joining her at the table.

'Where are they now?'

'Emily is in the living room watching one of her shows and Michael is upstairs.'

'How have they been?'

'They've been fine, stop worrying,' Margaret smiled. 'What about you, how was your day?'

'My appointment was okay. After that, I did some shopping and when I finally arrived home I, I think I had the strangest dream—'

A knock on the front door cut short the conversation.

'Afternoon, Mrs Davis.'

'Sergeant Burgess,' she smiled. 'Have you come to look around the barn?'

Surprised, the sergeant said, 'Er, actually no, Mrs Davis. I came to ask if you'd seen PC James. He came here earlier and we haven't been able to contact him since.'

'I haven't seen him, I'm afraid. As I mentioned last night, I had to go to York this morning and arrived back in the early afternoon. I suppose he could have come before I got home,' she said.

It was clear Sgt Burgess was concerned.

'Okay, Mrs Davis. I'm sorry to have troubled you,' he said.

'Please, call me Elaine. I hope you find him.'

Sergeant Burgess smiled. 'Thanks, I'm sure he'll turn up.' He went back to the police car.

She closed the door and leaned her back against it. *What was I thinking? Why didn't I tell him I might have seen the police car?*

Then again, she still couldn't be sure if she'd imagined or dreamed it. She certainly didn't want people to think she was some kind of crazy cat lady, not that she had any cats, yet. Everything would be fine; he'd turn up safe and sound. *Wouldn't he?* Elaine was so mixed up. She tried to dig deep to remember. It was moments like this that irritated her so. Her entire life, plagued by lost time here and there.

18

Tuesday, 8 August

In bed, fast asleep on her side with her head nestled in the comfortable pillow, Elaine opened her eyes. Something had woken her. She climbed out of bed, slid her feet into her slippers and put on her dressing gown. She raced along the landing and down the stairs to the front door. After a struggle with the bolt and a twist of the key, she stepped outside, turning to her right. The full moon highlighted the swing bench, now re-attached to the porch ceiling. She must have noticed it in passing earlier but not registered it at the time. But who fixed it? Taking advantage of the bright night, she scanned the grounds to the front and sides. Out by the old oak tree, she was startled to see a figure sitting on the rope swing.

Heart in mouth, Elaine walked hesitantly towards him. The figure did not budge as she neared. There was no doubt in her mind that somebody wanted to frighten her, but who would do such a thing? She assumed it was the same man who'd entered her house before. Wearing a round white mask with large black holes for eyes and an oversized, dark smile, he rose from the swing to face her. A towering, burly man. He took a single step forward and stopped. Elaine knew she should turn and run in the opposite direction but stood her ground. She had an overpowering need to discover who and why this person was pestering her. The man took another step forward and paused again. The way her legs felt, she would easily believe it was the ground trembling beneath her feet. He took one more step forward and Elaine's valiant endeavour was over.

As bravery deserted her, she started to run. Close to the house, she glanced back. There was no sign of him. Wary, her breathing deafening, Elaine headed back over to the tree, the swing gently swaying before her. She reached out to hold and steady the rope, and herself. A few steps ahead, his chilled breath cut through the night air behind the massive trunk. As terrified as she was, this had to end.

'Who are you?' she hollered. 'What do you want?' She dared to move another step closer and stopped.

'You should never have come back here, Elaine,' an angry, coarse voice snarled.

Breathless, paralysed with fear, short bursts of vapour swirled in front of her. She willed her legs to move and stepped backwards, one ungainly step at a time, her pace quickening as the dark figure stepped partly out from behind the trunk. He just stood there, only half of him in view.

'You couldn't keep away, could you?' he growled.

Elaine fell to the ground and jumped up, running as fast as she could back to the house, this time without hesitation. She leapt over the steps, skipped across the porch and was through the door in a flash, slamming it shut behind her. She bolted the door and rested her head against the back, panting.

Something crashed against it, forcing her to leap back with fright. Her heart banged in her chest as she anticipated the next assault. Another loud thump on the front door sent her into panic mode. She stepped back and froze at a presence immediately behind her. Too scared to turn around, she eased her head down until her chin rested on her chest. A pair of huge brown shoes were on either side of her feet. His chest brushed her shoulders and his breath skimmed her hair.

With nowhere to run, she turned to face her fear, tears rolling down her quivering cheeks.

'Please – please don't hurt me,' she cried to the imposing figure, stood *so* close, the air from his nostrils blew through two small holes in the mask onto her face.

The man's eyes, partially obscured, gazed at her. His large, weathered hands rose upwards, menacing and slow. Elaine edged back until her shoulder blades pressed against the front door. The man grasped her sobbing, wet face with his massive hands. A faint whimper escaped from her mouth. Through the wide smiling hole, his thick lips parted as he grinned at her. Elaine wanted to turn away but was incapacitated by a sense of foreboding. His thumbs caressed and wiped the tears from her cheeks before he removed his hands and stepped back. He pulled the mask from his face to reveal his identity. Elaine stared in astonishment as she looked into the face of – her father.

Her body hurled upright as she woke abruptly in sweaty disarray. This was a first for her. Until now, her father had never featured in any of her dreams. In fact, she was surprised she remembered what he looked like. There had never been any family photos for her to view. Her mother said they were lost after he died. But why now, after all these years, had he found his way into her mind? Furthermore, why was she so afraid of him? Things were bad enough at the moment and these disturbing new visions were not going to help.

19

Tuesday, 8 August

No cloud had exposed itself for days. As far as the weather was concerned, it was hot and getting hotter by the day. The sky above resembled a canvas of blue. Early morning and Elaine sat on the top step of the porch drinking a glass of ice-cold lemonade. Repairs were underway to reattach the swing bench to the ceiling (the only part of her earlier nightmare she wished to be true). She'd already made use of the stepladder and filled the hole. Now it was a case of waiting for it to dry.

Elaine monitored a police car coming up the drive, willing it to be PC James. Sgt Burgess climbed out after it parked.

'Good morning again, Mrs— Elaine.'

It was nice he'd remembered to call her by her first name. She loathed being called Mrs Davis, even more so since the divorce. She'd considered changing it back to her maiden name but there were more important priorities right now.

'Good morning, sergeant. It's a beautiful day,' she said, appearing happy.

'Oh, I can't stand it like this, hate it. The sunshine I can take, it's the damned heat I can do without. I can't recall the last time it was like this,' replied Sgt Burgess. He removed his cap and wiped his forehead with his arm to relieve the beads of sweat. 'Anyway, please, call me Tom.'

'Okay, Tom it is,' she smiled. 'Has your lost constable shown up yet?' Elaine said light-heartedly.

Tom's mood altered, a concerned look on his face. 'I'm afraid not. That's why I'm here.'

'God, has something happened to him?'

'Well, that's the problem. We don't know. We can't locate PC James or his patrol car.'

'Surely a policeman and his car can't just vanish from the face of the earth,' she said, baffled.

'I know how ridiculous it sounds,' said Tom, failing to conceal his embarrassment. 'If the press finds out, they'll have a field day, and find out they will if he doesn't turn up soon. You're certain you didn't see anything yesterday?'

Elaine stuck to her story and lied to Tom again as she pretended to think back to the day before. 'No. As I told you, Tom, I wasn't here in the morning. I got home in the early afternoon, had a nap on the sofa and woke up a little later. I did some housework and then you arrived. I wish I could be more helpful.'

Tom wiped the droplets rapidly reforming on his forehead, his thick silver hair, wilting in the heat. But there was more to it than that: tired eyes, a worried look on his face, the tension in his shoulders, his inability to stand still. From personal experience, Elaine recognised his extreme agitation from the mounting pressure he was under.

'Well, the only thing we're certain of is this was his last call before his shift ended. Then he simply – disappeared. All we have to do now is establish where he went from here,' said Tom. 'Have you been to the barn since yesterday, Mrs Davis?'

Tom had reverted back to calling her by her married name. She rose to her feet, realising how serious this had become.

'No, I assumed PC James had done that and hadn't found anything untoward.'

'Do you mind if I check the barn, Mrs Davis, take another look around?'

'Not at all.' Elaine wanted to appear as helpful as possible.

Tom walked around the side of the house, searched the shed and crossed the field. He approached the barn with trepidation and for a moment, dithered outside the door. It seemed there was more to it than just a missing constable. Tom placed one hand on his baton, pushed the barn door open, and inched his way inside.

A phone rang on the small console table in the hallway of Robert's sumptuous house in Aldersbrook Road, Solihull. Robert stepped through a doorway into the hall, laughing and pointing. 'Chloé, you're as bad as the kids. I knew playing Monopoly with you lot was a bad idea,' he smiled.

'Hello,' Robert answered.

'Am I speaking to Mr Robert Davis?' said a well-spoken, older sounding gentleman on the other end.

'Yes, that's me,' he replied.

'Ah, Mr Davis, I'm so sorry to trouble you. I have been trying to reach your ex-wife Elaine, but I'm afraid I'm failing miserably. You are the only other contact I have.'

'I see, may I ask who I'm talking to?'

'Oh, yes, of course, I'm so sorry not to have introduced myself. This is Dr Graham Walker, Mrs Davis's former psychiatrist.'

Robert had only met him once or twice over the years, his most prominent memory of him being both posh and eccentric. 'Dr Walker, yes. What can I do for you?'

'Well, I'm still in possession of your ex-wife's records and hoped to have passed them onto her new psychiatrist by now so that he is up to speed with her condition.'

'That is a little odd, Dr Walker. I saw her recently and everything seemed fine. She mentioned seeing a new psychiatrist. I'm sure it's just a mix-up or something, Dr Walker. I will get in touch and have her call you as soon as possible.'

'That would be wonderful. Thank you so much, Mr Davis.'

'Goodbye, Dr Walker,' Robert said as he put the phone down. He turned, startled to find Chloé standing right behind him. 'God, Chloé – you made me jump,' he laughed.

'Oh yes, Dr Walker, no problem, Dr Walker.' Chloé mocked him in her French accent, trying to mimic Robert's deeper voice. 'I take it that was Dr Walker,' she smiled, backing away from him and through the doorway to another room.

'You cheeky cow,' he laughed, and hurried after her.

Elaine filled a glass with water and stood at the back door of the kitchen to drink it, attempting to take advantage of any breeze in the air. She stared at the barn in the distance, wondering how Tom was getting on. Through the shimmering heat, she saw the large black hole from where the door was wide open. Apart from the occasional bird tweets, a deathlike silence lingered in the air. Tom charged from the darkend doorway looking a little worse for wear. He doubled over. She couldn't tell if he was struggling for breath or being sick. After a few seconds, he stood upright, removed his cap, and wiped his brow with his arm. As Tom staggered towards the house, she put down the glass and rushed out to him.

'Tom, are you all right?' She grabbed his arm and helped him back to the kitchen and onto a chair.

Elaine passed him the glass of water, which he guzzled down. She took the glass from him and refilled it. Tom drank some more, visibly a lot more comfortable than a minute ago.

'Thank you,' he said.

'What happened, Tom?'

He downed the rest of the water. 'I'm okay, just – so thirsty.' Tom was saturated, perspiration soaking through his shirt as he calmed down.

'I'll get you a damp towel,' said Elaine, and went to the nearby cloakroom.

She came back and passed Tom the cold, damp towel which he pressed upon his face.

'Oh, that's so good,' she heard his muffled voice say.

'Can I get you anything else?' she asked.

'No, I'm fine now, but thank you.' Regaining his composure, he placed the fresh towel on the back of his neck and sat up straight. 'There's no sign of anything untoward out there,' he said, much to Elaine's relief. The last thing she needed was a dead police officer found in her barn.

'It's hard to tell if he was right about someone making use of your barn. I couldn't see much in there to suggest it – just some old furniture and a big tarpaulin he could've mistaken for blankets in the dark. Andrew said he'd found a milk carton with a recent date on, but I sure as hell couldn't find anything.'

'Andrew,' she murmured. Learning his first name made it all the more real – more personal. 'His family must be worried sick, is he married? Does he have children?'

'His parents are being notified later today. He isn't married and fortunately, no children. He's only been working here for a few months,' he answered, getting to his feet. 'Would it be okay to use your bathroom?'

'Yeah, sure, it's out in the hall, first door on the right.'

Tom gave a smile of gratitude and headed for the cloakroom.

Elaine thought about the missing constable. Should she tell Tom about the car or not? How would she explain not mentioning it before? Too late now, best to stick to her original story.

Tom re-entered the kitchen looking more refreshed.

'I put the towel you gave me in the wash basket.'

'Thank you,' she replied. 'So, do you think anyone *has* been using the barn?'

'Hard to say. As I said, I couldn't see anything, but Andrew wouldn't make up seeing a recently purchased milk carton if he hadn't. Most likely kids, using it as a camp.'

'What – and they decided to come and have a tidy up, did they?' Elaine scoffed.

'Look, I know you're still worried about the intruder from the other night, Mrs Davis, but to be honest, finding Andrew is my priority right now.'

'You're right, I'm sorry. I shouldn't be so selfish.'

'Not at all, you're concerned for your safety, as am I, but I'm sure whoever entered your house is long gone,' he reassured her.

Elaine remained sceptical but appreciated his efforts to put her at ease. 'Are you feeling any better?' she asked.

'Yeah, thanks. It was most likely the heat and, well, I'm not getting any younger,' he joked. 'I guess I'd better be off.'

Out on the porch, as Tom was about to leave, he said, 'Thank you, Elaine, for – well, you know. I'm a bit embarrassed about coming over a bit peculiar in front of you.'

'Don't be silly,' she said, 'I'm just glad you're all right.'

A subdued silence lingered as they gazed at each other, both aware of something other than the current circumstances between them.

Tom broke the connection. 'Oh well, I should get on my way. Who knows, maybe he's reported back to the station,' he said, with a weak and unconvincing smile.

'I do hope so,' she responded.

He was on the first step when he stopped, and turned to ask, 'Elaine, why did you move back here?'

Taken aback by his question, she wondered how he knew she'd lived here before. She considered her answer.

'To start over,' she replied. 'To be closer to my mother.'

Tom gave a broad smile and left.

20

Tuesday, 8 August

Feet up, watching TV with a glass of Merlot in hand, Elaine had spread out on the sofa. It was a humid evening, not often the case out here in the countryside. Draughts had a way of finding their way inside these old secluded houses in the middle of nowhere. So far this summer, the nights had provided little relief from the day's intensity of the relentless sun.

The ringing of her phone startled her. Robert. It was unusual to get a call from him during the day, let alone after ten at night. She muted the TV and answered. 'This is a bit out of the blue,' she said.

'Hi, Elaine, it's me, Robert.'

As well as his name appearing on her screen, did he really think she wouldn't recognise his voice after all these years? 'I know who it is,' she said in a blunt tone. 'What's up?'

'I'm sorry to be calling this late. I meant to call earlier but lost track of time.'

'Why don't you just say you forgot?' Divorced for two years and he still couldn't find it within himself to be honest with her.

'If I'd forgotten, I wouldn't be calling you now.'

Elaine shook her head; she couldn't be bothered to go down this childish and argumental path with him.

'What do you want, Robert?'

'I had a call from Dr Walker today. He said you need to contact him or get your new psychiatrist to get in touch with him as soon as possible, something about forwarding your records.'

She took a moment, trying to think.

'Elaine, you there?'

'Yes, I'm here. It's, er, a bad line. I'm sure he has sent for them. Dr Walker clearly hasn't received the request form yet,' she faltered.

'Oh, I see. Well, I just said I'd let you know.'

Flustered, Elaine hoped it didn't come across on the phone. 'I'll give him a call and explain. Thanks for letting me know. Bye.' She couldn't get off the phone quick enough and dumped it on the sofa next to her. She hated when Robert got involved in her life. He frustrated the hell out of her.

Wearing nothing but his boxer shorts and sitting on a high stool at the breakfast bar, Robert contemplated, bemused by the agitation he'd detected in Elaine's voice. The sight of Chloé entering the room, donning an all too short cream nightshirt distracted him. The thin transparent material didn't leave much to the imagination. It showed off her long, toned legs and barely covered her peachy bottom.

'What's wrong?'

'I don't know, Elaine sounded a bit weird,' he replied, bothered by something, tapping his phone on the work surface.

Chloé huffed, 'Perhaps that's because she is weird. Why do we keep getting hassles from that crazy bitch? You said yourself she was loony tunes,' she fumed, circling her index finger at the side of her head.

'Hey, that's not nice,' Robert fired back.

'Well, she gets on my nerves. I'm sure she knows we were together long before you left her and that's why she continues to bother us and remain in our lives.'

'She doesn't know anything. She's part of our lives because of the kids and the business.'

'What if she knows what we were doing when Charlie went missing? What if she saw me by the carousel watching you, or saw us sneak down the side together?'

'She didn't see us and she doesn't know. She would have said something long before now, don't you think?'

'No, that's not how it works with crazy people. She will wait and play games until she destroys us, piece by piece.'

'Chloé, I promise you; she doesn't know anything about us. Besides, I doubt she'd remember if she saw anything, anyway.'

'Ha, so you admit it, she is a madwoman.'

'Maybe a little,' Robert grinned but was soon serious again. 'But it's still not nice to insult her.'

Chloé slinked over to him, talking in a soft, seductive tone. 'Ah, is Robert all protective, huh?' She moved between Robert and the breakfast bar.

'Did I make him all angry?' she continued in a sexy, suggestive tone, her accent appealing even more to Robert.

He couldn't resist her when she was like this and still found it adorable when she mixed up words and said things incorrectly in translation. She moved in close, her lips nuzzling at his ear. She grabbed his hand, placed it between her legs and laid kisses on his face before moving her lips to his neck. Robert was all smiles now as he put both hands under her legs and lifted her onto the breakfast surface in front of him. His phone under her back, Chloé reached a hand underneath to slide it away along the worktop.

He leaned forward and kissed her, sliding his tongue into her receptive mouth. He forced her back, raised her nightshirt and kissed her belly. His mouth moved upwards, teasing her skin and edging closer to her breasts. Robert's lips closed around her hardened nipple. He flicked and caressed it with his tongue. Chloé moaned, her head jerked back in excitement. He planted gentle kisses and licks on her body, his hands on her breasts, and eased down until his face was between her legs. She rested her legs on his shoulders, arched her back and moaned as his tongue found its target.

On the sofa, Elaine's watery eyes glared at the phone in her hand. She pressed the End Call icon. She'd heard everything and felt a cocktail of emotions ranging from shock to anger. Both assumed the other had ended the call until Elaine picked up her phone from the sofa. Dumbfounded, she didn't know how to react. Her son's death had been Robert and Chloé's fault!

Devastated, her head spun as she tried to process what she'd just heard. Out of nowhere came an explosion of rage. She pushed the coffee table onto its side and grabbed the table leg, lifting and tossing it across the room. She let out an almighty scream, followed by another until a stillness enveloped her. Elaine knelt in front of the open fire, her eyes captivated by the burning firewood, her mind lost in the smoke that swirled up the chimney. She held out a hand in front of her, unflinching as she moved it into the wavering flames. A desperate need to feel physical pain. Something to numb her senses to the indescribable emotional torture surging through her. She didn't bat an eyelid to the intense heat blistering her skin.

'Stop, Elaine! Stop that now!' a voice hollered. She drew her hand away from the fire. 'You don't need to do that, my girl.'

'Why not, Mother?' Elaine said, still on her knees.

'You shouldn't be punishing yourself for what Robert and that French whore did. One way or another, they will pay for what they have done,' Margaret stated.

Taking her mother's words on board, Elaine got to her feet and settled back on the sofa. She examined her mobile for the time: 10.33 a.m. She scrolled through the very short list of contacts to Lila and debated whether it was too late to call her. Elaine had an urgent need for a friend. She hesitated for a second then pressed Call.

'Hey, Elaine,' Lila answered, sounding pleased to hear from her.

'Hi, Lila. I'm sorry, I know it's late but can you talk?' she asked, wiping away the watery tracks from her cheeks.

For the next hour, they talked. Elaine explained about the phone call she'd had with Robert and some of the things she'd heard; however, she didn't discuss what she'd learnt about Charlie. That was too private to share with anyone. She briefed Lila about her life with Robert, the various times he'd cheated on her in the past, and other tragic events of the last few years.

They'd agreed to meet the following night at the same pub as the week before. Elaine felt better after speaking with Lila and sharing something personal with her. She was also pleased to have arranged another night out. Her fury with Robert needed reigning in. It was a devastating blow to have his betrayal confirmed by overhearing their discussion. Chloé's opinion of her didn't matter, but to hear Robert insult her was like a repeated kick in the stomach. It was no longer about an act of duplicitous behaviour; it was about how he'd come to lose Charlie, something no mother could forgive, and there would be serious repercussions.

Any feelings of love between them were long gone, but she supposed Robert would at least have some respect for her. Everything he had in his life was down to her, the business, the money, the big house. How quickly things can change, more so when people are seen for who they truly are. The ties that once bound them together weren't just broken – they were obliterated. As her mother had pointed out, he'd cheated on her before and in all likelihood, more than the four times she knew about. He had a way of making her forgive him, of exonerating himself and blaming her for his philandering ways. Elaine sat back, smiling, her anger fading. They'll pay for what they have done. She unmuted the sound to the TV and calmly took a sip of Merlot.

21

At the breakfast bar, Robert sipped coffee and tackled his rubbery scrambled eggs in the same spot where he'd made love to Chloé the night before. As he checked his phone for a missed call from a number he didn't recognise, Robert noticed his chat with Elaine had been longer than it should have been. His heartbeat raced, his breaths grew shorter and sweat formed on his brow. He rubbed the back of his neck at the horrifying realisation that neither of them had ended the call the previous night.

'Shit! No, no, no.' Robert was uncertain what he should do. He tried to remember what had been said and what she might have heard.

'Shit,' he said again as he dialled her number, mulling over what he would say. He'd just have to play it by ear. There was no answer the first time; he tried again.

On the porch, halfway up the stepladder, Elaine screwed the hook into the ceiling for the swing bench, paying no attention to her phone as it rang in her pocket for the second time in a matter of seconds. With the hook in place, she grabbed the chain and heaved the bench up and slipped the supporting chain over the hook. She loved doing jobs like this and had acquired a wealth of experience in various trades during her time on site. To test her handiwork, she eased her backside onto the bench. Success.

Elaine stared at her hand; she'd treated the burn, taken painkillers, and covered the blisters with a large plaster, but damn, it still hurt. Her phone went off again. Elaine pulled it from her pocket and saw it was Robert. She ignored it, smiled, and rocked herself back and forth.

After doing some more jobs around the house in the morning, Elaine set off for the annual Duncombe Park Steam Rally, held in Helmsley since 1990, an event she'd been looking forward to taking Michael and Emily to. She knew it would be something they'd love. Along with the immaculate full-size vintage steamers, were vintage cars, models, crafts, a funfair, and among the many entertainers, were the renowned Can-Can dancers.

Not so long ago, Elaine wouldn't have contemplated being amongst such a large crowd. After walking around for a while, browsing and taking in the attractions, the main event was about to get underway: the parade of steam engines. As they passed, smoke and steam filled the air. How she loved that smell. There was something incredible and unique about it, almost magical, harkened back to another age. For a second, Elaine was sure the mystery man from The Royal Oak stood across from her in the crowd. As she tried to take another look, a giant steamer rolled by and blocked her view. Elaine waited for another gap to scan the crowd opposite but couldn't see him.

Since the night at the pub, he'd drifted into her thoughts every so often. There was no doubt he'd had eyes for her that night but since yesterday, she'd also been thinking about Tom Burgess. Tom was not only rugged and handsome, he also had an air of genuine sincerity about him. There seemed to be a mutual attraction between them. So what if the blue-eyed stranger was at the rally. If he lived nearby, many of the locals were sure to visit at some point over the weekend.

Elaine settled down to watch the Punch and Judy show. How Emily loved puppet shows. After the performance, she headed over to the fair and wandered around, watching the children enjoying the rides while she took pictures with her phone. Now and again, she glanced around, suspecting someone was following her. It wasn't unusual for her to feel paranoid, another symptom of her illness.

With time getting on, Elaine headed home, happy and looking forward to a night out. She hadn't been this enthusiastic about something for a while. Reconnecting with Lila had been a positive step for her and it couldn't have come at a better time.

Robert had called four more times while she got ready to go out. Elaine continued to ignore him. She'd opened an unpacked box in the dining room and found an old white, long-sleeved summer dress with red roses scattered about the cotton material. It showed off more leg than she liked, but it went nicely with the shoes already set aside. It wasn't often Elaine showed off her legs but she knew hers were nice enough, so figured, what the hell. Her confidence was on the up.

She took a taxi into town, straight to The Royal Oak Pub and without hesitation, went inside. It was busy but not as lively as the Wednesday before. She'd arrived earlier this time and luckily enough, Lila was already there with Nicole. Ashton and Steve would join them a little later. The background music was low-key, so they sat and chatted at the same table as the week before.

Nicole went to the bathroom before going out for a cigarette, which gave Lila a chance to talk to Elaine.

'I was so glad you felt you could call me last night. It was great to catch up. We didn't get much of a chance to chat last week,' Lila said.

'It was nice, wasn't it? I wanted to call you all week. I just wasn't sure if you'd want me to or not.'

'I felt exactly the same way. I didn't want to come across as being pushy after all this time. You know, I've never stopped thinking about you over the years,' said Lila.

'I thought about you a lot too.' For Elaine, that was only a half-truth. There were plenty of lapses in her memory from her younger days.

Almost tearful, Lila put a hand on top of hers and before she spoke, noticed the plaster. 'Oh, it's nothing,' said Elaine.

Lila continued, 'It was horrible when you were sent away. I was devastated and nobody would tell me where you were.'

It was easy to tell losing her friend all those years ago still pained Lila. Elaine placed her other hand over Lila's and observed bruising on her friend's forearm. The bruises resembled grab marks of strong fingers pressing hard into the skin. When Lila saw her staring, she removed her arm from view. Both ladies bore marks caused by the men in their lives.

'On the phone, you mentioned we'd be doing something different tonight,' Elaine said, wanting to switch focus and not ruin the mood.

'Oh yeah!' Lila reacted with excitement. 'Well, Nicole persuaded Steve to be our chauffeur for the night and he agreed to take us to a club in York.'

'Wow!' Elaine pretended to be thrilled. She hadn't been to a club in – well, she couldn't recall. 'Should be fun,' she said, concealing her mixed feelings about the idea.

'Don't get used to it because it's not a regular thing for us,' Lila laughed. 'After what you heard on the phone last night, I had a feeling it could be just what you need.'

'I'm sure you're probably right. Wait a minute! You mean you arranged this just for me?' It had been a while since anyone had gone out of their way for her.

Lila grinned, 'It's what best friends do.'

Lila's gesture meant so much to Elaine. It helped push the negative thoughts from her mind. She would make a determined effort to enjoy herself now, considering her friend had gone to so much trouble.

Nicole returned and asked if the ladies were up for some tequila shots. Elaine and Lila looked at each other.

'Silly question,' they replied at the same time, laughing as Nicole went to the bar.

'So, what made you move back here?' Lila asked.

'You're the second person to ask me that this week,' Elaine smiled. 'I'm beginning to think nobody wants me here,' she added as Lila laughed. 'I don't know. I thought it would be good for me to come back. It was time for a change. If I'm honest, I know it sounds silly, but it was almost as though I was being drawn here for something,' she explained.

Lila smiled, 'That doesn't sound silly at all. Didn't I tell you? I have magic powers,' she said, motioning her hands and fingers as though she'd cast a spell to bring her back.

Nicole came back to the table with the drinks on a tray: vodka and cokes all round and six glasses of tequila shots with salt and lime wedges.

'I thought we'd do our shots properly this time, so ladies, let's get this night underway,' Nicole beamed.

Elaine had no idea what to do.

'Just copy me,' Lila said.

Elaine looked bemused as they licked between their thumbs and index fingers and poured on the salt, but she copied them anyway. They licked the salt, downed the shots, and sucked on the lime wedges, Elaine a few seconds behind. They repeated the process for the second shots. The vodka and cokes followed suit. They weren't messing about tonight, squeezing in plenty of drinks before Steve and Ashton arrived about nine. Elaine kept an eye out to see if the blue-eyed man who occupied her mind was about; there was no sign of him.

It took a little over fifty minutes for them to get to York. The club itself was well known for its revolving dance floor and cheesy eighties and nineties classics. They were lucky enough to get a VIP booth because of a no-show. More tequila followed and the cocktails kept on coming by way of a personal waitress. The girls danced on the crowded, rotating floor, having a fantastic time.

Ashton and Steve sat in the booth, lecherous in their behaviour towards the waitress. To be fair, it was mostly Ashton, who'd already had a few drinks himself, including half a bottle of brandy on the drive down.

Finding it all a little overwhelming, Elaine headed back to the booth. The evening was a new experience for her and although enjoyable, it wasn't something she pictured herself doing regularly. Elaine asked the waitress for a bottle of water. Steve, as the designated driver and bloated on Coca-Cola, excused himself and went to the bathroom upstairs. Ashton grinned at Elaine and blatantly ogled her breasts. As much as she wanted to stop him making her feel uncomfortable, she let it go. She wasn't going to spoil having a good time by making a scene. She pretended not to notice him leaning back, eyeing her legs and manoeuvring himself to look up her dress.

'You're a right sort, you know,' Ashton said, raising his voice over the music.

'Thanks,' she responded, remaining courteous.

He shifted himself around the booth to sit next to her as the waitress returned with her water. Elaine took a drink as Ashton asked the waitress to fetch him another bottle of beer.

'I saw you looking at me at the pub last week.' Ashton said, moving his hand to her bare knee.

'Why would you think I was looking at you?' She forced a smile as she brushed his hand away, remaining calm and pleasant.

He put his hand back on her knee, sliding it up her leg. 'I think you want me.'

'Really, is that what you think?' Elaine laughed.

The waitress returned with Ashton's beer, saw Elaine's discomfort, put the bottle in front of him and deliberately flicked it over into his lap. And apologised. The waitress winked at Elaine, who took advantage of the diversion and re-joined Lila and Nicole.

Elaine looked pretty in her dress tonight. Throughout the evening, she caught Ashton stealing glances when Lila wasn't looking, and she didn't care for it at all. As much as she was tempted to tell Lila, there was no way she would jeopardise their renewed friendship.

After declining a couple of offers to dance, Elaine was well aware she'd caught the attention of one or two men throughout the night. Granted, they were much younger, as were most of the clientele; nevertheless, she was flattered. The rest of the evening went by without further harassment from Ashton.

Elaine was the last to be dropped home. Steve had been eager to see the back of an annoying and tanked-up Ashton, so he took him and Lila home first. They may well be good friends, but even he could only take so much of Ashton. Nicole had passed out in the front, while Elaine struggled to get out from the back seat of the car. Steve went around to help.

'Come on, you,' he said, as he offered his hand to help pull her out.

She gripped on to his arm as she staggered towards the house, stopping to take off her shoes along the way. She stumbled up the steps, laughing, and would have fallen if not for Steve.

'What a gentleman you are,' she slurred as she rifled through her clutch bag for the keys to the front door, repeatedly failing to locate them.

Steve took it upon himself to delve into her bag and find them for her. He then opened the door and helped her inside.

'Are you sure you'll be okay?'

'Yes, yes, I'll be fine. Thank you kindly, Mr Steve,' she smiled, and closed the door, remembering to lock and bolt it.

22

Thursday, 10 August

Despite nursing a slight hangover, Elaine started work early the following morning. She'd scraped and sanded lots of the flaking paintwork on the porch. Dressed in a pair of tatty jeans and a red and blue checked shirt, she took out her phone and sent Lila a text to thank her for a brilliant night out. She browsed through the missed calls from Robert before going into the house.

'Hey, Mum,' she said, seeing Margaret seated in the kitchen.

She slid her phone across the table to show her Robert had called nine times. Elaine basked in the delight Robert knew or at least thought he knew she might have overheard his and Chloé's exchange.

'Robert won't be happy he can't get hold of you,' said Margaret.

'No, he won't,' Elaine said with a smug grin.

'He also won't be pleased when he finds out you know what he and that French slut did.'

'Well, he's not going to find out. At least not until I'm good and ready.'

'That's my girl,' Margaret responded with pride.

With her hangover fading, Elaine resumed work on the porch for a couple more hours before taking a much-deserved lunch break. After making a cup of tea and a peanut butter and banana sandwich, she made herself comfortable on the sofa, her eyes glued to the television. The disappearance of Police Constable Andrew James was all over the media.

Helmsley would become the focal point of the nation. A full-scale search was already underway in the area. A police helicopter had circled overhead earlier, no doubt in search of the patrol car or any other clues that might lead to the whereabouts of the young constable. Extra officers had been drafted in from other local constabularies to help conduct the search. The media circus had rolled into town which, on a personal level, Elaine could have done without. She didn't want her past being dragged back into the public eye. All she could do was hope to be left alone but knew it was unlikely, bearing in mind he'd been on her property the day he went missing. It would depend on how much information the police revealed to the press. The invasion of the small town and surrounding areas would continue for a while, until either they found Constable James – or they didn't. At least Elaine's house was a fair way from the town centre, away from the media circus setting up base there for the time being.

Sgt Tom Burgess had been kind enough to pay her a visit that morning to inform her that over the next few days there would be some officers poking around. He also said a couple of detectives would be visiting her to make further enquiries. She would tell them the same as she'd told Tom. She was in a no-win situation, and as for being honest – it was far too late. Elaine had been so confused at the time, passing out and not knowing if it had been her imagination or not. Now it seemed a distinct possibility Constable James had been there that day.

Robert had again tried to contact Elaine on the phone. This time he'd left a message for her to call him, without revealing what he wanted. She knew she'd have to take his call at some point. It wouldn't be possible to ignore him forever, which was a shame.

In recent months, things had been better between them; time had eased the tension and helped heal the anguish. Until she overheard his conversation with Chloé, that is. That was a game changer, Robert showing his true colours.

She'd forgiven his cheating over and over, including an eight-month affair. What if there were more women to add to the cheat list? Having discovered more details about his relationship with Chloé, all sorts of things went through her mind. How long had their fling been going on behind her back? Nothing would surprise her about the man she thought she knew, or the level he would sink to, to get what he wanted.

She'd taken an enormous bite of her sandwich when there was a knock at the door.

'Typical,' she said, with a mouthful.

On her way to the door, she attempted to chew at speed. Peanut butter and banana was not a great combination when you needed to eat fast. Two suited detectives showed her their warrant cards. Parked on the drive behind them were three other police cars. The detective in charge introduced them as Detective Chief Inspector Richard Fuller and Detective Inspector Samuel Pierce. DCI Fuller looked to be in his mid-forties, white and tall. A barrel of a man with greying brown wavy hair. His younger colleague, DI Pierce was black, shorter, and stocky with a shaved head. Elaine was still chewing her sandwich. She held her hand up to point out the obvious while at the same time exhibiting apologetic eyes. The detectives eyed each other. DI Pierce couldn't help but raise a cheeky grin, which disappeared when he saw his DCI didn't see the funny side.

When she could speak, she smiled, 'Sorry about that. I assume you've come about the missing police officer?'

'Yes, I'm afraid so, Mrs Davis. Sergeant Burgess said you've been most helpful and that we wouldn't need a warrant, so, would it be okay if our men searched the grounds while we come in and ask some questions?' He put his size ten black shiny shoe forward as though she had a choice in the matter.

'Not at all, it's fine,' she agreed.

DCI Fuller signalled to the other officers to begin their search before stepping inside.

'May DI Pierce take a look around the house while we talk, Mrs Davis?'

'Of course,' she answered.

DCI Fuller asked similar questions to Tom and she obliged by giving the same answers. She told the detective about the intruder, how he'd stood on the porch watching her before storming into her house, running through the front door and straight out the back. She also told him Sergeant Burgess had searched the grounds, and that PC James had informed her someone had recently made use of the barn. She was confident the detectives would have known all this, having read the reports at the station.

DI Pierce returned from searching the house and shook his head at DCI Fuller as if to express he'd found nothing of interest. Why would he? He sat on the sofa next to his colleague. The DCI took the name, address and telephone number of her psychiatrist in York and noted she'd used her maiden name of Bennett there. Needed to confirm her whereabouts they said, without making her sound like a suspect. She opened up to them about the trauma of her son, it wasn't at all something she liked to talk about, but it was the reason she gave for seeing a psychiatrist. They empathised and paid their respects.

Their enquiries over, for now, the detectives went outside to join the six uniformed officers and spent the next hour or so combing the grounds, the sun fierce above them. When they returned to the house, Elaine was back working on the porch. She removed her mask and offered them a drink, which they both declined. Before they left, DCI Fuller handed her a card with his contact details and asked her to call him if she remembered anything else that could help their investigation. Elaine hoped this would be the end of it. Most of all, she hoped they found PC James as soon as possible, alive and well.

With another interruption over with, she got back to work. No sooner had she begun, her phone started to ring. Robert. This time, she took his call.

Robert hesitated when he heard her speak, probably not expecting her to answer. Elaine wasted no time asking what he wanted, letting him know she was busy. He stammered and stuttered his way through the conversation, probing and trying to work out whether she'd overheard anything. Elaine did her utmost to play it cool, enjoying the sound of him squirming.

It wasn't often she'd had the upper hand over him in recent years or during their entire relationship, but this was good for her. At last, the tide had turned and Elaine had gained some control over her life. Torturing Robert in the process was an added bonus.

With Robert growing in confidence, it was clear he believed she hadn't heard the conversation between him and Chloé. He went on to ask if she was okay, saying she sounded strange on the phone the other night. The subject soon altered as Robert harped on about the missing policeman, claiming that was his reason for trying so hard to get hold of her. It was a good job he couldn't see the expression on her face. Lying bastard! Elaine knew full well the news only broke late last night. Robert had been calling her since yesterday morning. Had he always believed her to be such a fool? It wasn't worth thinking about how many times he'd tried to pull the wool over her eyes during their marriage.

She explained to Robert the circumstances of how she'd met the police officer the night before he went missing. Robert was angry and expressed his concern, wanting to know why she hadn't told him about the intruder. Elaine played it down and said she didn't want to keep putting her problems on him. He insisted she called him if anything like that happened again. Listening to him babble on bored her to the extent of picking flaky bits of paint from her hair. When the call ended, she was pleased with herself for not letting on what she knew, but why hadn't she told him the truth? Why didn't she tell him what a horrible, conniving bastard he was? Maybe she was saving it for another time; a more fitting moment.

She spent what remained of the afternoon scraping and sanding more of the porch, making one hell of a mess, most of which had fallen onto large, white cotton dust sheets. Fixing up the house was a colossal job for her to take on but as she'd told Robert, she wanted to do it by herself. It was personal, and a challenge she was relishing. She would pour blood, sweat, and tears into getting the house right for her and the children.

23

Thursday, 10 August

After putting in a hard shift, Elaine called it a day and carried the folded dust sheets over to the shed. She pulled out a galvanised incinerator bin and emptied the debris from the sheets into it and dragged it back inside. While she swept the remainder of dust and flaked paint from the floorboards, a man wearing a police uniform walked up the drive.

'Not again,' she said, reluctant to have yet another visit from the police after a good few hours work in the exhausting heat. Hot, sticky, and far too tired for any more questions, what more could she tell them? Other than the truth.

As he drew closer, her eyes lit up. In an unbelievable twist of fate, the blue-eyed stranger from the pub approached. Gobsmacked, it was hard for her to believe the man who'd been on her mind was a police officer. Elaine found it intriguing and a bizarre coincidence, not that she was a big fan of coincidences.

'Mrs Davis?' he asked, his accent giving little away about where he was from.

'Yes, that's me,' she beamed, a little let down he didn't appear to recognise her.

'I'm Police Constable Roy Kell. If it's okay with you, Mrs Davis, I've been asked to take another look around your premises with regards to the missing policeman.'

Captivated by his remarkable eyes, she gazed down from the porch. They'd without question cast their spell on her, or was it something else, his familiarity? It troubled her.

'Two detectives and some uniformed officers have already been around today,' she said, trying not to be obvious she was using her advantageous position above to steal secret glances of him in his uniform.

'Yes, I'm aware of that, we're just trying to be thorough, Mrs Davis. I'm sure you understand.'

'Well, I suppose you have to be,' she said. Self-conscious about her appearance, Elaine made a discreet attempt to brush the dust from herself. 'Well, you're welcome to have another look. Would you like me to come with you?'

'Thank you, Mrs Davis, but that won't be necessary,' he replied, much to Elaine's disappointment. As he started to walk away, he hesitated and turned back. 'If you'd like to tag along and it's not an inconvenience, I guess it wouldn't be a prob—'

'No,' she jumped in, failing to conceal her delight. 'It's no bother. I, er, just need to clean my brush and roller.' Elaine did well to come up with an excuse to go and make herself a little more respectable.

'I'll catch you up,' she said, and dashed along the hallway to the cloakroom.

A glimpse of her reflection in the mirror made her want to scream. Her ratty hair, sweaty face and neck, covered in dust and flaky bits of paint.

'Oh my God, look at the state of you,' she muttered.

She ruffled her hair in a bid to shake off at least some of the mess and fixed it to appear more presentable. She cleaned up as best she could before joining PC Kell.

While walking alongside him during his search of the grounds, he apologised again for disrupting her day. Elaine wasn't inconvenienced at all. She was glad to meet him at long last, of course, she didn't tell him that. The sun blazed above them, the temperature at a ridiculous level as it scorched the ground they walked on. It was more extreme out in the open and clearly bothered PC Kell. He removed his cap, the sweat dripping from the strands of his hair.

In the shade of the line of trees to the rear of the house, he scoured the ground for any trace of PC James. 'Where are you from?' he queried, 'your accent doesn't sound as though you're from around here.'

'I was born in London but my parents moved here when I was little. I moved away for a while and well, decided to come back.'

'Oh, by here, you mean in town?'

'No,' Elaine smiled. 'Here, this house.'

'Wow, that's amazing. You bought back your childhood home?'

'No, it's been in the family for years.'

As they drifted beyond the line of trees, Elaine let him know they were no longer on her property and this land belonged to the next farm over. PC Kell ignored her comment and kept on going, searching through the long grass. Elaine followed. It wasn't long before they came across the pond.

PC Kell took a good look around. 'I assume the pond belongs to the owner of this land?'

'You assume right, but it doesn't look like he's worked this part of the property for some years. I used to come out here and feed the ducks when I was younger. I probably shouldn't tell you this but I sometimes bring my daughter out here.'

'Why shouldn't you tell me?'

'Well, you being a policeman and all. You could arrest us for trespassing,' she smiled.

PC Kell laughed, 'Oh, I reckon I can overlook it, just this once mind,' he joked. 'It's secluded, hard to find I'd imagine.' He raised his head to the sky. 'Looks like the heat is making the water recede,' he said, pointing to where the water level had subsided significantly.

'Yeah, I think it's always done that when there's been a dry spell. Once it almost dried out completely.'

'Is it deep?' PC Kell seemed to have a keen interest in the pond.

'About six or seven feet— Oh my God, you don't think your PC is in there, do you?'

He laughed, 'I doubt it, but I'll let the detectives know it's out here.'

They headed back onto her property, walking in the shade of the trees towards the barn. A police helicopter flew low over their heads. PC Kell waved as it circled above them, surveying the area before moving on, exploring the land along the line of the road.

'This will probably sound silly, but have we ever met before?' he asked.

The question took Elaine by surprise; considering she'd presumed he had no recollection of her whatsoever. 'We have sort of met,' she smiled, pleased he'd remembered her.

'Where was that?'

She explained they'd exchanged glances at the pub in town the Wednesday before last, which he recalled in an instant. That pleased her even more.

'I did wonder though, if we'd met before that night, like years ago?' she said.

'Maybe,' he said. 'I did grow up around here but moved away before I reached my teens.'

'That must be it,' said Elaine, her curiosity somewhat satisfied.

'Did I see you at the Duncombe Park steam rally on Wednesday?' she enquired.

'You sure have a lot of questions considering I'm the police officer here.'

'Sorry.'

'I'm just kidding,' he said. 'I was working that day, so unless I have a twin I don't know about, it wasn't me. I would love to have gone, though. How was it?'

'It was good fun. My children love that kind of thing.'

'Children?' he asked, sounding surprised.

His response worried her; she hoped having children wouldn't put him off asking her on a date. 'Did you know PC James?' she asked, wanting to steer the conversation in a different direction.

'No, not at all, I'd only met him the once,' he replied. 'I should check in there,' he said, gesturing towards the barn.

They were about fifteen feet away when Elaine felt a sharp pain behind her eyes. She heard a high-pitched continuous tone in her head, getting louder. Her anxiety kicked in and she had no idea why. She didn't feel right at all. She fought hard to hold herself together, but the closer they got, the worse she felt. She lagged a few steps behind him as they walked around to the front of the barn.

'You not coming in?' he asked.

Her panic attack well underway, she could feel her heartbeat accelerated, accompanied by an urgent necessity for more air in her lungs. Her legs had become cumbersome and unwilling to take another step. Blurred images entered her mind, nothing she could make sense of or see clearly enough. The phone rang and vibrated in her back pocket. Whoever it was could not have picked a better time to call: apart from Dr Walker, her former psychiatrist. As much as she didn't want to take his call, it was a sacrifice worth making if it saved her from embarrassment in front of PC Kell.

'I'm so sorry, I have to take this,' she said. 'I'll meet you back at the house.'

PC Kell smiled, waved a hand, and carried on to the barn.

She took the call and walked to the house. Elaine told the doctor she'd been meaning to call him but had been so busy with the move. Dr Walker stressed the need for her to supply the address of her new psychiatrist so he could send on her records to continue her treatment. She made the excuse she wasn't at home and didn't have his details with her, but promised to send them on.

Elaine thought it was an overreaction from him. She understood he had her best interests at heart, but she didn't want her new doctor to know about every single aspect of her life. She wanted a fresh, unbiased approach. Yes, her dreams were bad, but she would tell him about those at the next session.

Convinced coming back here had helped, Elaine was content, even optimistic about the future.

About fifteen minutes later, PC Kell was out front by the open doorway, shouting up the hall.

Elaine rushed from the kitchen along the hallway. 'I'm so sorry I had to rush off like that. You all done?'

'Yep, I couldn't find anything to report back.'

'Apart from the pond,' she reminded him.

He laughed, 'Yeah, apart from the pond.' An awkward pause followed as they both stood there, not knowing what to say next.

'Was there something else?' she asked, hoping to convey confidence as the constable lingered on her doorstep.

'Actually yes. I don't want to overstep any boundaries here, but I wondered if you'd like to go out for a drink sometime?' he asked, bashful.

Yes! About time. 'I'd love to,' Elaine answered without hesitation.

He took out his notepad and pen and jotted down his phone number. He tore the paper from the pad and handed it to her. 'My name is Roy,' he stated and backed away. 'I hope to hear from you soon.'

'Oh, you will,' she said, containing herself. She loved how shy he seemed.

Bursting with excitement, she watched him stroll down the drive. 'Look back. Please, look back,' she mumbled.

Wearing his charming smile, Roy did look back, right before he headed out onto the road. She placed his number in her jeans pocket and went back inside the house.

*

In the living room later that night, Elaine told her mother about her prospective date, the coincidence of it all, and about him being a police officer. It had been an odd few days for sure. She told Margaret she'd wait a while before calling him, at least until the missing constable business was cleared up – the next few weeks would be a busy time for the police.

A knock on the front door had Elaine and her mother contemplating who it could be this late. Surely not the police again?

'Who is it?' she called out from behind the door.

No reply.

Calling out louder the second time brought nothing but more silence. She opened the door a little way and peered out through the crack. When she couldn't see anyone around, she stepped out uneasily. She walked along the front of the house, looking down both sides for any sign of who was responsible. Was Tom right, could it be teenagers messing around?

'Little shits!' she fumed and went back inside the house, closing the door.

After re-joining her mother on the sofa, she was infuriated by another knock. Somebody was taking the piss. Elaine ran into the kitchen and grabbed a large knife from the block on the worktop. She opened the front door and stormed out of the house, waving the gleaming blade. She wanted whoever it was to see she was armed and angry.

'Who's out there?' she shouted into the night, her pulse racing.

Only the sound of crickets, frogs, and the rustling of the trees disturbed the quiet night. She didn't care if it was youngsters mucking around; this wasn't something she wanted to continue.

As she patrolled the porch, her thoughts were all over the place. Was it in her head? Was she hearing things? She dismissed the possibility as absurd; her mother had also heard the knocking. She went back inside, securing the door behind her. In the living room, Elaine grabbed her phone and was about to call the police when she stopped herself. Instead, she scrolled through the list of names down to Robert. What was she thinking? To be fair, he'd asked her to call him if anything else happened, so with a sly grin, she did.

Snuggled with Chloé on the sofa watching TV, Robert's mobile rang. He grabbed it from the side table and they both saw Elaine was calling. Annoyed, Chloé sighed, glaring at him before he'd even answered. She edged closer, making damned sure she was close enough to hear, irritated by so much contact with his ex-wife.

'Hi, Elaine, what's the matter?'

She explained, and Robert told her she should call the police right away. She responded by saying it was likely to be kids playing silly buggers and assured him she'd call them if it happened again.

'I'm only letting you know because you told me to,' she said, sure Chloé would be within earshot.

Now on the edge of the settee, Chloé scowled at him, shaking her head.

'Okay, well, make sure everything is locked up and don't open the door to anyone tonight. I'll call you first thing in the morning.'

The call ended and Chloé stood, fuming. She threw a cushion at Robert's head and stormed off. Robert cut a frustrated figure and buried his face in his hands.

24

Friday, 11 August

Elaine started work first thing, having already mixed up some filler and made a start on smoothing over the cracks on the porch. Sure enough, Robert called her earlier to see if there were any further incidents during the night. He also took the opportunity to complain about Chloé having a moan. No doubt looking for sympathy. He wasn't going to get any from her. That she'd caused a rift between them gave her a great sense of satisfaction , getting her day off to a perfect start.

Reports on television forecast the stifling weather was set to continue. The heat never usually bothered Elaine; however, the extreme conditions of late were taking a toll on her. Another helicopter flying overhead caught her attention. With the sun in her eyes, it was difficult to make out if it belonged to the police or the press. She assumed police but suspected it wouldn't be long before the media had one up in the air. Like everybody else, Elaine doubted the outcome would be positive. It had been five days now since the policeman's disappearance.

As she thought about making some lunch, two police vehicles came up the drive, an all too annoying and familiar sight. A further intrusion she could have done without. Her anger subsided when she saw Tom Burgess driving one of them. The other vehicle was a van belonging to the dog unit. Tom explained they'd brought the dogs in to see if they could pick up a scent of anything that could help locate PC James. Elaine had no problem agreeing, guessing the investigation wasn't going at all well and they were desperate.

While the two officers went off with the dogs, she invited Tom inside for a cold drink. He didn't need asking twice. She opened the back door, hoping for a draught to blow through the house. Elaine snapped ice from the tray and stacked the cubes into two glass tumblers as Tom talked about the search and the commotion in town from the press. The ice popped and cracked as she poured cold lemonade into the glasses and passed one to Tom.

'Do you think it's going to turn out bad, Tom?'

Elaine was comfortable around Tom. Having seen him numerous times in the past few days, albeit not under the most pleasant of circumstances, she regarded him as a friend.

'Yeah, I think so,' he conceded. 'It's been too long. The worst thing is, we have nothing to go on. Nothing at all.'

'It's all so strange. Anyway, thanks for the heads up about those detectives. They did come yesterday.'

'Huh! They couldn't detect a spot on a kid with acne,' a disgruntled Tom jumped in.

Elaine smiled at his comment.

'I know I shouldn't make jokes, but the top brass has made a complete mockery of this. I filed a report two hours after he'd gone missing because something wasn't right, and those at the top did nothing. They wanted to wait it out and see if he showed up, didn't want any embarrassment.'

'What embarrassment?'

'They were worried he might've gone on a bender, or run off with somebody's wife. They're all barmpots. They should've had search dogs in the area the next day. They'll be lucky if those dogs pick up on anything now,' Tom went on as he stood from the table.

He took his lemonade and walked over to the back door and watched the officers with their dogs in the distance. Elaine was sympathetic to Tom's point of view; he had every right to be angry. The investigation should have started much sooner than it did. Tom was an experienced policeman and had worked with PC James. If he had an inkling something wasn't right, they should have listened.

'Another police officer called here yesterday afternoon. He came not long after the detectives had left.' Elaine hoped Tom could give her the low-down on Roy.

'Is that so,' said Tom, perplexed. 'I certainly never sent anyone out here. Did he give a name?'

'PC Roy Kell.'

'Never heard of him. Must be one of the officers brought in from elsewhere.'

'I got the impression he was from around this area.'

'I may well be knocking on a bit now, but I'm still able to remember the names of the officers I work with,' Tom smiled.

'As I said, it was most likely one of those brought in to help with the search.'

Elaine was disappointed not to uncover any new information on Roy.

'Well, thanks for the lemonade,' said Tom as he placed his glass next to the sink. 'I suppose I should go and see how they're getting on. See you in a bit,' he smiled, and headed out of the back door.

Dr Neville Brown had just finished seeing a patient when his assistant Louise, passed on a message to call Detective Chief Inspector Richard Fuller. Seated at his desk seconds later, and to some extent baffled, he dialled the number on the paper. The detective enquired about an appointment Mrs Elaine Davis had with him the previous Monday.

'I don't have a patient of that name,' Dr Brown said.

'Ah, sorry, the lady did say she used her maiden name for the appointment – Ms Bennett.'

'Ms Bennett? Yes, I did see her last Monday. Is there a problem?'

'No problem. Just needed verification of her whereabouts.'

The call ended and Dr Brown was puzzled more than ever about his patient. He failed to understand why she hadn't used her real name or why the police had called to verify her appointment. He'd considered she was withholding something and this only added to his suspicions. Despite her denial about seeing any other therapists, he was convinced she had, particularly from what he'd observed about her behaviour so far.

The detective's call further piqued Dr Brown's interest in Elaine. She'd mentioned her recent move from North London. It was a long shot to contact the four offices in Central and North London where he'd previously worked, but he was desperate to learn more about her past, he wanted to find out if any of his former colleagues had treated her. Because he'd have to do this between patients, Louise offered to assist by making some calls.

Before Tom and the dog unit left, he returned to the back door of the kitchen.

'I was right about the dogs. Nothing. Reckon we're finished here and you should be left in peace,' he said.

'That's music to my ears, Tom.'

As soon as Tom departed, Elaine went back to work. With the wood filler drying fast, she began the sanding. A few holes would need longer to dry, but she was eager to make a start on the painting that afternoon. A couple more hours of rubbing down where she'd made good, followed by a good dusting, and Elaine was ready to get the first coat on. Emily appeared out front with a paintbrush in hand and insisted on helping her mum. They started to go over the rendering with a new coat of white. She cut in with Emily's help first, letting her loose on a part of the wall she'd eventually go over with the roller. The fresh paint made an instant impact.

Elaine heard the crunching noise of a vehicle on the sparse layer of gravel. She didn't recognise the blue Ford Fiesta but guessed it wasn't the police and hoped to God it wasn't a journalist. She was thankful when she saw Lila, donning a pair of oversized sunglasses – an unexpected but welcome surprise.

'Wow!' Lila said as she reached the bottom of the steps. 'I can see you've been busy.'

'Yep, me and ...' Elaine looked around for Emily but she was nowhere to be seen. She smiled and continued, 'Yeah, extremely busy. It's great to see you again.'

Lila stepped up to greet her and they made a half-hearted attempt to put their arms around each other. Elaine didn't want to get any paint on Lila's clothes. She led her through to the kitchen and fetched two cans of Coca-Cola from the fridge.

At the table, sipping their drinks, they chatted for a while before Lila said, 'Anyway, the main reason I came over is to invite you to my impromptu barbecue. Thought I'd take advantage of the fantastic weather,' said Lila.

'When is it?'

'Tomorrow afternoon until late.'

'I don't think I can make—'

'Yes you can. I'm not taking no for an answer.'

After a short pause Elaine smiled, 'Then I guess I'm coming.'

'I've made calls and lots of people are up for it. I thought it would be a great way for you to meet some new faces.'

While Lila nattered, Elaine wondered why she hadn't removed her sunglasses. Yellow bruising around Lila's eye as she turned sideways told the tale. Elaine coaxed the truth out of her, horrified to learn Ashton had picked a fight after their night out in York. Lila went on to reveal the full extent of his handiwork and confirmed what Nicole had told her about the scars, beatings, and the awful stories behind them. She'd tried to leave him on more than one occasion, but every single time he'd convinced her to stay. As so often happens with women who suffer physical abuse from their partner, she made excuses for him, saying how things hadn't always been bad and they'd had some brilliant times together. She added he'd always provided for their children.

Ashton was six years older. They'd been together since she was eighteen. He'd pursued Lila relentlessly, not giving her much option but to be with him. She'd found his persistence endearing. Within a few months, he'd persuaded her to leave the university in York where she was training to be a midwife. A decision over time she'd come to regret. It sounded as though she wasn't at all happy with many of her choices in life and things hadn't turned out quite how she'd anticipated.

They reminisced for a while about the old days and people with whom they'd gone to school. Lila filled in lots of blanks about some of their old friends she'd befriended on Facebook, where they were and what they were up to. Elaine had never jumped on the social media bandwagon and stayed away from sites such as Facebook. She'd toyed with it once for a few months and found all it did was make her anxious, frustrated, and confused. She didn't understand why people she hadn't met or spoken to for years contacted her out of the blue. If they'd been good friends, surely they'd have kept in touch? She thought back to all those deleted friend requests, one of which was Lila's. Elaine wished she'd clicked confirm rather than delete.

There were other things she couldn't comprehend; like why people posted pictures of a meal they'd cooked or had eaten in a restaurant. Did anyone honestly care? She understood it had its good points but was a tad old-fashioned when it came to social media. While Elaine struggled with her own life, everyone else projected images of how marvellous their lives were, which comes back to why she got rid of it in the first place. It was in no way conducive to her bouts of depression.

Elaine enjoyed Lila's surprise visit, disappointed when she said she needed to go. It had been a while since she'd had a proper one-to-one with a friend and was thankful Lila had accepted her back into her life with open arms. It felt good to have a second chance at their friendship; a friendship which should never have ended.

Dr Neville Brown made some calls but had no luck finding any information on Elaine. It occurred to him he may have spoken to someone who'd treated her but they were unwilling to breach doctor-patient confidentiality. As Neville finished talking with an old friend, his assistant Louise dashed into his office in a blaze of excitement. She'd called some of her former colleagues and discovered she used to work with Dr Walker's current assistant. Unfortunately, he was away and only a few weeks from retirement. He had, however, left instructions with *his* secretary to forward Mrs Davis's records should her new psychiatrist get in touch; to use his exact words "Post Haste." Her former co-worker also revealed Dr Walker was under the impression Elaine had been avoiding the matter. The notes were to be sent by courier first thing Monday morning.

25

Friday, 11 August

That same evening, after another roasting day grafting out front followed by some late tea, Elaine settled on the sofa ready for an evening of relaxation and TV. Sleep took hold during a series she liked on Sky Box Sets called *Bones*. She drifted off almost as soon as she put it on, an indication of just how exhausted she was.

A continuous knocking on the front door disturbed her. With an irritated sigh, she went to answer.

'Who is it?' she called.

Unlike the other occasions, this time there was a reply, 'Sergeant Burgess.'

'Tom?' How strange! As Elaine opened the door, she asked, 'Why are you here at this time? Do you have some news about PC James?'

Tom wasn't standing on the other side – nobody was. The bulb in the porch light flickered, and with a loud ping, the front of the house was cloaked in darkness. Convinced she'd heard Tom, she stepped out of the door.

'Tom?' she called, and walked to the end of the porch.

Hearing an intermittent squeak behind her, she turned sharply. A presence radiated from the swing bench.

'Is that you, Tom?' Elaine stepped forward with caution.

The short squeak every time the bench swayed unsettled her. As she edged closer, a voice pierced the gloom.

'It wasn't your fault, Mum.'

'Charlie?' Elaine moved gingerly towards the bench, startled by the buzz of the outside light flickering on. There he was – her boy. Although sitting in front of her, she remained vigilant and sceptical. How she wanted to touch him, to hold him again, wanted this to be real, but she didn't know what was anymore.

'It wasn't your fault, Mum. You can let me go.'

'No, Charlie. I can't,' Elaine said with a sad determination.

'You have to let me go,' he repeated. 'You're in danger, Mum. He's coming,' Charlie said and pointed to somewhere on the porch behind her. 'Beware zero six four two,' he said with urgency, his voice fading. 'I have to go. You need to wake up. Now!'

An assortment of love and perplexity poured out of her as she watched his manifestation fade away.

'Charlie, please – come back,' she cried out, but he was gone. The hidden uncertainty of a pitch-dark night returned as the light sputtered off.

Elaine turned, looking where her son had pointed. 'What did he mean, beware zero six four two?' she said, puzzling over why those numbers were important.

As she walked over to where he'd indicated, the squeak of the bench recommenced behind her. Instinctively, she knew it wasn't her son returning. A bitter chill shrouded her. Shuddering, she resisted the compulsion to turn.

"He's coming," Charlie had warned her. He'd tried to wake her, wanting his mother to escape her appalling dreams.

Elaine thought back to when she'd seen him in the mist. Charlie had wanted to leave then. Was keeping him with her holding him back, holding herself back? It didn't matter. She couldn't let go, didn't want to let go, not now, not yet, not ever. She needed him. To her, those precious encounters were worth the price of her hellish nightmares, if only to see him for a few seconds.

An extremely slow and intimidating whistle filled her ears. She recognised the tune as 'Thunder and Blazes,' the usually fast and chaotic music commonly played as an introduction to the clowns at a circus. The beast was taunting her again. The moon reflected off his familiar dark outline as he eased himself back and forth on the bench, his loathsome red, cracked shiny skin, his freakishly oversized black eyes glowering at her. Her body trembled as she waited for his next move.

'Come on, you slimy fucker!' she screamed. 'Come on!'

He didn't move, nonchalantly swaying and whistling, mocking her. Elaine made a move for the front door but stopped short when the whistling ended abruptly. Her eyes flicked to see the monster had gone. Ahead of her, the front door slammed shut. She tried the handle; it wouldn't open. Complete silence surrounded her: not even the usual noises of the nocturnal creatures echoed.

A deliberate, continuous scratching noise emanating from beneath the wooden floorboards broke the eerie silence, starting from the end of the porch behind the swing bench and drawing nearer. Elaine reversed, distancing herself from the hideous scraping sound until her back pressed up against the rail.

Long fingernails emerged between the gaps of the boards. Elaine's eyes followed the fiend's sharp curved nails as they raced towards her feet, the scratching noise amplified by the second. She closed her eyes and let out a scream, anticipating the razor-like claws about to slice through her bare feet.

Her terrified eyes opened and she looked down. The claws had stopped a hair's breadth from her toes. Elaine watched as they retracted unexpectedly beneath the floor. Out of the corner of her eye, she saw the front door creak open and made a dash for it. With that first step, she bawled out in anguish as the beast's nails, *thrust* through the floorboard and the middle of her foot, ripping through flesh and bone. Ignoring the excruciating pain, she moved her other foot forward. Punctured as soon as it hit the floor, she grimaced in horror at her wrecked feet. Elaine prised her right foot from the nail, letting out an enormous scream in the process. Blood welled from the open wound and saturated the boards below. She moved her damaged foot forward and placed it down quietly, hoping to evade a further onslaught. No such luck, the beast struck again.

Ever weakening but determined to make it inside, Elaine yelled in horror as she ripped both of her feet free, listening to the atrocious sound of her tearing flesh. She sank to the floor, resting on her hands. Claws pierced the softness of her palms with ease. A shriek of agony burst from her lungs, tears free-falling as the red drops splattered upwards, slapping against her face before raining onto the floor. Vomit spewed from her mouth and mingled with the red stickiness of the floor.

She watched and yelled aloud as the monster's claws slowly withdrew, her strength fading fast. With supreme effort, Elaine crawled and hauled her ravaged body. So close to the door, she could go no further, too weak from her brutal injuries. She'd scarcely any fight left in her as she fought to remain conscious. A sanguineous trail portrayed her traumatic journey across the porch floor.

No sound passed her lips as Elaine rolled onto her back. Despite everything, her eyes remained focused on the open doorway. She arched her back and shuddered as a pointed claw ruptured the skin at the front of her neck. Blood gushed from her mouth and throat. Her body broken, she summoned the fortitude to go on, raised her legs, and attempted to slide herself backwards. Two large hands burst through the floor either side of her, thwarting her. The beast's curled talons plunged down, slicing and tearing into her stomach.

26

Saturday, 12 August

Clutching her chest as though awakened from near death, Elaine gulped in an immense intake of air. This went beyond anything she'd experienced previously. She checked her hands and feet; the residual pain imaginary, she knew it wasn't real. Slumped on the sofa, she inhaled deeply and exhaled slowly until she calmed down and her heart rate recovered. Did this show the extent of just how damaged she was?

The Breakfast Show on BBC1 television was on; the clock on the screen read 06.42. She laid her clammy head back and closed her eyes, overflowing with relief. Her eyes fluttered open and she looked back at the clock on the TV, transfixed by the numbers.

'Zero six four two,' she murmured. Charlie's warning. Why were those numbers important and what meaning did they have?

'What was he pointing at?'

Elaine sprung up from the sofa and headed outside. She went straight to the bench and positioned herself where Charlie had been sitting in her nightmare. She focused on the dream and the area of the porch he'd pointed at and walked over. Moving closer, one of the floorboards bore the numbers 0642. Emily must have painted them, but why, why would she paint those particular numbers?

All through her early breakfast of rubbery scrambled eggs on burnt toast, Elaine tried to make sense of the numbers— 'Oh crap!' Robert dropping by had escaped her mind again, a shorter visit than usual, which suited her. She was excited about going to Lila's barbecue later that day. First, she had a salon appointment in town and wanted to pick up a couple of bottles of Prosecco for later and it would be nice to buy something new to wear.

As she arrived in town, she saw for the first time how busy it had become since the story broke about the missing constable. Elaine would've preferred not to have come here. She had hoped the drama might have died down to some extent because they hadn't found a single clue to his whereabouts. She couldn't have been more wrong; there were still plenty of news vans and police cars around. Maybe people were there out of curiosity; everybody loves a mystery. The summer holidays made it difficult to distinguish between those here about the policeman and the regular influx of visitors flocking to the medieval town. She was grateful she lived on the outskirts, under the radar of reporters asking questions, potentially dragging up her past. Out of sight, out of mind was the perfect philosophy.

Her first stop was the salon to get her hair washed, trimmed, and blow-dried. Then she shopped for a new dress and found one she liked at Pennita, a fabulous boutique in Castlegate. With only groceries left to buy, Elaine knew she'd better get a move on to greet Robert.

At the counter, Elaine paid the lady and picked up her two bags of shopping, ready to leave. Upon hearing a deep voice ask for a pack of twenty Silk Cut King Size, she glanced sideways to the next counter and saw a scruffy older man with a thick mop of dirty grey hair staring back at her, a curious expression on his face. He failed to hear the checkout lady calling him. As the person behind the man politely drew his attention to the assistant, Elaine turned and made a swift exit. She walked across Bridge Street to Market Place car park.

She reached her car and heard a gruff cockney accent call out behind her, 'Mrs Elaine Davis?' For a split second she froze. The man from the shop. He shouted her name again but she ignored him, placing her shopping in the boot.

There was only one person who said her name in that awful way. She'd hoped he hadn't recognised her in the shop. She detested his voice and wasn't at all happy to hear it again. Elaine didn't want to acknowledge the man who would take her back to a dark place. She kept up the pretence, paid him no attention and closed the boot of the car.

'Mrs Davis?' he called again.

Elaine purposely blanked him, pretending not to know the name. As she opened her car door, he was within arm's reach.

'Excuse me, miss,' he said, finally getting her attention.

She faced the slovenly man in his long, crinkled black leather jacket and crumpled trousers.

'Hello, can I help you?' she smiled, keeping up the charade.

The man scrutinised her as if thrown by her veil of self-assurance.

'Mrs Elaine Davis?' he said, his mind depositing uncertainty into the words creeping from the back of his throat.

'I'm sorry, no. You must have me mixed up with somebody else,' Elaine answered with a persuasive smile.

'In that case, I'm sorry to have troubled you. You reminded me of someone I used to know,' he said, backing away with his hands up in an apologetic fashion.

'No problem,' she said.

Elaine got into her car, concealing her drawn-out sigh of relief, trying so hard to keep it together before driving off. She hoped she'd convinced him but couldn't be sure. It had been five years, she'd aged a little and her hair was different. A fifty-fifty chance. Elaine remembered him, though. Lenny Grey was not an easy man to forget.

Probably in his mid-fifties, he hadn't changed much from the suited journalist she recalled. Apart from the fact he no longer looked as presentable as he once did, it was obvious the last five years hadn't been too kind to him. Good! Why should she care? He'd got what he bloody well deserved. Now here he was. She should have guessed he'd show up. He loved nothing more than exposing lies and conspiracies, sometimes to his own detriment. A missing policeman story was right up his street. All she could do was hope their paths didn't cross again.

She would never forget or forgive how ruthless he'd been when he hounded Robert and her, convinced they were behind the death of their son. In court, Lenny admitted to harassing the family and accepted an injunction preventing him from going anywhere near them for twelve months. Elaine went on to renew it for the subsequent two years; she wished she'd kept on renewing it. She'd hoped never to see him again. Was that too much to ask?

Elaine revelled in the fact Lenny was going through a rough time. He should have thought about the repercussions of pestering the grieving family of a murdered child. After his court appearance, she learned he'd been blacklisted by many of the newspapers that used to buy his tawdry stories. They'd distanced themselves, with one paper writing a column about him being the most unethical journalist they'd ever had on their books. The fact he was here told her someone was still willing to pay for his lies.

Robert was sitting with Emily under the shade of the porch when she arrived home. Excited, Emily ran over to her mother. Elaine wasn't over the moon about seeing Robert after what she'd heard but there wasn't much she could do about that. Preoccupied as she was by a certain reporter, telling Robert that Lenny Grey was in town was out of the question. He'd go straight into town to find him, which would bring Lenny to her doorstep. It was better to pretend everything was well. She greeted him with a spurious smile.

Michael wasn't around today, having joined a local football team and playing in a five-a-side tournament. Robert enquired about the number 0642 he'd seen painted on the floor. Elaine fobbed it off as a paint colour serial number she'd thought about using. Robert expressed how well she'd done out front. Patronising prick! Why wouldn't she have made an excellent job of it? She was probably better than he was at decorating anyway.

After a cup of tea and a bite to eat inside, Emily announced she wanted to go and feed the ducks again. The three of them strolled out to the pond together. Elaine explained to Emily about the receding water level; that if it dried out because of the hot weather and lack of rain, the ducks would have to find a new home. Emily was sad for the ducks as they tossed in more defrosted peas. Robert passed the bag to Emily but it fell from her grasp. His gold watch slipped from his pocket and into the long grass as he bent over to pick up the bag.

Emily ran ahead as they wandered back to the house, chatting about Michael, his football, and various other things. The usual silence fell between them and Robert decided this was the perfect time to break some news to her.

'El – Chloé and I,' he hesitated, 'we're thinking of having a baby next year.'

Elaine was nonplussed and deep in thought. 'I see, and this is something you felt the need to tell me because?'

'I just thought you should find out from me first.'

'Why, Robert? I don't understand.'

'I didn't want you to be upset or anything.'

Elaine frowned. 'No, I mean I don't understand why you think I'd give a shit. Do you need my permission or something? You can have as many kids as you bloody well please.'

A short, unpleasant pause ensued before she said, 'I bet you won't lose her child.' As soon as the words came out, she wished she could take them back. The truth about how Robert came to lose their son had left a rage simmering inside of her, information she didn't want to divulge, not yet anyway.

'That's not fair, Elaine,' he said, turning his head to her.

'You're right. I'm sorry for saying that,' she said.

'I'm sorry too. I didn't mean to—'

'Mean to what, Robert, upset me? We were over so long ago and the fact you even have the nerve to think I'd be upset about it, shows what an arrogant arsehole you still are,' Elaine struck back harshly.

Few words were exchanged between them until Robert left a little over thirty minutes later.

27

Saturday, 12 August

Stepping out of the taxi at Lila's, the fabulous aroma of meat already sizzling on the barbecue whetted Elaine's appetite. She'd made an extra effort with her appearance: her hair looked terrific and the new long-sleeved summer dress showed off her shapely figure and legs. Mid-heeled wedges completed her chic look. Music blared from the garden at the back in competition with raucous laughter and raised voices.

Lila's house was an attractive end-of-terrace. Her mother had left it to her when she passed away from cancer six years ago. Elaine went through the side gate with a haphazardly taped A4 sheet of paper reading 'BBQ This Way.' Topless men wearing shorts confronted her, their shirts discarded no doubt almost as soon as they'd arrived. Vest tops, shorts, or skirts seemed to be the order of the day for the ladies.

It was a beautiful day for a barbecue and there was a good-sized crowd, about twenty people or so. Another gathering in the company of mostly strangers that not so long ago would have been avoided. Of late, though, her self-confidence had increased. She'd made a determined effort to break down the barriers that had previously restrained her. Lila saw her from the kitchen window and rushed out to greet her. After showing Elaine where the kitchen was and putting the bottles of Prosecco in the fridge, Lila poured her a large glass from an already opened bottle. Elaine gratefully took a sip. Lila then gave her the grand tour of the house and introduced her to some of the other guests, including her eldest son Jack, who was on his way out the front door to visit his girlfriend. Nicole and Georgia, she already knew, which helped put her more at ease.

After a quick chat with the ladies, Elaine strolled over to fetch a burger from where Ashton and Steve stood over the smoking charcoal, cans of Stella Artois in hand. They said their hellos and straightaway Ashton leered at her cleavage with a big grin on his face. He was so blatant about it. She'd disliked him from the first second she'd laid eyes on him. After finding out how he treated Lila, she had even less time for him. Elaine wanted to shove his face into the hot coals.

She allowed her imagination to run with it and, oh it felt so good, so right. Her hand holding his head in place, his face burning as she made him promise never to hurt Lila again.

Steve calling her name as he held out a burger brought her out of her delightful daydream. The fantasy was fun while it lasted, but it was time to continue the façade of being the perfect guest. A never-ending supply of cold cans and bottles from a big barrel filled with ice and water fuelled the fun. A nice touch. People danced, fooled around and played silly drinking games, which Elaine was happy to watch, but not quite ready to participate in. She surprised herself by finding the experience enjoyable. She'd been to the odd barbecue before; however, they were usually a little more formal, where lobsters and scallops replaced sausages and burgers, with cocktails and wine being the main drinks.

As the evening set in and some guests began to leave, Elaine approached Lila coming out of the kitchen door where Ashton lingered with Steve and another friend.

'Lila, you wouldn't happen to have some after-sun I could use? I did put sunblock on earlier but I'm starting to feel burnt.'

'Yes, of course. It's in the cabinet above the sink in the upstairs bathroom you saw earlier.'

After closing the door, Elaine noticed that unlike the downstairs bathroom, this one had no lock. She opened the mirrored cabinet and found it straight away.

Bottle in hand, about to apply the soothing lotion to her legs, she was startled by Ashton's appearance in the doorway.

'I see you've found it?' he said.

'Yes.' It wasn't worth wondering why he was there; she had a good idea why.

Normally, her stress levels would have blown the roof off as he entered the bathroom, shutting the door behind him. She didn't know how or why, but her nerves stayed steady. The Elaine from a week or so ago would have left the bathroom in a blind panic. She'd heard the stories about Ashton and how nasty he could be, and seen the bruises to prove it.

'What do you want, Ashton?' she asked, acting with a dash more confidence than she actually had.

She'd had a fair bit to drink but remained aware of her vulnerable position, seated on the edge of the bath ready to rub the after-sun over her legs.

'I thought I'd give you a hand,' he suggested, impudently taking the lotion from her hand before kneeling in front of her with a lecherous grin.

Elaine cringed as he rubbed the lotion onto her shin and calf with a lewd glint in his eyes. As much as she tried to hide it, she wasn't at all comfortable with the situation. She couldn't believe what an arrogant pig he was. He moved on to her other leg, roughly caressing the cream into her skin.

'Okay, that's all I needed,' she said, to put an end to it and to hide her mounting uneasiness.

'No, don't be silly,' he asserted. 'Best to do the top of your legs as well.'

He squirted more lotion onto his hand and rubbed it into her upper left thigh, meticulous as he worked his big rough fingers into her skin, his unrushed hand sliding higher and higher under her dress. She struggled not to slap away this loathsome man's hands touching her body. She hoped he would be happy now and leave before things went too far. He removed his hand and squirted more lotion onto it and massaged it into her other thigh. His hand moved under her dress, much further than needed, his fingers touching the outside of her knickers before he rested them against her crotch. Elaine flinched and caught him glancing into her eyes, trying to gauge her reaction.

Ashton's excitement greater, heavy breaths escaped his open mouth, smelling of beer and char-grilled meat, mingling with the repulsive body odour of stagnant sweat on his skin. Elaine remained utterly still, did nothing to stop him, even though no more than a few moments ago she was repulsed by this man and his inappropriate behaviour. What had changed? Was she now willing to accept his advances – even enjoy them?

Elaine looked him in the eye and smiled. Calm and unhurried, her face close to his, holding his gaze, she reached down, took his hand, and eased it from under her dress. She rose to her feet and reached for his other hand, lightly brushing her breasts against the side of his face. Elaine pulled him to his feet and rotated him until his back was to the bath, not once dropping eye contact. She placed his hands by his sides and squatted down in front of him, easing his shorts and pants past his knees. Rising back up, she encouraged him to sit on the edge of the bath. His pupils dilated and he let out a heavy, expectant sigh as Elaine moved her right hand down to stroke his inner thigh.

'I knew you were a dirty bitch,' he muttered.

Elaine responded with a sultry grin. With her left hand, she caressed the side of his face and rubbed her finger over his lips. In one swift move, she placed the palm of her left hand over his mouth while her right grabbed and squeezed his testicles, hard. She forced him back, into the empty bath, his head smacking against the wall tiles, her hand preventing him from yelling out. She had him right where she wanted him: paralysed as her vice-like grip tightened on his throbbing scrotum.

An unexpected turn of events for both Ashton and Elaine. Her angry and evil glare incited an irrational fear within him, a look of disquiet evident on his face. Nobody had ever put a literal squeeze on him like this, and there was nothing – nothing – he could do about it. Elaine's manner unyielding, if he budged a tiny fraction, she viciously strengthened her grip. She moved her face close to Ashton's, gripping tighter still, delighted to see tears form in his eyes.

'Now you listen to me, you bastard,' she hissed with disconcerting quietness, furiously spitting as she spoke, a woman possessed. 'You will never, *ever*, fucking touch me again. Do you understand?' There was no reaction from him. 'I said, do you understand?' She squeezed tighter.

Ashton nodded energetically in agreement as she continued to restrain him in the bath with her hand over his mouth, his neck forced against the curve and his legs dangling over the edge.

'*If*, under any circumstances, you hurt Lila again,' her grip ever compressing, 'I will rip this sack of tiny balls from you and push them one after the other into your *fucking* sleazy mouth.' She pulled hard on his scrotum, his testicles clenched in her hand. He was lucky she hadn't ripped them off there and then.

Elaine first removed her hand from his mouth, her eyes locked on his. Next, she released her grip on his testicles. He rushed his hands to shelter his boys and ease his discomfort and embarrassment.

'Stay!' she demanded, like an order to a dog.

Ashton slid down into the tub to rest on his side. Elaine, so in control and relaxed, washed her hands as if nothing was out of the ordinary for her.

'Bet you weren't expecting that, were you?' she said, staring at his mirror image in the cabinet door. She clutched the towel and turned to him, drying her hands with meticulous care.

Ashton winced with pain, shocked by his predicament.

'You crazy bitch,' he muttered, his voice betraying his torment, much to her delight.

Elaine tidied her hair in the mirror before glancing over at him, still crippled and cowering in the tub. She made a rapid fake lunge towards him; he flinched like a nervous dog.

'Thanks for applying the sun lotion,' she sneered, before casually walking out the door and closing it behind her.

It wasn't long ago she'd fantasised about hurting Ashton, and now it had become a reality. Did she feel good about it? Damn right she did.

She filled a glass with Prosecco from the fridge and joined Lila in the garden, thanking her for the use of the upstairs bathroom and the lotion. A good twenty minutes or so later, Ashton re-joined the barbecue, slightly worse for wear. For the rest of the evening, he was a grumpy ass and made sure to avoid any eye contact with Elaine. About ten o'clock, she called a taxi and went home.

In the back of the cab, she was both surprised and pleased with her actions. Where had all that aggression come from? It felt like it had been building up inside her for a long time. She wasn't knocking it. It had made her feel more assured, stronger, and she hoped Lila would reap the benefits of her actions.

28

Sunday, 13 August

'What do want, Robert?' Elaine asked, not expecting his call in the early afternoon.

'I don't suppose you've seen my seen my pocket watch?'

'No, I haven't.'

'I'm pretty certain I lost it when I was there yesterday. Would you mind having a look for it?'

'Of course, I will, Robert. I know how much it means to you.'

'Thanks, El, I really appreciate it. Let me know if you find it, I'll pick it up next time I'm over,' he said.

'Okay, no problem. I'll go and look for it right now,' she said, and hung up. *As if*! 'Come over and find it yourself, you prick.' She wasn't going out of her way to find his blasted watch. Why would she?

A knock at the door came as no surprise; of late there was always someone or other showing up. She was surprised, however, to see PC Roy Kell standing in front of her when she opened the door.

'Hello again, Mrs Davis,' he smiled, removing his cap to greet her. 'The porch is looking good, it's amazing what a bit of paint can do,' he said, admiring her work.

'That's what everybody says – but it is true.'

Elaine considered why Roy was there. Perhaps he wondered why she hadn't called him. She hoped not. 'I'm sorry I haven't called you yet, it's just, what with everything going—'

'Yet?' he interrupted, smiling. Responding to Elaine's bewildered look, he continued, 'You said yet, which indicates you were going to.'

Roy looked pleased with her accidental disclosure. 'You'll be a detective in no time, picking up on things like that,' she joked. 'What brings you out here? I thought the police were done with searching my place,' she said.

'I happened to be in the area and thought I'd, well – here I am,' he smiled. 'I hope I'm not intruding.'

Quietly pleased, Elaine said, 'No, of course, it's fine. Would you like to come in for some tea? I was about to make myself a cup.'

'Sure, that would be great.'

Roy followed her along the hall to the kitchen, where they made small talk before Elaine made an excuse to go and tidy herself up.

Hands hugging the warm cup, Roy glanced around, spotted Elaine's phone on the worktop and went over to it. The screen lit up with a picture of two children, which he guessed to be hers. He scrolled to the picture gallery and deftly fingered his way to the photographs Elaine had taken at the steam rally, grinning to himself as he browsed through them.

When she re-entered the kitchen, Roy was sipping his tea at the table. She invited him to sit outside with her so they could enjoy the splendid weather. Although attracted to Roy, she didn't feel entirely at ease in his company. She couldn't work out why.

'What was it like growing up here?' Roy asked.

'I wish I could remember,' she answered.

'How come you don't?'

Elaine wasn't a fan of questions; that's what her psychiatrist was for, but truth be told, it wasn't a question she could answer with full confidence.

'I recall parts of my childhood, just not as much as I'd like to. What about you, I know you said you grew up here, but whereabouts?' She wanted to get away from talking about herself and find out more about him.

'Actually, not too far away at all,' he replied, short and sweet.

'That's not giving much away.'

'I don't like to give too much away,' he smiled.

'Ah, a man of mystery, eh!' she laughed.

'Something like that.'

'Not every woman likes a mystery, especially ones that are hard to solve.'

'Do you think I'll be hard to solve?'

'Time will tell, Mr Kell. It always does, in the end.'

The small talk trickled on, with more laughs as they got to know each other.

'I lied before,' he said.

'About what?'

'I pretended not to remember seeing you that night in the pub.'

Elaine grinned and shoved his shoulder. 'I knew you must have recognised me when you came here. Why didn't you say?'

'I didn't want to look like a desperate fool,' he laughed.

'And you don't now?'

Smiles faded as their eyes asked questions. A composed Roy leaned in, his lips closing on hers. She'd thought about this moment from the first time she'd laid eyes on him. She let her lips move towards his until they fused together. Roy placed his arms around her as their lips parted, tongues playful. Something felt distinctly wrong. Elaine wasn't comfortable; it just didn't feel right. She pulled back, breaking their kiss. She rose to her feet and stepped away from him to conceal her awkwardness. Elaine gathered herself and turned to Roy, forcing a weak smile to offer some reassurance.

'I'm sorry, Roy, I should be getting on. I have so much work to do,' she said, making her excuse.

'Is everything all right?' he asked.

'Yes, it's just, it's been a while for me, that's all.' She tried not to meet his gaze.

'Okay,' he said. 'There's no rush. I should be getting off anyway or they'll have a search party out for me as well,' he joked.

She followed a little way behind him to the steps. 'I'll call you soon,' she said.

'I look forward to it,' replied Roy, leaning in to kiss her again. She offered her cheek.

As he headed off down the drive, Elaine waited until she could no longer see him, dropped her sham smile and dashed for the downstairs cloakroom. She only just made it to the pan as the contents of her stomach emptied. It wasn't anxiety – she knew that feeling all too well. This was different.

*

By the time late evening came, she was in much better shape as she mulled over her encounter with Roy earlier in the day. Possibly her sickness had nothing to do with him: maybe the heat, or even something she'd eaten. Nevertheless, uneasiness cloaked her about the whole situation and whether to pursue her interest in him. She'd been hoping for fireworks – there were none! No matter how much she wanted their first kiss to be unique, it wasn't; it had entirely failed her expectations. Rather than the sensual effect she'd hoped for, she'd found it ineffective, but also – unsettling, and she didn't understand why. She certainly couldn't elicit something that just wasn't there. Elaine looked up to see Margaret seated in the armchair across from her.

'You know, don't you, dear?' her mother said, telling rather than asking.

'What do I know?'

'You know!' Margaret repeated in a cryptic tone.

'No – I don't, I don't know anything or what you're even talking about,' she argued.

'Yes, you do, child.'

Frustrated with Margaret, Elaine rose from the sofa. 'Do you know what, Mother? Sometimes you don't half get on my bloody nerves. I'm going for a bath,' she fumed and left the room.

Small tea light candles flickered around her as she relaxed in a bath full of bubbles. Her eyes opened when she heard a knock at the front door. An irritated sigh crossed her lips, giving voice to her annoyance. It was late, so she ignored it and hoped whoever it was would disappear. She wasn't in any mood for visitors. At a second, louder knock she stood and reached for the towel, wrapping it around her body as she stepped out of the bath. Another knock came as she headed down the stairs.

'All right, I'm coming. Hold your horses.' A combination of not thinking straight and anger led her to open the door without questioning who it was. 'You better have a good reason—'

29

Sunday, 13 August

Dazed and disoriented, Elaine stirred. She lay on her back by the wide-open front door. Instinctively, she raised a hand to her aching face and nose. A fusion of wet and dried blood covered her fingers when she pulled her hand away. Elaine lifted her head, alarmed to see the white towel stained with dark red. Disconcerted and out of sorts, she rolled to her right and attempted to stand. Her heart skipped a beat.

A masked man lay a couple of feet from her, a knife buried in the side of his neck. Blood enveloped the top half of his body and covered the hallway rug. Elaine raised a hand to her mouth, aghast as she stared into his open, dead eyes. She clambered to her feet and wiped her hair away from her face, which was stuck to a now drying red crust. What had happened? She was in the bath. There was a knock at the front door, she went to open it and now this grim sight confronted her.

She surveyed the appalling scene in front of her. Had she done this? Was she capable of such a thing? The man's belt and the button on his jeans were unfastened. A sign of his intentions? His eyes stared at her. Her nerves rattled, she reached down and removed his balaclava.

Ashton.

'Well, this doesn't look great, does it, my girl?' Elaine glanced over her shoulder to see her mother standing at the foot of the stairs. Hysterical, it took a slap from her mother to calm her down and convince her of what to do next.

Rushing along the hall to the cloakroom, Elaine looked in the mirror. Various shades of red covered her hair, face, and chest. She turned on the taps to wash, her hands moving ferociously to scrub the stains from her body. Splashes of red contrasted with the white porcelain sink and ceramic tiles above.

Cleansed, her skin revealed a contusion, already turning blue and purple, and a nose bleed. Ashton must have hit her in the face. She reached up to touch it and frowned at the pain. No doubt there would be more bruising to follow. After assessing her injuries, most of the blood on her must have been Ashton's.

His body lay in the hallway of her home. Elaine hoped it was a nightmare or hallucination. She couldn't deny her perception of certain things was, at times, erratic. Any vague hopes of this being a dream were scuppered as soon as she re-entered the hallway. There he was. This was not a mere twist of her mind. This was bad – this was real.

She approached the body, still in disbelief. Ashton must have attacked her and she'd defended herself. But if he'd knocked her out, how did she get the knife from the block in the kitchen? How did it end up in his neck? It was hard to make sense of anything; it must have been self-defence. She went to her phone in the living room and the first thing she noted as the screen lit up was the time: 11.57 p.m. It was at least two hours since she'd answered the door. She tapped 999 into her phone and stopped her finger short of pressing Call. Elaine marched into the hallway, her brain in overdrive.

A finger hesitated over the Call icon, her thoughts churning as if they were in a cement mixer. She glowered at Ashton's corpse with contempt. It was doubtful he would've told anyone he was coming here, especially if he'd planned some vicious revenge attack. Calling the police would undoubtedly bring a new level of hell down upon her. It had been hard enough with the constable going missing. It would also bring a magnitude of reporters to her doorstep, including Lenny Grey. She couldn't go through all that again, opening up all those old wounds, it would finish her.

Margaret had suggested she knew what to do, and Margaret was right: Ashton had to disappear. Elaine knew that two men going missing in the same small town within a week of each other was madness, but what choice did she have? Who'd miss this piece of shit anyway? Not Lila, not in the long term anyhow. It occurred to her it would categorically put an end to their friendship if it came out, even if she had been defending herself. How would she begin to explain why he was alone at her house in the first place? Lila would suspect they'd been sleeping together and so would the police. They'd all think she'd killed him. She'd begun to settle here, make a go of things. It wasn't supposed to be like this. She needed a friend, she needed Lila, but sadly, that wasn't an option – not right now.

In all honesty, Elaine reached a decision the second her mother slapped her across the face. It just took one part of her mind longer to catch up and convince the other part. She put her phone on the side, moved Ashton's feet, slammed the front door shut, and scurried upstairs to change into some old clothes. When she came back down, she put on a pair of yellow marigold gloves and got to work. She lifted Ashton's legs and shifted them to the middle of the rug, repeating the process with his arms until his body was centred. On her knees, she gripped the handle of the knife and eased it back and forth, not batting an eyelid at hearing the squelching sound it made as she removed it from his neck. She took it to the kitchen and dropped it in the sink.

Returning to Ashton, she lifted the remainder of the rug and folded it over him, grateful for the non-slip sheeting underneath, which helped prevent blood from soaking onto the floorboards. Elaine fetched a Stanley knife from a toolbox under the stairs, slipped the blade in the back pocket of her jeans and opened the front door. Grabbing the corners of the rug and the sheet underneath, she hauled him outside. Only a small red puddle remained on the floor. Elaine dragged the rug across the porch to the steps and down, his body thumping as it whacked every step. Not an easy task to drag a dead weight, but seclusion and time, she had plenty of.

Elaine peered over at her car. If only it were possible to get him in the boot; unfortunately, Ashton was a tall and well-built man and there was no way she'd be able to lift him.

'Come on girl, think,' Elaine said, taking another glance at the car, homing in on the tow bar at the rear.

She went to the shed and came back with a length of rope. She lifted the end of the rug and wound the rope twice around his legs, tying a knot. She ran back inside the house to fetch her car keys and a roll of black refuse bags.

Elaine reversed the car towards the body and got out to tie the rope to the tow bar. With the headlights switched on, she drove forward, nice and slow, successfully dragging the rug. So far, so good. She went past the shed and over to the boundary fence where the old track was, which led to the back of her property. It was fenced off now, but at least she'd get the body up to the line of trees. When she'd driven as far as she could, the headlights illuminated a slanted, four-foot-high wooden fence that blocked the way to the next farm. She popped open the boot and got out of the car with the black bags.

Removing the rope, she put it in one of the bags. Elaine heaved the rug across the dry dirt and grass to beyond the line of trees. After a few more stops to take a breather and regain her strength, she reached the pond. The water glistened, reflecting the glimmer of the moon in the clear sky. She plonked the body at the sloping edge of the pond and uncovered him. She eyed Ashton and hesitated.

'My God, woman, what are you doing? This is crazy,' she said, pacing up and down, agonising about how she came to be in this predicament. 'All you wanted was to start over.'

She searched around, collecting big stones from the ground and putting them into Ashton's front pockets. She unzipped his fly and frowned at him as she stuffed more stones inside his trousers. The ringing of a mobile phone sounded out from somewhere on his body.

When she retrieved it from his back pocket, guilt consumed her. It was Lila.

'It's all your fault, you tosspot,' she cursed and scowled at Ashton. 'You just couldn't keep your filthy fucking hands to yourself. Could you!' Elaine kicked him in the side. Ashton's body rolled off the rug and down the slope into the pond.

Open-mouthed, Elaine watched as he floated a little way out before sinking below the water, bubbles trailing to the surface. His phone rang again. Lila was obviously concerned. Infuriated by what he'd driven her to, she hurled the phone out into the pond.

As she dragged the rug back to the car, she heard a rustling in the long grass and stopped, listening, waiting. A fox? At least that's what she hoped. After a minute, she carried on pulling the rug behind her, failing to see Robert's pocket watch, glinting in the moonlight beneath her feet. At the car, she put the non-slip sheeting in a bag and used the Stanley knife to cut the rug into small pieces. With three black bags full of evidence in the boot, she drove back to the house to finish cleaning up.

First, she washed the knife and scrubbed it with bleach before returning it to the block. She cleaned and scrubbed the floor in the hall and attended to some stains smeared on the porch. After that, she wiped down the cloakroom and put the bloodstained towel, the remnants of the non-slip sheeting, and the dirty cloths she'd used into a bag. She fetched the other bags from the boot and carried all four over to the shed, dropping them on the floor outside. Elaine disappeared inside and re-emerged, dragging a galvanised metal incinerator behind her. She dropped pieces of the cut carpet into the burner and poured in a tiny amount of petrol from an old red metal can. She struck a match and tossed it in. Elaine stood back, cloaked in a golden radiance of shining light in the blackness that encompassed her, her mind and body on autopilot while she wandered around inside her head.

Elaine appeared almost self-congratulatory on how she'd managed to clear everything up in such a calm and quick manner. She loaded more and more pieces of carpet into the flaming bin, followed by the sheeting, the bloody towel, the rope, and the dirty cloths. Elaine gazed into the hypnotic flames before removing her clothes and throwing them into the fire, along with the black bags. She took off her bra and knickers and threw them in, leaving nothing to chance. Lastly, she peeled the marigolds and deposited them triumphantly into the flames. She placed the lid on the top to leave the evidence to incinerate overnight. Naked, she walked unperturbed back to the house.

30

Monday, 14 August

Elaine had managed a little sleep, about forty minutes in all. Awake, she fretted about the madness of the previous few hours, trying to justify her actions. He was a violent man who'd attacked her; did that excuse her for sticking a knife in his neck? Perhaps, but dumping his body in an abandoned pond and burning all the evidence? Probably not. It was too late now. It was her only choice. That she couldn't remember killing him, worried her more. How could she blank out such an ordeal?

Lying in bed thinking about everything wasn't going to get her anywhere, so she got up. In the upstairs bathroom, the mirror revealed the nasty bruise on her face; if, at all possible, it would be best to keep away from everybody. Downstairs, Elaine paused for a second or two, the image of Ashton's lifeless body imprinted in her memory. She was quick to disregard it and carry on to the kitchen to make some tea and toast.

Not quite your typical Monday morning, but she couldn't treat this week differently from any other. She had to act as though nothing out of the ordinary had happened. Everything must continue as planned, apart from going to see her psychiatrist.

Having someone digging about inside her head right now was the last thing she needed. Too much had gone on and there was too much work to be done. Elaine called and left a message cancelling her appointment. She'd chosen to make an early start painting the floorboards. Good job, seeing as there were a few spots of blood she'd missed. She blocked off the porch steps with thick, bright yellow tape and set to work. With the primer coat done, it was time for a tea break.

Margaret, Michael and Emily were all seated at the kitchen table. Elaine went straight over to the kettle, switched it on and prepared her cup of tea.

'Mummy, can I go and play on the swing?' asked Emily.

'Yes, but use the back door.'

'Okay,' said Emily.

'Why the back door?' asked Michael.

'Because the front door is out of bounds today. I'm painting the porch floor,' said Elaine, her back to them, tired and confused.

'Yes, your mother is going to be very busy today, so best not disturb her,' said Margaret.

She poured the hot water into her cup, strained the teabag and turned around to an empty room. Thankful to be left in peace.

The parcel arrived nice and early at his office by courier. Dr Brown had anticipated its arrival all through the weekend. As soon as he was at his desk, he opened the large envelope and pulled out a manila folder containing the records of Mrs Elaine Davis.

Unable to mask his shock at what he read, he called Louise into his office and asked her to cancel his afternoon appointments.

Elaine cancelling her session had thrown a spanner in the works, which meant a trip to Helmsley was in order. It was essential to speak to her in person, as soon as he could.

Lenny Grey opened the door and entered his hotel room in town. He put a carrier bag on the table and pulled out a bottle of Teachers. He fetched a mug from the tray containing the kettle, a small assortment of tea bags, coffee sachets, and a couple of insufficient milk portions. Once he'd poured the whisky, he took a nice big swig and let out a contented sigh. His mobile phone rang and he reached into his jacket pocket: Ken Wainwright, one of his contacts from the police. He'd been waiting for this call. He sat on the edge of the bed and answered. Ken wasn't the only person he'd reached out to for information on Elaine Davis, but he was the first to get back to him. He also found out PC James's last known location – Sablefall Farm.

Lenny had been digging for information ever since bumping into the woman in town he believed to be Elaine. Now he had confirmation, an unmistakable delight filled his smug, fat, craggy face. Lenny thanked Ken and hung up. He went back to the table and poured out more whisky, gulping it down in one. Lenny left the mug, picked up the bottle of whiskey, and lay on the bed with his back against the headboard. After another swig, he sat the half-empty bottle on the bedside table next to the dog-end laden ashtray and reached for the packet of Silk Cut. He pulled out a cigarette and with his gold flip lighter, lit up. Lenny was on a different plain as he inhaled the tobacco fumes and held them in his mouth before finally freeing an abundance of smoke. For a few seconds, he may well have believed he was the happiest man alive, but when he clocked himself in the dressing table mirror opposite, he saw a sad bloke in his fifties with no purpose or direction. A man without means.

Elaine finished applying the undercoat to the floorboards and placed the tray and roller on the hallway floor. A gleam from underneath the console table caught her eye. She reached under to find a thin gold chain with a linked, oversized capital *A*. The shiny gold letter was stained with dried blood. What else had she overlooked? As she put the chain in her pocket, something else dawned on her. How did Ashton get to her house? He'd have used some mode of transport and his car wasn't on the drive. Elaine ran out of the back door and searched around for any sign of the blue Fiesta, but nothing. Did someone give him a lift? That would mean he wasn't alone. The other person might have seen her kill him and fled the scene. She paced around, desperate for an answer to magically pop into her head. It didn't. This could change everything.

Elaine's mobile rang. It was Lila, and she was a mess, crying and mumbling about Ashton not coming home the previous night. Even though Elaine was disinclined to show the bruising on her face, going to see Lila wouldn't be such a bad idea; it would give her the chance to find out if Ashton had driven to her house or not, and she did feel sorry for Lila.

*

When she arrived, Lila was effing and jeffing, ranting he'd slept at some tart's house. 'It wouldn't be the first time,' she said. Poor Lila was so distraught, she didn't even notice the bruising on her friend's face. Elaine had done her best to mask it with make-up, but it remained conspicuous. When Lila did eventually comment on it, Elaine told her she'd slipped on the tread of the ladder while decorating the porch ceiling and caught her face.

Stressed, Lila said she'd called his mobile umpteen times and that he'd either switched it off, or the battery had died. Elaine sat in the armchair and let her friend rattle on. All she could do was think about Ashton's car: there was no sign of the Fiesta outside or anywhere on the street. She did her best to keep her frustration hidden from Lila. *Shit*! Did they have two cars? If she wanted information, she needed to stay calm and ask the right questions.

'Could he be with Steve?'

'No, I tried Steve, he's at work. He hasn't seen him since the barbecue,' Lila explained, pacing up and down, fuming that she'd kill him when he came home.

Elaine knew he wasn't coming home, and while it hurt to deceive Lila, it was a relief to find out Steve hadn't been with him last night.

'Perhaps he stayed at another friend's house, hung-over or something?' said Elaine.

'What other friends? He doesn't really have any friends other than Steve. They're as thick as thieves those two. If he doesn't have a clue where Ashton is, you can bet he's shacked up with some whore.'

Elaine hoped Steve had no idea Ashton was going to her place last night. It was also pleasing to find out Ashton wasn't a popular man. Why would he be? He was a complete prick.

'I'm sure there's a reasonable explanation,' Elaine stated. 'Do you think he might have gone for a drive or something?'

'No chance, he wouldn't have got far in that piece of crap. The pig knew I needed to use the car this morning.'

As Lila spoke, Elaine noticed the letter *A* of Ashton's chain protruding through the stretched material of her jeans pocket. She casually concealed it with her hand.

'Take a seat and let me make you a cup of tea,' Elaine said and went off to the kitchen.

It was good to know Ashton had used the car last night, but the question on her mind was – where the bloody hell was it? She'd searched the area near her property on the way to Lila's; there was no sign of it. After a soothing cup of tea, Elaine gave her friend a lift to pick up her son from a sleepover party. She dropped them back home and promised to call her later.

On her way back to Sablefall farm, Elaine thought about Ashton. Since she'd met him, he'd done nothing but leer at her, touch her inappropriately, and to top it off, he'd smacked her in the face. Was that why it hadn't affected her in the way she would have thought? It wasn't so much to do with whether he deserved what he got; it was more to do with how she'd taken it all in her stride that concerned her. She took another look around the surrounding area to see if she could spot the car – no luck.

31

Monday, 14 August

Turning into her drive, Elaine was surprised to see an old, battered black Renault Laguna parked near the house. There didn't appear to be anyone seated in the car. After parking, she glanced through the windows to see it littered with takeaway cups, food cartons, and junk food waste on the back seat and floor. Her curiosity waned as it occurred to her exactly whose car it was.

Access to the front steps was still cordoned off, so she assumed her uninvited guest was waiting for her around the back. Elaine let out an embittered sigh as her teeth crunched together in anger. She opened the unlocked kitchen door and walked inside.

'Still breaking into people's property, I see,' Elaine said, barely taking a glance at the man seated at her kitchen table as she placed her keys and handbag on the worktop. 'What are you doing here, Lenny?' She had so much rancour for this man.

Lenny grinned. 'How you doing, Mrs Davis, or seeing as we've known each other so long, Elaine?'

How she hated Lenny's gravelly cockney accent and the way he said her name. She'd believed they would never meet again after she moved away from London. Even after their fleeting encounter in town, she'd hoped he hadn't recognised her, and yet, here he was. The smell of whiskey exuded from Lenny. No surprise there.

'I said, what do you want?' her voice echoed the intense emotions that had washed over her before she stepped into the kitchen.

'You almost had me fooled at the car park, bit older, different hair, and it's been a while, but it's rare I forget a face.'

'Oh, how lucky for me,' she replied, filling the kettle and switching it on before taking a seat opposite him.

'Don't be like that, Elaine. It may not be so unlucky for you that our paths have crossed again.'

'Our paths crossing has always been unlucky for me, Lenny. Why would it be any different now?'

It was difficult not to be a little curious about Lenny. Sometimes he would get straight to the point when he had something to say, and other times, he liked to play his silly little games.

'You'll see. You mind if I smoke?' He pulled a cigarette packet out from his jacket pocket.

'I'd rather you didn't but if you must,' she said, and fetched an old ashtray from a drawer, sliding it across the table.

'Indeed, I must. A filthy habit I've never been able to rid myself of, but I suppose to rid yourself of a bad habit, you have to at least try. I, unfortunately, to my own detriment, love it.'

He put a cigarette in his mouth and threw the packet on the table. He lit his cigarette with his gold flip lighter and savoured the first deep puff before releasing the smoke through his mouth and nostrils.

'First off, I want to apologise for my behaviour and some of the accusations I made. It doesn't happen often but I'll admit on that occasion, I was barking up the wrong tree. I see that now and I'm sorry.' Lenny took another puff on his cigarette.

'Oh, you see that now do you? You're sorry?' she said, her rage escalating. 'Well, it's too fucking late to be sorry!' She banged her fists on the table, stood up sharply, jerked the chair back, and paced the kitchen. 'You hurt my family, Lenny, deeply. Just fuck off and leave me in peace,' she stormed, pointing at the door.

'I wonder if that injunction is still against you, shall I call the police and find out?' she said, pulling her phone from her pocket.

'Good try but we both know it isn't. Anyway, don't get your knickers in a twist,' said Lenny.

'Get my knickers in a twist! Don't you dare fucking grin at me, you bastard!' Elaine ran at him, slapping him over the head repeatedly.

Lenny stood, holding his arms out to fend off the blows and backed away. As Elaine retreated, Lenny started to cough and stubbed out his cigarette in the ashtray.

He ran his hands through his greasy mop of hair to put it back in place.

'All right girl, you calm now?' he panted, with a slight smile on his face.

Elaine looked a fatigued and defeated woman. It was so hard for her to have Lenny here in her kitchen, he resurrected so many bad memories.

'Lenny, please go. If you truly are sorry, just leave me be,' she begged, taking a seat and burying her head in her hands.

Instead of doing as she asked, Lenny sat down. 'Look, I may well have been wrong about things back then, but you see, I get these instincts, especially when there are secrets people don't want getting out.'

Elaine eased her head up to gaze at Lenny.

'Thing is, I know what you've been hiding now. I also know this was the last place that copper called at before he disappeared. I think you get my drift.' Lenny glared straight at her in such a cocksure manner.

'I don't know what you're talking about, Lenny.' Elaine didn't want to think about how she disposed of Ashton's body in a confrontation with Lenny; he'd see right through her. But how did he know? Was it him in the long grass at the pond that night?

'I had a feeling you'd say that, so I'm gonna leave a deal on the table for a couple of days, after which, I'll come back and get your answer.'

He put both his arms on the table and leaned forward. 'I don't make much money anymore because the top papers won't touch me. Therefore, I'm stuck selling my stories to local rags for peanuts. Hence I'm still driving about in that old banger outside. Now, what I suggest is, you buy my complete and utter silence, and I promise you, the story I have will never see the light of day. Not by my hand at least. Of course, I can't guarantee someone else wouldn't find out, although I'd imagine it unlikely.' With a calm and cheeky expression, Lenny settled back into the chair. 'So, what do you reckon?'

Elaine was staggered by his offer to stay silent. It wasn't like Lenny at all. She wondered how much this old has-been would want.

'Let's say I do have something to hide, and I'm not saying I do, mind. How much would we be talking about?'

Lenny let out a broad grin from across the table – he liked where she was going with this. 'Ten bags of sand.'

'Speak English, Lenny. I'm not up on all your cockney bollocks.'

'Ten grand.'

'Ten thousand pounds?' Elaine's repeat sounded like a question.

Lenny grabbed his cigarettes, put them back in his pocket and got to his feet, sliding the chair underneath the table. 'I got debts, what can I say.'

'If you do have something over me, why would you keep it quiet?'

'Because I've had enough. I'm too old and I'm tired of all this shit. Plus, I reckon I owe you from before. Anyway, as I said, you have a think about it and I'll see you in a couple of days.' He walked past her and out of the kitchen door, closing it behind him.

It must have been him that night, rustling about in the long grass, observing her dispose of Ashton's body. What she couldn't get her head around was why he only wanted ten grand to keep a murder quiet; she would have paid a hell of a lot more. Was he going soft or did he honestly have some form of regret for causing her family so much hassle five years ago? For the next few minutes, she considered Lenny's proposal. If she paid the ten grand, would it be enough to buy his silence? Knowing Lenny, probably not. He'd come crawling back for more at some point. The shrill ring and harsh vibration of her phone interrupted her train of thought. Not having heard from her husband, Lila had alerted the police. Being the dutiful friend, Elaine drove over to spend some time with her.

Lila was pretty hysterical, more so than earlier in the day, as would be expected. She had no idea why he hadn't come home yet. This wasn't normal behaviour, even for Ashton. When he'd cheated in the past, he'd usually come back with his tail between his legs by now. If he'd gone off to do one of his dodgy deals, often involving stolen electrical goods, he would have called. Elaine kept the tea flowing and tried to console her, which wasn't easy with guilt traversing through her veins. But her guilt wasn't for Ashton; no, she'd been surprised to discover how unremorseful she felt about killing the wife-beating bastard— *His chain*! Still in her pocket.

The dull lull between light and darkness at dusk, where colour fades from everything, settled around Dr Neville Brown as he parked his silver BMW in front of Elaine's home. He grabbed the manila folder from the passenger seat. Neville Brown took heed of the tape blocking access to the front door and walked around to the back. He tapped on the glass of the kitchen door and waited. No response. He tried again, this time knocking louder, still nobody answered. He'd hoped to arrive earlier but a road accident on the way delayed him for well over an hour. Neville decided to go back to the car and wait a little longer. He hoped it wasn't a wasted journey.

As he walked down the side of the house, he heard a door slam to his right, from the vicinity of the shed.

'Hello!' he shouted, and walked across. 'Elaine!' he called. Her first name was the only one he could be sure of getting a reply from.

Cautiously, he pushed the shed door open and stepped inside. Visibility was poor but light enough to see there was nobody inside. As he stepped back on the half-turn, a blow to the left side of his head drove him to the ground; the folder dropped from his grasp and landed beside him.

On the floor, prostrate, his senses all over the place, he tried to crawl forwards without knowing why. Dazed and oblivious, he scrambled to his knees, resting on his hands as he tried to push himself up. A steady flow of blood streamed from his head, running into his left eye and down his face, dripping from his chin onto the dusty ground. He raised his head to glance briefly into the eyes of his assailant. The last thing he saw was a shovel swinging towards his head again.

32

Tuesday, 15 August

Far too hot to work in the afternoons, Elaine made the most of the marginally cooler mornings. Dust sheets covered the floor and the ceiling above had received its first coat of white. She hoped to get away with two coats; time would tell. She was pleased with her work on the porch so far; it was progressing well. She just wished all the aggravation of recent days hadn't happened. Life, though, was never that simple.

For a change, it had been a quiet morning. Elaine sat peaceably on the swing bench, appreciating a cup of tea. White paint speckled her face where the baseball cap and mask hadn't covered. She perused her handiwork before turning her attention to the tops of the trees across the grass to the front. Temporarily engulfed with a sublime serenity, she enjoyed their gentle sway. How she'd longed for a tranquil moment such as this. This was how it was supposed to be, so far though it had been anything but. She evoked memories of her childhood and living here with her parents. Why was there so much from her past that evaded her? It astounded her how much of her adolescence she'd forgotten, especially when it came to her father. Her memories of him were sporadic, most of them from before they moved to Sablefall Farm.

She tried to summon anything relating to her life here: of her father, his heart attack. So much missing. So much she wanted to see. Needed to see. A drastic change in her mood overcame her, calmness disrupted by an indescribable deep-seated uneasiness building within. Elaine glimpsed something, the outside of the barn before its deterioration. She heard talking and laughing coming from within. Now she was inside the barn and there he was; her father – but wait, there were other men. Who were they? One of the men turned to face her. He grinned to parade his horrid yellowing teeth with a large gap between the front two. She knew that face; just seeing it made her cringe. All the men were cheering, smiling and gesticulating. What were they looking at? Her mind's eye turned to see—

The thud of her almost empty cup hitting the floor and spilling what remained of its contents, abruptly ended her vision.

Watching nearby, Michael said, 'Are you all right, Mum?'

'Yes, I'm good,' she said, rallying a smile to play it down. 'My mind was – elsewhere.'

'Do you need any help?' he asked, sincere in his offer.

'Sure, go and get some old clothes on. You can help with the next coat on the ceiling.'

Michael went inside and never resurfaced. *Teenagers*!

When she completed rolling the final coat on the ceiling, she removed her cap and mask, tossed them onto the sheet, and stood back with her hands in her pockets to check her work. Her fingers connected with Ashton's neck chain. Elaine pulled it from her pocket and examined it in the palm of her hand. It would be a good idea to get rid of it as soon as possible. She cleaned her tools and headed off back to the pond.

Using the bottom of her shirt, Elaine wiped the gold necklace free of any fingerprints and nearing the pond, flung it out into the water. Going closer to the edge, her mouth dropped open in shock. Visible just above the surface of the water, were the lights on the top of a police car. She knew at once it was the missing police car. It had to be.

'Oh my God,' she muttered in disbelief and horror.

The intense heat of late, coupled with the lack of rain, had seen the water line gradually drop. She walked around the edge to get a closer view of the troubling sight. Elaine presumed the police constable's body was down there with the car. She stood as close to the edge as she could and strained to see through the green, leaf-covered water. Only the top of the roof was visible, the rest of the car hidden beneath the murky water. It was most likely noticeable on the night she dumped Ashton's body, but it was dark and more pressing matters commanded her attention.

In turmoil, Elaine's heart thumped and blood rushed to her head. This couldn't be happening. What was she going to do now? Under ordinary circumstances, she would call the police. However, things were anything but ordinary. If she did report it, they would find Ashton's body. The wheels in her mind turned, overloaded with questions begging for answers.

Elaine analysed the day it all started to go so wrong, from the second she arrived home and saw the police car parked out front. The shopping she put away, the cup of tea she drank. Her stroll out to the barn to locate the police constable. A vague recollection of somebody appearing through the barn door as she passed out. Then she woke sometime later on the sofa. What if she hadn't fainted at all but gone through some form of psychotic episode and killed PC James? After all, she couldn't conjure up the memory of killing Ashton either, yet she knew she must have. Murdering Ashton in self-defence she could understand, but as far as the young PC was concerned, there was no logic to it. What could he have possibly done to deserve such a fate?

Elaine knew she had to tell the police; it was the right thing to do. She was so conflicted and confused. What about her children? They didn't deserve any of this. Why should they suffer? A desperate desire to find a way out of her predicament overcame her. It would surely rain soon. The water level would rise and the bodies would remain concealed. Thoughts raced, voices in her head – all of them her own, talking over each other, telling her what to do and quarrelling about why her plans wouldn't work.

'Stop!' she shouted long and loud, placing her palms on her face.

PC Kell was going to report the pond, something else she'd forgotten about. It would soon be all over for her anyway. Elaine wandered back to the house in disbelief at what she'd found. Her next move must be carefully thought out. The most probable outcome was she'd have to call Tom and accept the consequences.

The next couple of hours indoors were spent pondering over every possible outcome. What if PC Kell hadn't reported the pond? It was a long shot, but it was possible. She'd researched the weather for the coming days on her laptop: rainfall would not be her saviour. Perhaps she should wait and let the police find the car; it wasn't on her land. What would she gain from turning herself in now and making it easy for them? If charged with these murders, it didn't matter whether she was arrested in a few hours, a few days, or a few weeks. She deliberated over and over, unable to come up with a single scenario that would have led her to kill PC James and go to the extremes of hiding the police car in the pond.

Her phone rang and she saw Lila's name, the voices in her head finally fell silent – relief. Her heart rate slowed, the sharp pains in her chest eased. Elaine sighed. The sound of Lila's voice soothed her, saved her from loneliness. She welcomed Lila's invite; getting out of the house for a while was what she needed.

When she arrived, Lila was still upset and pissed off with Ashton, maintaining her belief he'd shacked up with another woman. Drinking copious amounts of wine wasn't the answer but for a brief respite, it certainly helped. They were both desperate to drown their personal crises. Lila verbally ripped Ashton to shreds, telling Elaine how he'd mistreated her and the kids and how they'd all be better off without the bastard in their lives. She went as far as to say she hoped he'd never return. Elaine fervently hoped she meant it. If she were imprisoned for his murder, in some inexplicable way, she'd feel vindicated she'd given her friend a chance at a better life. Lila would never suffer at his vicious hands again.

They prattled on drunkenly into the night, again about the old days and individual events in their lives. Lila told more horrific tales of the beatings and harsh treatment she'd suffered, which only reinforced Elaine's justification. Well into the third bottle of Chardonnay, Elaine saw how late it was and decided it was time to go. A disappointed Lila offered her a bed for the night, but Elaine was insistent on getting home. There were plenty of other things on her mind right now; in the morning, she had a big decision to make regarding her future. Lila offered to call a taxi, Elaine refused, determined to drive herself home. Lila had been drinking before she arrived and was far too drunk to think about stopping her. With her head all over the place, Elaine's clear thinking had gone by the wayside. The consequences of her actions now were non-existent compared with what she might face in the coming weeks.

33

Tuesday, 15 August

Elaine thought she'd done well on the journey home, a notion ruined when she swerved into the drive too fast and hit the already detached wooden swing gate at the entrance. Her electric wing mirror dangled by the wire. Elaine pulled up to the house and switched off the engine. She puffed out her cheeks and expelled a long breath, wishing all her worries and problems would vanish into the night air along with it. Out of nowhere, she yelled and bashed her hands against the steering wheel. She closed her eyes, trying to take everything in. All she'd wanted and dreamed about was to create a lovely family home for her children. A dream now in shreds.

Past midnight, Elaine gazed at the star-filled sky as she walked from the car to the house. She snatched at the tape blocking the way to the porch and swayed up the steps. Slumping onto the swing bench, she kicked off her shoes and took in the close moon, a moment's escape from a mind consumed by chaos.

She glanced across the lawn and saw something over by the oak tree. Puzzled, Elaine staggered to her feet. 'What is that?'

Looked like a raggedy old sheet thrown over a branch. Alarmed, nerves tingling, she went down the steps to investigate. Nearer, she grasped the reality of what lay ahead. Her walk turned into a sprint. 'No, please, no!' she shouted as she closed in on the hanging body of her mother.

Frantic, Elaine stood beneath her. The wooden swing seat dangled, resting on the grass, held up by only one piece of rope, the other wrapped around Margaret's neck. A wooden ladder lay propped against the bark of the tree. Unsure what to do, she grabbed her mother's feet and tried to push her upwards to relieve the pressure on her neck, but soon realised how useless an idea it was. She climbed the ladder and tried to grab the rope, almost falling in the attempt. Elaine reached out, her fingers scraped against Margaret's torso. A cracking sound broke the silence of the night. Her mother's neck progressively twisted around, bones grinding grotesquely together. The skin on her face, grey, crumbly, and shrivelled. Margaret's eyes opened wide to reveal two white, glowing orbs.

'Beware zero six four two,' were the whispered and choked words, groaned from her dead mother's mouth.

Stupefied, Elaine's feet slipped from the step of the ladder. Both hands held on tight to a round wooden tread until she regained a foothold and descended. Her eyes awash with agony, she looked up at her mother, hanging there. She ran back to the house, retrieved her phone from her handbag on the bench and called the emergency services. Elaine raced back down the steps and back to her mother.

'Michael – Emily.' She stopped dead in her tracks and ran back to the house to check on them.

She scurried up the stairs and along the landing, pushing the door to Michael's bedroom wide open. To her dismay, his bed was empty. Panic-stricken, she ran to Emily's bedroom, only to find her bed empty too. On emotional overload, she searched the house, crying out their names over and over again. There was no sign of Michael or Emily anywhere.

In the kitchen, she collapsed in a heap, the only sound the pumping rush of blood as her heart palpitated against the cold stone floor. She bawled aloud as a flurry of tears swept over her cheeks as she cried, 'What have I done to deserve any of this?'

Sitting up, red-eyed and wet-faced, she half-expected Charlie to appear at any instant, or perhaps the repulsive beast would come to tear her apart again. Elaine slapped her cheek to see if she was awake or not. She dropped to the floor in a crumpled heap attempting to protect herself from whatever was coming next.

'It must be a dream – it must be,' she cried.

After a minute or two in the same position and with nothing happening, Elaine clambered to her feet, traipsed out to the front porch and sat on the bench to wait, her eyes fixed on the corpse of her dangling mother.

Little over ten minutes later, the flashing blue lights of a police car approached up the driveway. She realised this was no dream. Her mind in uproar, she rushed towards the vehicle as it parked. Tom and a female officer stepped out of the car.

Crying hopelessly, Elaine ran straight to Tom. 'Help me, Tom. Over here.' She hastened to the tree with the officers following close behind. A few feet from the tree, Elaine slowed to a halt, a bewildered look about her.

'Elaine, what's the matter, what's going on?' Tom asked.

'There!' Elaine pointed to the tree where she had seen her mother hanging not long before. Except now – only a lonesome swing rocked mildly before them. 'She was there, Tom.'

'Who was there, Elaine?'

'My mother. She was – there.'

Tom stared sympathetically into Elaine's eyes and stepped closer. 'I know she was, Elaine, I know she was. Come on.' Tom put his arms around her to comfort her and led her back to the house.

'Liz, could you go on ahead and make some tea, please?' Tom asked his colleague.

Elaine was in such a traumatic state. She couldn't think straight at all. 'Someone's taken my children, Tom. I can't find them anywhere in the house.'

'The kids are fine, Elaine. They're with their father,' Tom assured her. She relaxed, relieved they were safe.

Tom smelled the alcohol on Elaine's breath. He guided her up the steps, sat her on the bench, and went into the house to fetch a blanket. When he sat next to her, he placed his arm around her once again. The other police officer approached with two cups of tea.

'Thank you, Liz. Can you check the house over, please? Make sure it's secure,' he asked, reaching for the cups. He eased one into Elaine's trembling hand. 'Here you go.'

They sipped their tea in quiet until Elaine, puzzled, asked, 'Why does Robert have my children, Tom?'

'They live with him, Elaine. As far as I know, they visit you on Saturdays,' he explained.

Her head was all over the place. 'And my mother?'

'It was a long time ago, Elaine. Don't you remember?' He paused, waiting to see if she did. Instead, she appeared even more flustered. 'You were fourteen. You found her over there,' he gestured with a nod of his head towards the tree.

Elaine looked back over. Her memory fired off a series of short and hazy muddled visions. Her mind went through the gears, placing all the pieces together before replaying them for her to see.

She'd been dropped home from school by Lila's mum. As she was about to ascend the steps to the house, she paused for a second or two, at first not believing her eyes. She raced over to the oak tree to find her eyes hadn't deceived. Hanging from the tree was her mother. Lila's mum was halfway down the drive when Lila heard Elaine's agonised screams and alerted her. Lila's mother was first to reach Elaine. She consoled her as best she could and led her away from the sorrowful discovery, back into the house.

Elaine wept as the stark realisation engulfed her. 'I remember,' she whispered.

Tom pulled her closer to him. He explained how the house had been boarded up not long after that day.

The minutes on the porch passed in silence until Tom asked PC Liz Morgan to help get Elaine settled in bed. He went down the steps to examine Elaine's car. While he comforted her, apart from conjecturing how much alcohol she'd had, he also detected damage to her car. A closer inspection revealed a broken wing mirror, smashed headlight, a significant crack on the bumper, and a huge scrape along the side of the car. Although she'd driven home drunk, as long as nobody else was involved, there was no way he'd report it.

Tom knew a fair amount about Elaine's history from when she grew up here and the events surrounding her mother's death. He learnt more about her later life from the report the detectives had made during their investigation into the missing police officer. This was how he knew her children lived with their father. Yes, Tom was all too aware she'd had a very troubled life.

He still couldn't understand why she'd come back to her family home, no matter what reason she gave. Why hadn't she buried all this in her past and left it there? How could returning possibly help her? Tom found himself attracted to Elaine but hadn't fully grasped how damaged she was, until now. It had crossed his mind to ask her on a date. With the missing policeman business, that thought was on the back burner. His mindset was different now, more along the lines that it wasn't such a good idea. Tom, however, had a gentle soul and decided he would try to look out for her in any way he could.

The two officers stayed for a while until a call came through Tom's radio. He believed it best for PC Morgan to remain with Elaine for the rest of the night. He didn't want her left alone in the house and intended to call Robert Davis first thing in the morning. Maybe her ex-husband could shed some light on her situation, and more specifically, her mental health. He presumed she'd be on medication; an excessive amount of alcohol might have had something to do with her present delusional state of mind.

34

Wednesday, 16 August

Almost nine in the morning, Elaine stirred, still dressed in her work clothes from the previous day. Her mind wandered in uncertainty and then the previous day's events punched her repeatedly in the stomach, at least that's how it felt. Waking to the reality she was all alone was hard for her to believe. She'd imagined her children lived with her and worse still, her deceased mother. The conversations, their voices so clear and their faces – so vivid. Hallucinations of her mother had happened before. She'd hoped all that was behind her now. It was a shock to the system, to go through the trauma of losing her mum all over again. Even though twenty-eight years had passed, it felt as raw now as it did the first time, and this was her second relapse to this extent.

Downstairs in the living room, she saw the back of PC Morgan asleep on her sofa. She'd forgotten all about her being there. The police constable must have stayed awake well into the early hours to be sleeping this long. Her duty belt, bowler hat and radio were on the coffee table beside her. She left the officer snoozing and slipped quietly into the kitchen. She carried on with her morning routine: putting the kettle on and sitting in her usual chair.

A devastating blow, having to come to terms with something that had happened so long ago, coupled with the discovery her children lived with Robert. She must have known. It had all been part of her plan, to get better and in the near future have them back living with her. Where had the line been crossed? It was hard for her to acknowledge she'd been hearing sounds and seeing visions that weren't there. If she indeed was this bad, how could her children ever come back to live with her?

She pulled the phone out of her pocket and tapped through the photos she'd taken at the steam rally. There were photos of the funfair and the steamers, her children, though, did not appear in any. What about the family trip to Rievaulx Abbey; she didn't have the children with her on that day, either. In reality, the only time she had seen the children was when Robert brought them on a Saturday. What about Michael? He didn't even come the last time, instead choosing to go to some football tournament. It wasn't that she blamed him for doing so; it was more that she'd never be part of certain aspects of her children's lives: sports, music, or dance. Whatever hobbies they chose to take up, she wouldn't be involved, and she knew that would slowly cripple her mind. How useless she'd become – and she hated herself for it.

Elaine went to the cloakroom and splashed her face with cold water. She studied herself in the mirror, puzzled about how she'd managed to convince herself everything was well when it blatantly wasn't. It was tough for her to accept she was still so unwell. Elaine thought coming back to the house had been a good idea, the right thing to do. How wrong she'd been.

Other doors creaked open in her mind, revealing various realities hidden from her. She'd regarded it peculiar at the time when she poured her mother a glass of water in the kitchen. She watched her drink some of it, only to notice the glass still full when she'd picked it up later. She thought about her tears out on the porch when Robert drove off. They weren't for that arsehole; they were for her beautiful children, leaving her to go home. The numbers she'd believed Emily had painted on the porch floor, obviously put there by her own hand, but why 0642? What was the significance of those bloody numbers?

Now would be a good time to let Dr Brown know her story and get those records transferred. Her former psychiatrist, Dr Walker, had emphasised how important it would be to do so. She could see that now, but it was far too late for help. The enormity of her current situation brought her crashing back to Earth. None of it mattered anymore; all her hopes and dreams for the future – lay in ruins. PC James was almost certainly dead, and now it was even more probable that she killed him. Then there was Ashton. Only a crazy person would have murdered him and disposed of his body in the way she did. Lenny Grey witnessed the whole thing and was now blackmailing her. Was it time to accept who she was? To admit she wasn't getting better at all? Over the years, she'd always known her mental state wasn't on an even keel, but now things had escalated to a level beyond anything she could have imagined.

More painful memories emerged, this time of the children moving in with their father and that French slut when Elaine was admitted to the hospital. *Hospital*! Looking at her right arm, she rolled up her sleeve and there it was; a four-inch scar on the wrist along the forearm. She looked at her other arm: a mirror image. She recalled the nightmare she'd had when the beast slashed her wrists with his long sharp nails. It was her subconscious re-enacting the terrible moment when she'd tried to end it all, to rid herself of the irreparable grief she could no longer live with.

Robert had taken the kids to the zoo for the day. Luckily, he found her by chance because Emily had forgotten her favourite teddy bear, the one that belonged to Charlie. She wouldn't go anywhere without it. They returned to the house around twenty minutes later. Emily ran to the door, knocked, but didn't get an answer. Eventually, Robert let himself into the house and found her lying on top of their blood-soaked white satin sheets.

Elaine developed a form of blindness to the scars, always wearing long sleeves to cover her embarrassment, her shame, and mostly – her pain. So much had gone on in such a short space of time and now she was at a crossroads. Should she come clean and confess to the murders of Ashton and PC James? It was only a matter of time before it all unravelled – just as she had. She'd either be sent to prison or to a secure psychiatric unit for the rest of her life, never again allowed to see her beloved children. Maybe that would be for the best. What she deserved. There was an almighty tussle going on in her mind over PC James. Killing him was destroying her. She couldn't live a free life with that on her conscience. There was only one thing to do: turn herself in.

35

At 9.30 a.m. Tom arrived alone at the scene of a car reported dumped in the River Rye. It was a few miles from town, off the main road and down a long dirt track in the middle of nowhere. Someone jogging along the riverbank called it in. Tom would have put money on it being some kids out joyriding; it wouldn't be the first time. He parked up and peered over the edge of the bank to see a silver car about fifty yards along the river. He drove across the grass to get closer and noticed the number plate missing from the back, which he thought odd. He assumed the car had been rolled over the edge of the steep bank, its front submerged in about three feet of water.

Without having a clear view through the car's tinted windows, he knew he'd have to get wet. With a sigh, he took off his duty belt, placed it on the grass and trod with caution down the riverbank. All was fine until his foot slipped and he fell into the water. Tom scrambled to find his footing. Soaked through and not at all happy, he waded through the river to the car and pulled open the passenger door, stunned to see the body of a man lying across the front seats. He leaned forward to feel the man's neck for a pulse – he was still alive.

*

Her coffee finished, Elaine took a quick peek at the sleeping policewoman and went upstairs to freshen up and change into her red and blue checked shirt, and jeans. Back downstairs, she paused in the hallway and poked her head around the living room doorway. The police officer still hadn't budged. She debated whether to wake her; uncomfortable and embarrassed about the previous night, she decided to leave her be.

In the kitchen, Elaine put away the cups on the draining board the officer had washed up at some point. The battle in her head raged on about how damaged she'd always been and the awful things she'd done. Her poor children. Would they become as messed up as her? She flung the tea towel on the worktop and walked out of the back door to get some fresh air; a pointless exercise, it was already hot and humid.

Elaine rubbed the side of her head in frustration. She looked out to the line of trees at the back. Thinking straight with so much uncertainty in her life was difficult. She walked over for a further examination of the pond to see if the water level had receded any further. Maybe she was crazy enough to have imagined it all and there would be nothing out there but water and ducks. Her gut said that was improbable. At the pond, not only had the water receded to the point where the roof of the police car was fully visible, the roof of another vehicle broke the surface. The roof of a blue car. Her instincts screamed that it must be Ashton and Lila's car.

The cogs in her muddled mind crunched and ground as, in desperation, she gathered and examined every piece of information. Unequivocally, she couldn't have been the one who'd put Ashton's car in the pond. When she came around, she was on the floor in the exact spot where she'd struggled with him. It didn't add up. Something wasn't right. If someone else had put the car in the pond, she might not have killed Ashton after all, and there wasn't a good enough reason why she would have murdered the constable.

What if someone else had done this and she hadn't killed anyone? It would mean she'd gone to great lengths to cover up somebody else's crime. Two victims, two cars, in a pond near her home. Was someone trying to frame her? It would all come out about her mental health history. Both police and media would jump to the conclusion she was guilty. Why wouldn't they? She'd be an easy target. Let's all blame the mad woman for the murder of her best friend's boyfriend and the police officer. The voices bellowed in her head, hateful and accusing. The police would want answers quick. They would latch onto her like leeches. When it came down to it, she believed she hadn't done too much wrong. Granted, she'd disposed of Ashton's body and cleaned up the evidence, but he'd attacked her. She had to tell the police, talk to Tom, explain everything. He'd understand, wouldn't he?

Elaine dashed back to the house to act upon a decision that would wreck her plans and bring unwanted media attention, but at least she was confident in her own mind she hadn't murdered anyone. She ran through the kitchen and along the hall to the living room to wake PC Morgan. Puffing and panting, she called out her name and gently nudged the officer to wake her. Elaine leaned down and pulled the officer towards her, only to be confronted by a deathly blank stare and deep purple bruising around her neck. She stepped back in alarm, trying to take in the enormity of the dead police officer on her sofa. Controlling her rising hysteria, she looked around and saw the young officer's radio on the table and grabbed it, wildly pressing the buttons.

'Hello,' she repeated, 'somebody, help me.' There was no response. She dropped it back onto the table. About to run into the kitchen to fetch her phone, there was a knock at the front door.

'Tom,' she said, and hurried to open it. It was PC Kell.

'Roy!' She flung her arms around him. 'Quick! The police officer – I think she's been killed.'

PC Kell rushed behind her into the living room and checked for a pulse. He looked despondent and shook his head. 'You're right, she is dead. I'd better call this in.' Roy headed outside.

At the River Rye, Tom stood wrapped in a towel, given to him by a paramedic. There was now a fire engine, an ambulance, more police cars, and an air ambulance about fifty feet away. The rescue team had carefully freed the injured man in the BMW and moved him to safety inside the helicopter, hovering upwards, about to deliver him to Scarborough General Hospital. The man had no identification and both number plates were missing from the car. Alarm bells jangled. Until the man was conscious, it would be difficult to find out who he was and how he came to be in the river. Fuller and Pierce would investigate this case as well as that of the missing police officer, no doubt checking for any connections between the two; but first, they'd need to discover the man's identity.

Although still wet through, it wouldn't take long for Tom to dry off in the early morning heat. He could do with getting off home to shower, change and, if possible, get some rest. It had been a long and troubling shift. He also needed to speak to Robert about Elaine.

As Tom walked back to his car, his phone rang. 'Thanks for calling back, Daniel. What did you find out?'

'Well, I can tell you there is no PC Roy Kell registered at any of the North Yorkshire police constabularies. However, a sixty-two-year-old farmer was found dead in his home some miles away near the village of Crayke. It was assumed to be a robbery gone wrong. A few things were missing, including the farmer's 12-gauge shotgun.'

'And the farmer's name is?' asked Tom, already knowing the answer.

'Royston Kell.'

36

Wednesday, 16 August

Both Elaine and PC Kell waited in the kitchen for the arrival of Sergeant Burgess, the detectives, and an ambulance. A downcast Roy mentioned he'd only come by to pick up the constable. Distraught about the poor young woman, she still had to tell Tom and the detectives about the two dead bodies in the pond. She trusted Tom and wanted to tell him before anyone else.

'You okay?' PC Kell asked.

In response to his preposterous question, Elaine glared across the table at him. 'No, of course, I'm not. There is a dead policewoman on my sofa.'

'You're right, I'm sorry. I was just trying to help.'

She stood up and went to the sink to get a drink of water, gulping it down in one. Resting her hands on the edge of the sink, she took some deep breaths to calm herself and regain some self-control. She refilled the glass and turned to face the PC.

'How long do you think they'll be?'

'I'm sure they won't be too long,' he replied, gazing down at his wristwatch.

As Roy checked the time, her eyes were drawn to something that sent waves of terror surging through her body. Stunned, momentarily immobilised, the epaulette on Roy's shoulder transfixed her: the shiny silver digits – 0642. Nauseous, she brought a hand to her mouth. The numbers activated a kaleidoscope of images which circled fast around her head. One by one, they came into view before rotating to the next, encouraging her to see what her subconscious had deciphered.

Zero six four two, the numbers painted on the porch floor. The exact time on the TV when she woke from a nightmare. The same horrid nightmare where Charlie had tried to warn her. "Beware, zero six four two," he'd said. Her mother, hanging from the tree had repeated the same phrase. Lastly, her fleeting glance of the badge number on PC James's epaulette as he stepped forward to tell her about someone using the barn, the light on the porch highlighting the digits. All along her mind had been trying to warn her and there – sitting at her kitchen table was a man wearing the uniform of Police Constable Andrew James.

'Elaine, what's wrong?' Roy asked.

Mesmerised, she wanted to turn her head, look away, not meet his gaze, not let him know she'd worked out he wasn't who he claimed to be. Frozen, she saw him glimpse over his shoulder to work out what her eyes had fixated on.

The sound of smashing glass broke her trance. The tumbler had slipped from her hand and crashed to the floor, sending droplets of water splashing over her jeans and trainers. She inspected the pieces of glass around her feet and instinctively reached under the sink for the dustpan and brush. Frightened though she was, knowing this man was an imposter, she did her best to carry on as normally as possible. Every single thought, a sucker punch to her head. Who was this man and what did he want with her? Was he the one responsible for the mounting body count?

The revelation that she was in the same room as the man who'd conceivably murdered three people made her tremble with fear. She wanted to run, get away from this maniac, but for her own sake, she had to remain calm. An uncomfortable dryness in the back of her throat assailed Elaine as she swept the glass.

Roy stood up from the table and went over to her. 'Here, I'll help you,' he said, fetching the tea towel from the worktop. He knelt beside her, dabbing at the water and carefully picking up the larger pieces of glass, placing them into the dustpan. Elaine couldn't prevent her hands from shaking. Roy noticed and positioned his hand on top of hers, stopping it in its tracks, detecting its tremor beneath his.

'Why don't you go and sit down? You're in shock,' he said, taking the brush from her.

Her nerves shattered like the glass tumbler, Elaine managed to force a half-smile. 'Yeah, you're probably right,' she mumbled, her lips quivering as she spoke.

She stepped over to the table, careful to avoid any remaining shards of glass and sat with her back to Roy, to conceal her terrified expression. Elaine stared at the clock on the wall. It was almost ten forty-five. She knew it wouldn't be long now. She had to hold it together for a little longer until Tom—

You stupid idiot! Tom isn't coming, nobody is coming. Roy, or whoever he is, wouldn't have called the police.

All she could do now was wait and trust Tom or someone would show up soon. Over and over, she asked herself the same questions. What did this man want? Why was he playing these games with her? Was he the silhouetted figure who'd scared her senseless and ran through her house that night? And the constant knocking at her door. This could all be his doing. It no longer seemed a coincidence he was at the pub the night she first saw him; it might have been his intention all along. She was sure he'd been at the steam rally too. Was he some kind of crazed stalker? She had to focus on the assumption he was an extremely dangerous man.

'That's all swept and wiped up now,' said Roy, placing the tea towel on the worktop.

She could sense him standing close. 'Thanks,' she said, fighting to hide the tension in her voice. Perhaps she was trying too hard; after all, she had discovered a dead body in her house, surely that would mask the real reason for her angst.

'What do you want me to do with the glass?'

'Er, the bin, over there,' she pointed towards the pedal bin. She spotted her handbag on the worktop. Her car keys were in there. 'No, sorry, there's a recycling bin just outside the back door.'

As soon as Roy stepped outside, she bolted from the chair for her handbag and rummaged for the keys. After what seemed like an age, she retrieved them and ran to the front door.

She pulled open the door, flinging it wide, only to be greeted by Roy standing at the bottom of the porch steps with a shotgun dangling by his side.

'Where are you going, Elaine?' he questioned with a wide smug grin.

Elaine slammed the door shut and sprinted to the back door, locking it. She pulled a gleaming knife with a long, serrated edge from the block; the same knife she'd pulled out of Ashton. She held it out in front of her, contemplating her next move. Glancing back at her handbag, she placed the knife on the worktop and searched for her phone. It wasn't in there.

'Fuck!' she cursed.

She cast an eye to the back door; Roy stood on the other side, amused, as he watched her through the glass panel. She grabbed the knife from the worktop and held it out in front of her for him to see.

'Searching for this?' he smirked as he held her phone up to the window, tapping it on the glass. He must have taken it when she'd had her back to him.

'What do you want?' she shouted.

'I thought it would be good to get to know each other,' Roy replied. 'You've no idea how long I've waited for this.'

'Go away!' she screamed.

With pouted lips and sad, mocking eyes, he said, 'Ahhh, don't be like that, Elaine.'

'Please, just go!' she whimpered.

'Okay. I'll leave you alone if that's what you want.' Roy disappeared.

She knew full well he wouldn't leave, but it didn't stop her from edging over to the door to check.

'Boo!' Roy shouted as he reappeared at the glass, startling her into a backwards jump. 'You didn't *really* believe I'd gone, did you?' he laughed.

Shaking, Elaine backed further away from the door.

'Okay. I am going this time.' Roy vanished once again.

Elaine held her gaze on the door, waiting for him to show his face. Thoughts raced through her head. What did he mean by he'd waited so long for this? Out of nowhere, she heard music playing in the house, no, not music, a song – a song she knew. Justin Timberlake's 'Can't Stop The Feeling'. Where was it coming from? The tune echoed along the hall – PC Morgan's mobile. Elaine raced to get there before it stopped and before Roy heard it. She searched the pockets of the officer's uniform and just as she retrieved it, the ringing stopped. The screen showed Sgt Burgess had called. Elaine tried to return his call; it was busy. The phone pinged. A text alert displayed for a message on the answerphone. She touched the on-screen button to listen:

"Liz, this is Tom. If you're still with Mrs Davis, I'd like you to stay with her. Don't leave her alone. I'll be there soon."

She tried to ring him again but was disturbed by the sound of breaking glass. She peered around the doorframe into the hall: Roy had smashed the bottom glass panel of the kitchen door. He used the butt of the shotgun to knock out the remaining glass so he could climb through.

With the knife in one hand and the mobile in the other, held tight to her ear, she sprinted upstairs. Elaine's nightmares were loathsome at times; in comparison, this was terrifying. There was no answer from Tom as she ran into the bedroom at the front of the house. Having cleared this room, all that remained was the bed she slept in, a tiny bedside table with a couple of drawers, and a large, heavy wardrobe: nothing to push against the door. At least the old house had rim locks with keys on most of the doors. Elaine turned the key and crouched with her back against it.

The handle of the bedroom door squeaked and she looked up to see it slowly turn. Frantic, her call went to Tom's answerphone. 'Sergeant Bur— Tom, it's Ela—' Her body shuddered and jolted forward as Kell kicked the door hard. The phone flew from her hand and slid along the floor, coming to a stop under the wardrobe. Elaine kept her body weight firmly against the door and gripped the knife. Sweat streamed down her terror-stricken face. Her body jarred forward again as Roy continued to force his way inside. She stayed strong, using her legs to push her body against the door.

'The pond, Tom. Look in the pond!' Elaine cried out, hoping the phone was still recording her message.

37

Grateful he'd found time to go home, Tom wandered into his bedroom, a towel wrapped around his waist having just stepped out of the shower. Something much needed after his unexpected dip in the River Rye. His phone bleeped on the bed next to the spare uniform he'd laid out ready. He sat down and found a message from Liz, which he listened to straight away. He heard a rustling, static sound, then finally, a voice, "Sergea— it's—" was followed by a loud banging noise. He listened on, thinking there was nothing more until he heard, "Pond, Tom – the pond." The connection was bad and left Tom baffled.

'Did she say pond? What on earth is she going on about?'

He was about to call Liz back when his phone rang: an unknown number. He answered to find it was Robert.

'Mr Davis. Thanks for returning my call. I'm sorry to trouble you,' said Tom.

'Your message said you wanted some information on Elaine. How can I help?'

'I'm concerned about Mrs Davis's mental state. Last night, she had an episode involving her mother and children.'

'Oh, she's not seeing her mother again?' said Robert.

'It's happened before?'

'Yes, a couple of times.'

'When you say, seeing her mother, do you mean she believes her to be alive?' asked Tom.

'Yeah, kind of. If Elaine isn't taking her medication, when she's stressed or lonely, she will somehow imagine her mother is with her and have entire conversations. It's never happened with the children, though, that's new.'

'So, she's schizophrenic?'

'That's one of her disorders, yes. We went through some traumatic times together, but that doesn't include the issues from her childhood which, to be honest with you, I don't know much about. I know about her finding her mother, but I get the impression there's a lot more to her past, and I don't think she recalls events from back then. Obviously, her doctor never shared any details with me,' explained Robert.

'No, he wouldn't. I'm aware of her history and suicide attempts, but I didn't realise the extent of damage to her mental health. Is she safe, I mean, should she be living alone?'

'Sergeant, when she's on her meds, you wouldn't know there was anything wrong with her. I mean, depression finds its way through now and then, but she manages. Plus, she has therapy, which helps a lot. I actually believed things were different this time and she was stronger, doing okay. What with the move and starting over, she seemed happy. Determined. I thought things were looking up, obviously, I was wrong.'

Robert's tone worried Tom. He didn't know what powers Mr Davis had over Elaine and it wasn't his intention to make her life more difficult by instigating her being committed to a hospital or something.

'I'm probably overreacting, Mr Davis. She'd had quite a lot of alcohol last night and maybe that was more to do with it,' said Tom, attempting to play the situation down.

'She shouldn't even be drinking alcohol, Sergeant Burgess. Not with the kind of medication she's on.'

Tom worried he was making matters worse. 'Well, I'll be seeing her shortly. I'm sure she's in a much-improved state of mind today and I've blown things out of proportion. I'll check on her and if you'd like, I can give you a call to let you know how she's doing,' said Tom.

'That would be great, thank you.'

'Okay then, goodbye for now, Mr Davis.'

It sounded feasible to Tom that she'd had an emotional breakdown. She'd been through so much in her life and losing one child was enough to send any parent over the edge, but with her other children living with their father, she'd pretty much lost an entire family. He threw his phone on the bed and finished drying himself before getting dressed. He'd forgotten to call Liz back.

Robert saw Chloé stood in the living room doorway, scowling at him, a look he was all too familiar with after any discussion involving Elaine. She'd caught the end of his phone conversation.

'Who wants to know about Elaine now?' Chloé's voice made it clear how exhausted she was with his ex-wife and all the problems that came with her.

'The police,' Robert said, blunt in his reply.

'What has she done now, burned down her house?' she said, drifting closer.

'I have to drive up and see her,' he said. The look on his face implied he had an idea what Chloé's reaction would be.

'Oh, no, not anymore. I am sick of this. Every time there's a call from her, you go running. She is nutty as a fruit bat.'

'Cake,' Robert corrected her. 'Nutty as a fruitcake.'

'I don't think you should talk about Mum like that,' Michael said from the open doorway.

'I didn't mean it. I was correcting Chloé.'

'You do mean it. I hear you talk about Mum all the time and you both call her names. I don't like it.'

'Michael, please go to your room.'

Michael stared at his father with contempt.

'Now!' Robert ordered him.

'You're such a wanker. I fucking hate you – I hate you both!' Michael fumed as he stormed off.

With no time to consider a comeback, Robert turned to Chloé.

'What's a wanker, Daddy?' Emily asked innocently, now standing where Michael had been.

'Emily, go to your room, please, sweetheart. We'll talk in a bit, okay,' Robert said softly.

'I fucking hate you both as well,' shouted Emily, storming off, mimicking the actions of her big brother.

Astounded by her reply, Robert didn't know whether to laugh or be annoyed, but this was no laughing matter.

'Look, Chloé. You know how Elaine is.' Robert checked to make sure the kids weren't there. 'She's mad as a hatter,' he whispered. 'But lots of stuff has happened, you know that. I've tried to explain this a hundred times; it won't be like this forever. Either she'll get better and leave us alone, or she'll end up in a mental hospital.' He put his hands on her shoulders in a desperate attempt to pacify her.

Chloé wasn't having any of it as she shoved his arms away. 'You know what I believe. I think the bitch does it deliberately to pay us back,' she argued.

'I've told you before, she has no idea we were having an affair, and to be honest, I don't think she would even care about that now,' he said.

'What if she did overhear us on the phone call, huh?'

'I told you already, she didn't, she'd hung up the phone.'

'What about when she slit her wrists? I'm telling you, she knows.'

'For Christ's sake, Chloé, we've been through this.'

Chloé made straight for the living room door. 'Yes, we have, and always it's Charlie! Charlie! Charlie!' she yelled and slammed the door hard behind her as she left.

Robert called after her but it was no use. The next bang was the front door.

Now Chloé had gone, he had to make other plans for someone to take care of the children while he went to see Elaine. He called his mother to ask if he could drop them there for a little while. Robert thought about Elaine. He had loved her once and in his own way, he still cared, but somewhere inside, he hoped she'd finally cracked and gone over the edge. It was plausible the time had come for permanent care. For him and Chloé, Elaine being committed would be a godsend. It would mean they could legally dissolve the business partnership and have Elaine's name removed as a director; something he'd already made enquiries about.

38

There had been a long and unnerving lull since the second assault by Roy on the bedroom. With her back pressed firmly against the door, Elaine assessed the window. The roof of the porch was just below and she considered whether it was possible to jump onto it, climb down, and make a dash for the car.

Keys!

She checked her pocket, relieved as she caressed the bulging outline. It had to be worth trying to escape. There was no telling how long it would be before help arrived. Yes, Tom said he'd be there soon, but it could be too late by then.

Elaine shifted away from the door, desperate not to make a sound. On her hands and knees, she padded stealthily along the floor towards the sash window. There were one or two insignificant creaks, but eventually, she made it to the window. Elaine slid the fastener across to unlock it, gently raised the bottom sash, and poked her head out. The minor slope of the porch roof was a tad unsettling, but it wasn't far. If she hung by her hands and dropped, there would be hardly any distance to fall.

It appeared all clear below as she glanced around the yard. Quietly, she climbed out of the window. 'Can't Stop The Feeling' rang from the phone under the wardrobe.

'Damn you, Justin!' she growled.

With a loud crash, the bedroom door flew open and hung precariously by a single hinge. Roy stood in the doorway, holding the shotgun. He advanced towards her. Practically out of the window and scared senseless, Elaine let herself drop, hitting the tilted roof on her side. She let out a yelp as the blow knocked the wind out of her. She rolled onto her back, gasping for air. Above her at the window, Roy smiled.

She rolled over to the edge and dangled over the side, placing her feet on the horizontal rail of the porch. A fleeting glance at the window revealed Roy was gone. She jumped down and made off in the direction of the car. At the same time, Elaine pulled the keys from her pocket and clicked the car door open. Inside, she locked the doors and slipped the key in the ignition to start the engine. Elaine lifted her head ready to drive off, only to see Roy in the rear-view mirror standing a few feet behind – blocking her exit, the 12-gauge, double-barrel shotgun pointing at her.

Yanking the gear into reverse, she put her foot on the accelerator. A thunderous bang sent her diving low across the front seats for cover. Glass from the rear window rained down on her. She brushed the small fragments from her face, leaving traces of tiny cuts behind and sat upright. The car had stalled. Elaine searched for Roy but couldn't see him to the front or behind through the blown-out rear window.

Starting the car again, she reversed out of the parking area. As she manoeuvred into the driveway, she slammed on the brakes, terror sending adrenaline coursing through her. Roy stood in the middle of the drive, waiting for her. Their eyes met; a mini stare off ensued. She shifted the gear into neutral and squeezed the accelerator, revving the engine, hoping he would get out of the way. Regardless of whether he did or not, she had to go for it. Either he would jump out the way, or she'd plough right through him.

Elaine slipped the car into first gear and sped towards him. Roy raised the weapon, aimed, and fired. Elaine ducked, screaming as the windscreen imploded, sending glass hailing over her. After a few seconds, she raised herself, the small particles of glass on the seat cutting into her hands. Blood spots sprang from grazes and cuts behind glass fragments, propelled into her head and face from the impact.

The car had rolled onto the grass. It had also stalled again. Turning the key, her peripheral vision picked up something coming directly at the driver's side window. Instinctively, she huddled down. Another loud crashing noise, as the butt of the shotgun sent more glass flying into the vehicle. She sat up fast, still desperate to escape, the back end of the gun rammed hard into the side of her head.

39

Tom pulled onto Elaine's drive just as his mobile rang. He stopped the car, left the engine running and answered. An update from DI Pierce at the hospital about the as yet unidentified man he found in the river. He'd come round but fallen back into unconsciousness. The detective told Tom their inquiries were along the lines that the man might be the person responsible for both the missing PC and the death of local farmer, Royston Kell. Tom wasn't so sure he agreed.

After the call, he placed his phone on the passenger seat next to his duty belt and stab vest, and drove up to the house. Elaine's car wasn't there so maybe she'd dropped PC Morgan home in her battered vehicle or arranged for it to be towed to a garage for repair.

Tom parked up and called Liz on her radio but didn't have any luck. Something crunched under his feet as he stepped onto the drive. Bits of glass were scattered on the ground, he assumed from the damage to Elaine's car the previous night. He walked up the steps and knocked on the door. When there was no answer, he tried the handle; locked. Tom looked through the dining room window and saw covered furniture, boxes, and building supplies.

Curtains obscured the window to the living room. He stared across the grounds to the front but could see nothing untoward.

The message from Liz mentioned a pond. He hadn't noticed a pond on any of his previous visits but headed off to the left of the house and along the old trail. He came to a four-foot-high fence blocking the entrance to the next property. Tom knew Elaine's land only went up to this point. The fence leaned precariously and thin rope secured it to a post. Tom went closer and looked over the top. The gravel and dirt behind had been scraped from the fence being pulled back, but he couldn't tell whether it was recent or not. He walked along the tree line, then detoured through the small wooded area beyond the trees into the next property, appreciating the shade. Back in the open, overgrown grass, bushes, and more trees stretched before him. The exceptionally muggy heat took its toll on Tom: enough was enough.

In the wooded area on the way back to Elaine's house, Tom heard a quacking sound and spotted a small duck waddling along. 'What the?'

The duck waddled into the long grass, close to where Tom had just come from. He wanted to see where the little fellow would go and followed. Some of the grass was flattened. Someone had recently trampled through here. The duck kept going and Tom continued his pursuit. Is this what his career had come to? Tailing ducks! A large pond came into view. He watched, smiling as the small duck swam to join its family.

Tom's smile faded to a grim look of disbelief. Above the surface of the water were two vehicles, one unquestionably a police car. Tom was distraught. He hurried around the edge for a closer look, stopped short by a glimmer, the sun reflecting off something on the ground. He brushed the long stems of grass aside to see an old pocket watch. His disposable gloves were in his duty belt which he'd left in the car, along with his phone. Taking a clean tissue from his pocket, he bent down and carefully picked it up. He flipped the watch open and a quaint musical jingle played. He closed it, wrapped it securely in the tissue and stowed it in his pocket.

Tom got as close to the edge of the pond as he could. In total shock, he understood the scrambled message from Liz. She'd tried to tell him about her find, but how had she come across it right out here? He needed DCI Fuller here fast. Divers and a forensic team would also have to be organised. Tom hoped to God young PC James wasn't in the car or somewhere in the pond, however probable.

Back at the car, Tom opened the passenger door and grabbed his phone from the seat. There was no reply from DCI Fuller, so he left a message on his voicemail about finding the missing police car, followed by the location. Tom slipped the phone in his pocket, about to call in on his radio when he detected the distant sound of an all too familiar song. It was Liz Morgan's ringtone, coming from the open window above the porch. Tom dropped the radio on the seat, put on his stab vest, and retrieved the baton from his duty belt. He ran straight for the front door and rammed the bottom of his foot against it, breaking it open.

'Liz!' Tom shouted before dashing upstairs and along the landing to the front bedroom. The ringing had stopped.

Wooden debris from the splintered door lay on the floor. There was no sign of Liz or her phone as he scanned the room. He lowered to his knees to check under the bed and about to rise when he spotted it under the wardrobe. Tom grabbed it and left the bedroom.

'Liz!' he shouted again, going from room to room before he raced back down and straight into the living room, where he saw her on the sofa.

'Oh, please, no.' Tom traipsed over to her, fearing the worst. He placed his baton and Liz's mobile on the coffee table and leaned over her body. With a tender look in his eye, he touched the back of his fingers against her cheek: her skin was cold. Tom could tell she'd been dead for a few hours. Sorrow coursed through him. Liz was a much-valued colleague and a good friend who hadn't long since married.

A sombre Tom stood upright, stepped back and retrieved his phone from his pocket to call DCI Fuller. He heard a clicking sound behind him and slowly turned. In the doorway of the living room, a man dressed in a police uniform aimed a shotgun at him. PC Kell.

Tom raised his right hand in a calming motion. 'Now just take it ea—'

A deafening sound filled the room and the smell of pungent Nitroglycerin burned his nostrils, his stab vest ravaged by the impact. Hit in the midriff and involuntarily knocked back, the wooden coffee table collapsed effortlessly beneath Tom's falling weight. A red mist hung in the air as his head landed with a thud on the charred wood of the open fireplace. Ashes rose upwards to merge with the descending spray of his blood. Tom lay motionless with his arms fanned out either side of his body. As he watched the ash cloud dissipate, his eyes stared straight up into the black abyss of the chimney, his lips slightly parted as red fluid trickled from his mouth. A lone tear escaped from the corner of his eye, sliding down in slalom fashion, dodging around the droplets of sweat and spatter covering the side of his face. Tom's eyes closed.

40

Wednesday, 16 August

Gagged with duct tape and bound with a thin rope to an old wooden chair, Elaine's eyes flickered open. She took in her blurred surroundings as they adjusted to the bright ray of sunlight that streaked down through the partly caved in roof. Disorientated and drenched through from the intense heat engulfing her body, she quickly recognised the barn. She had no idea how long she'd been unconscious. Dark, crusted blood left a thick, sticky trail from the side of her left brow down her face, under her chin, neck, and onto her white undershirt. Tiny splinters of glass were still embedded in her skin. The gravity of her circumstances began to sink in. She tried to scream: the only sound a restrained, muffled murmur. Her hands tied around the back and her feet fastened tight to the front legs of the chair, she wriggled to see if she could loosen the knots. Her anxiety levels increased as her breathing gathered pace.

From out of nowhere, Elaine felt a surge of cold water running down her face. She spluttered, shaking her head to clear the water from her eyes and glared angrily at the culprit standing in front of her. He eased the tape from her skin and removed a cloth from her mouth. She gasped for air and let out a squeal of desperation and fury. Roy unscrewed another bottle of water and held it to her mouth. As much as she would love to decline his offer of refreshment, her thirst was too great. She noisily gulped it down. He poured the remainder over her head to cool her.

She glowered into those mesmeric eyes that had once captivated her. Elaine's apprehension increased in tandem with her helplessness. Her eyes widened to their full extent, her heart beating fierce and fast. The veins in her neck strained as she fought for every intake of air, nasal mucus mingling with perspiration and tears, her eyelids closing, her body in shutdown mode.

More water slapped her face to keep her from passing out. He dropped the empty plastic bottle to the floor and went behind Elaine to shift her chair into an area of shade. He reappeared, dragging an identical wooden chair with a manila folder resting on the seat and positioned it in front of her. He reached for the folder, sat down, and studied the pages. Perplexed, Elaine's mind wanted to ask the questions her voice, silenced by fear, couldn't.

She struggled to set free the words trapped in the back of her throat. Elaine fought hard to retain what little resolve she had left, until at last, she uttered, 'Who are you? Why are you doing this?'

Silence.

He continued sifting through the pages with an occasional look of amusement on his face. Not once did he raise an eye in her direction. Elaine's agitation was evident, along with her burgeoning anger.

'What do you want?' she raged.

Roy looked at Elaine with a smug grin. It all but revealed he knew something she didn't. She'd envisaged the reality of the outcome here, likely to result in her death. Somewhere inside, hope lingered. It was conceivable Tom would come looking for Liz. Someone might have heard the gunshot. Gunfire, however, wasn't unusual out in the sticks; farmers often used firearms to control vermin. Clay pigeon shooting was also a favourite pastime, so even if someone had heard the shot, it was doubtful it would be reported. She couldn't think straight. Hope was a desperate thing to cling to but it was all she had right now.

'Do you need some more water?' he asked.

Despite her state of confusion, she agreed with a nod. Roy put the folder on the floor, stood, and disappeared behind her. He re-emerged, unscrewing the lid from another bottle and held it to her lips. Again, she gulped away, the water lashing down her chin and neck as it fell from her mouth. The bottle almost empty and taking in vast amounts of air through her nose, she exhaled, relieved to have appeased the horrific thirst that had made the back of her throat feel as though it was full of dried sand.

Roy drank what was left in the bottle, tossed it away and retook his seat in front of her.

'I suppose I should introduce myself. My name is Harper Darmody. I'm sure that means nothing to you and there's no reason why it should.'

Elaine listened, immersed in uncertainty.

'How do you feel to be inside the barn, Elaine? Any unwanted stirrings come to mind?'

Unsettled with a strong sense of foreboding, she said, 'I know I don't want to be in here. I-I don't know why.'

'All will become clear soon enough. First, let's go through this file the good Dr Neville Brown brought to your door.' He picked up the folder from the ground beside him.

The mention of her psychiatrist's name disconcerted her. 'Dr Brown was here?'

'Not for long,' Harper said with a wink and a soft smile.

'Did you hurt him?' she demanded, concerned for his well-being.

Harper Darmody glared at her, bringing her to an immediate silence, letting her know who was in charge.

'You've had plenty of troubles in your life, past and present, but from watching you—'

'You've been watching me?'

Again, he scowled at her; his eyes revealed a far more malevolent side than she could ever have imagined.

'I can honestly say you've both surprised and impressed me with how you've reacted to certain situations, specifically, dumping the body in the pond and cleaning up the scene afterwards. You were lucky I was around to take care of him; he was going to rape you,' he said. 'I wanted you to believe you'd killed him. It was my knife that went into his neck. I swapped it for one of yours in the kitchen.'

Although she'd worked out she couldn't have murdered Ashton, it was still a relief to hear.

'This folder coming into my possession has opened my eyes to a whole new you. A history of mental health problems going right back to before you found your dear old mum hanging from that tree out there.'

His words tied her in knots; she couldn't begin to comprehend what any of this meant.

'You had the odd episode here and there until you reached your mid-twenties and went through a long spell where you were fine, but then your depression returned. You stalked your husband, found him cheating on you, and decided to be a silly girl and take an overdose. Was that to make him feel guilty and sorry for you?'

'You don't know anything about me,' Elaine countered.

Roy looked pleased to get a reaction from her.

'Again, you were all right for a while – but then came little Charlie's demise.' Harper grinned, provoking her further.

'Fuck you!' she blasted. Her disquiet transformed to rage.

'It must have been horrific, someone taking your child from right under your nose. What a silly boy though, to go off with a stranger like that. Dressed as a clown, wasn't he?'

Elaine was furious. The audacity of this animal, to mock and torment her. 'Don't you dare talk about my son,' she snarled.

'Not exactly the fun family day out you had wished for. You should have made him watch the movie *IT*. I think Pennywise would've made him more aware of clowns,' he smiled.

'You think it's funny to joke about something so dreadful?' she retorted.

'I'm not amused, believe me – maybe a tad,' he said without remorse as he gestured his index finger and thumb about an inch apart and steadily widened the gap.

'Shut the fuck up!' Elaine yelled and then screamed for a few seconds, blocking out what she was hearing.

'I see I've hit a nerve,' he said with satisfaction.

*

During Elaine's deafening scream and his focus solely being on her, Harper failed to hear a car pull up to the house. It was a deep red Aston Martin and driving it was Chloé. She had come to confront Elaine about the hassle she'd caused between her and Robert. She noticed the fresh paint on the steps and porch floor. She made sure to dig her high heels into the wooden treads and give a forceful little twist to scuff the paint.

She knocked on the front door and tried the handle, locked. She noted there were no cars around and guessed Elaine wasn't home. Chloé wasn't the type of woman to come all this way for nothing, so she sat down on the swing bench to await her return.

A brew of emotions traversed Elaine's body as she sat helplessly bound to the chair, forced to listen to the cruel taunts of this psychopath.

'Moving on, things went from bad to worse. Your darkness returned with a vengeance, didn't it? Wow!' he said, running a finger over the paper as he analysed her life. He could barely contain himself, getting pleasure from tormenting her.

'You really went for it the second time around, slashing both wrists, the right way as well. It's surprising how many people get that wrong,' he said, looking up at her. 'You spent six months in a mental health unit where you had electroconvulsive therapy, followed by divorce and losing custody of your children. Another breakdown and before you knew it, you were back in a secure unit for another six months. And there was me thinking I had it bad.'

Harper threw the folder on the floor, stood up and paced in front of her. She could do nothing but watch and wait for whatever was to come.

'I know you haven't taken your anti-psychotics in a while. Plenty of unused Risperidone in the drawer next to your bed. You don't take your anti-depressants either, you naughty girl. I bet you kept that from Dr Brown.'

More rattled with every word he spoke, she sobbed, 'Why are you doing this to me?'

'We're coming to that now, Elaine. For that though, we have to go back a long way. Do you remember when you first moved here?' He spread his arms and spun around in a gesture of where they were. 'To this place?' he emphasised.

'Yes – most of it.'

'Do you, Elaine, you sure about that? Because I don't think you do.' He pointed a finger either side of his temples, 'Probably all those electric shocks from way back helped block it out for you,' he mocked, and shook his body to suggest shock therapy.

'Come on, Elaine. Think!' he shouted in her face, making her flinch.

She looked afraid and clueless.

'It's in your file there, right at the beginning.'

He put his face close to hers, peering into her eyes, trying to read her. He eased away from her with a look of total surprise. 'My God – you really don't remember, do you? They did a real number on you, didn't they? They actually made you forget,' Harper said, his voice dropping.

'Forget what? I don't know what you're talking about,' Elaine whimpered.

Harper moved his chair to within a foot of where she was seated and sat in front of her. 'I have it as well, you know,' he said.

'What?' The increasing intensity of the situation and the unbearable heat and humidity added to her unrest.

'Schizophrenia,' Harper stressed in a blunt tone.

Elaine shook her head, annoyed, 'No – I'm getting better!' she argued, resolute.

Harper grinned at her, shaking his head. 'No, Elaine, people that have it as bad as you and I don't get better, we get worse – until it completely consumes us. Then we use it as a means to destroy ourselves and those around us.'

He leaned forward, cupped the side of her face and used a thumb to wipe away the salty trail coursing down her cheek. 'You know, I came here to take your life, only to find that you and me, we're the same.'

'What do you mean?' Elaine didn't know what to think anymore. Her emotions had besieged her to the point of wanting everything to stop.

He put his hands on her shoulders. 'Damaged, Elaine. Broken. Beyond repair.' Harper rose to his feet, pacing again, almost excited. 'Let's get to the important stuff, shall we? Do you want to know why you're so damaged, Elaine? Why you don't like this barn?'

In the silence, every nerve ending predicted something momentous was around the corner. Something that could shatter her world. Everything that had come before now, were mere tremors leading to this point.

'Your father used to bring you in here. I bet you don't remember that, do you?'

She shook her head, crying as he sought to resurrect something buried deep within her. If a memory was suppressed somewhere in the depths of her mind, it was no doubt hidden away for a good reason, and she had no intention of helping him locate it.

'Your father and his friend, Mr Denley Parker. Anything?' Harper asked, his eyes intent on hers as he searched for some hint of recollection.

She sobbed aloud, moving her head side to side in a frenzy, not wanting to hear where this was headed.

'Hmmm, I think I see a glimmer, Elaine. You don't want to hear or see it, but it's there,' he beamed, as though he believed he was making the breakthrough he wanted. Harper moved behind her and grabbed hold of the chair, turning it around until she faced an old rickety, wooden double bed frame.

As soon as her eyes focused on the bed, myriad inquietudes gushed through her. A portion of her mind fought with vigorous tenacity to protect the rest, but the defenders of her sanity were sadly losing ground as the incomprehensible, unwanted memories stirred within.

Elaine saw herself as a young girl crying softly. The girl wept in physical and emotional pain as she yielded to the suffering, while her father and a man of similar age took their turn with her on the bed. Elaine screamed out longer and louder than before, repulsed by the visions forming before her. A memory years of therapy and medication in her childhood and adult life helped to protect her from. For so long, it had stayed buried deep within the catacombs of her subconscious, and now it was over. The battle to protect her – was lost. A manic roar escaped her.

Elaine's horrendous, agonising scream captured Chloé's attention. It wasn't hard to work out something was seriously wrong. The grievous sound came from the vicinity of the barn.

She went straight to her car, opened the boot, and pulled out a long chrome tyre wrench. She kicked off her heels and placed them in the boot before going to the barn to investigate.

The reality of what Elaine had locked away for all those years hit her like a battering ram. How could her father have done that to her? She loved and adored him, or at least presumed she had. She wept. Her unbearable despair was profound. But wait, another memory manifested. She'd hoped there was no more to come. Elaine saw – a boy.

Younger than her, he bore a striking resemblance to her son, Charlie. Where had he come from and what was he doing there? The boy foolishly and to no significant effect tried to attack her father and Mr Parker, while a young Elaine lay on the bed dazed, disoriented, and no doubt drugged. She gazed upon the frail and incapacitated younger version of herself, her falling tears mixed with the dried ones that had faded to a salty crust. Not a sound passed the lips of the terrified and innocent young girl as she lay there.

The back of her father's hand struck the boy with enough force to knock him to the ground. With a stubborn and determined resolve, he scrambled to his feet and went at the men again. They were hurting the girl and he was desperate to protect her. This time, Mr Parker punched him hard in the face. He pinned him down while Elaine's father lifted her like a ragdoll from the bed and placed her on a chair. It wasn't beyond the realms of possibility she was sitting in the same chair now. Elaine observed this shocking event through the bleary eyes of her younger self, as the boy replaced her on the bed, severely beaten as he struggled. The young boy resolutely fought until he had no fight left in him. There wasn't a thing the helpless and adolescent Elaine could do to help as the blackness descended from the tops of her eyes until she could see no more.

A despairing Elaine wept uncontrollably.

'You almost know everything now,' Harper said.

She shook her head from side to side, 'No more, please, no more.' Her chin fell to her chest. What had transpired so far was odious enough.

'You saw yourself, didn't you?'

She gave a slight nod of her head.

'Did you see the boy, Elaine? Did you see – me?' said Harper as he sat on the bed frame to face her.

She glanced at him with a look of incomprehension. 'You – who are you?' The desperate need to know, apparent on her face, taunted her unlike anything she could ever have imagined.

'Once upon a time you had a brother, Elaine. A brother you were forced to forget.'

41

Elaine's pulses danced to the rhythm of her throbbing arteries as she tried to take in his last statement. Was it true, could this man be her brother? She would have known – wouldn't she? She recalled the moment she'd first laid eyes on him in the pub, the irksome feeling of familiarity. Had she known all along? The manifestation of her mother had told her she knew. When their lips touched, she couldn't deny something felt wrong. Had he been playing games all along, testing her to see if she genuinely had forgotten him, trying to induce some long-forgotten memory?

'I tried to stop them.' Harper's emotions broke through his, before now, unyielding exterior.

Was this man truly the monster he'd portrayed himself to be? Elaine watched as he thought hard to hold back the tears, but it was too much even for him as they descended. She emphasised with his misery and memories, leaving him with the scars and sadness of years gone by.

He continued, 'I always wondered why they kept taking you to the barn and made me stay in the house. I thought I might be missing out on something. I asked Mum – she wouldn't say.'

'Mum didn't know! She couldn't have. She would never have let it happen,' said Elaine in vehement defence of her mother.

Annoyed at her suggestion, Harper fired back: 'Oh, she knew, Elaine. She knew damn well what Dad and that fucker were doing to you and in time, she knew what the hell they were doing to me.'

Elaine shook her head in disbelief.

'One day, I slipped out of the house unnoticed. I had to find out, it's what kids do. I spied through a gap over there.' He pointed to the opposite end of the bed. 'I was able to pull a couple of slats free and squeeze myself through. I tried to stop them and they beat me, they beat me bad – then they both took their turn with me.' The tears he hadn't wanted to share continued to fall. 'They never used you for their pleasure again. I don't know why and it's something I've never understood but unfortunately for me, they decided I'd satisfy their evil desires. I tried to fight them at first, but eventually, I stopped. I don't know why. Maybe I was so physically and mentally broken, I no longer had the strength. They'd stopped hurting you and that was all I wanted.'

Harper stood and walked over to a wooden support post that rose from the ground and up to a cross beam. He leaned against it. 'I tried to tell Mother on many occasions but she always turned a death ear. In the end, she must have told Dad. They must have worried that I'd tell someone because they brought me back to this barn and threw me to the floor – right here.' A solemn-looking Harper surveyed the spot beneath his feet. 'Dad beat me unconscious and when I awoke, I found myself tied to this post.' He placed an arm around the column.

'Later that night, Denley Parker showed up. They slapped, punched, kicked, and used me. They finished off by urinating over me.' Harper was visibly overwhelmed with pain as he relived the abuse, the scars, without doubt, etched deep into his soul.

'As they did those despicable things, they made threats and said much worse would happen if I told anyone, not only to me but to you as well. I couldn't think of anything worse they could possibly do to me but I certainly wasn't going to risk finding out.'

Harper left the beam and strolled back to her. He leaned down in front of her. 'In the end, I couldn't have told anyone, not even if I'd wanted to. They kept me in here … tied to that post like an animal, for their amusement. So you see, Elaine, that's who our parents were – *Godless creatures.*'

He got to his feet and paced around the barn.

As Elaine listened attentively, she thought back to her nightmare where her father unmasked his face. The beast of her darkness? So many things started to make sense. She could understand Harper's tribulation.

'I wasn't even allowed back in the house. Fifteen nights, I spent, tied to this post,' he said, kneeling next to it. 'These marks in the wood right here are how I kept count.' Pensively, he moved his fingers over the engraved lines. 'On the sixteenth night, Mother finally caved. She couldn't take it anymore. Guilt maybe, who knows – who cares! She should never have allowed her children to suffer at the hands of those monsters. They had plans for both of us that night, and it wasn't only our father and Denley Parker.' Harper walked over, turned her chair away from the bed and sat opposite.

For a moment, Elaine was elsewhere, her mind, ravenous for long-forgotten memories of the atrocities that had occurred; the horrific things that had happened to them. Her little brother's pain, her pain, their tears, their scars. These awful events had been buried so deep within her and now – Harper had exhumed them. Elaine wasn't certain she wanted to hear anymore, but the choice was not hers.

'They'd found more men who'd also acquired a particular taste. Three other men, in fact. They came to do unspeakable things to us that night. Finally, for whatever reason, Mother intervened.' Harper rose to his feet, upset and angry. 'The police surrounded the barn and restrained them all. They saved you from a fate worse than death.' His eyes filled with a deluge of sadness. 'For me, it was too late.' He turned and glared at her. 'Your brother died that night, Elaine.'

Devastated by Harper's revelations, rendered numb by the flood of memories, the tears kept on coming. Not for her suffering, but for her brother's.

Harper retook his seat and continued, 'After that night, the police took us to a special hospital for children who'd suffered from the most obscene traumas. The doctors said they could help you with some form of intensive treatment. As for me, they considered I was too far gone – irredeemable. They were probably right, what kid could recover from that sort of thing and go on to live a normal healthy life?'

'What happened to you? Where did you go? How did I end up with Mum?' Elaine had so many questions and a strong urge to know more.

With the extent of the trauma, along with some unconventional treatment, her mind had somehow blocked out the cause of so much suffering in her childhood. Erasing the memory of her brother during the process was intentional, or unfortunate. The unlocking of her mental vault had set everything free. She now understood her mother's suicide. Margaret could no longer live with what she'd let happen to her children. She was their mother: she should have been the one to protect them, keep them safe, and if that meant from their own father, so be it. Margaret had more than failed her children; she had abetted an evil man and his accomplices. No wonder she couldn't live with herself.

'After a few months, we were separated and treated in different places. When you were eleven and deemed well enough, they returned you to our dear mother. I was nine, Elaine. Just a nine-year-old boy with nobody. I was taken to a psychiatric unit, where they promised to make me better and one day send me home. How was I to know that would never happen? It was never their intention to consider me for release – not ever. They changed my name. I assume to make it impossible for anyone to find me and to ensure I'd get lost in the system.'

Elaine wanted to deny everything she'd heard but deep down, she knew it to be the absolute truth.

Harper got to his feet and paced around once more. 'So there it is, you were sent home and me, well, I've been alone all these years, forgotten, a life destroyed. Which brings us to where we are now,' said Harper, arms wide to gesture at their surroundings, 'back to where it all went wrong and our lives were changed forever.'

'Liam – your name – you're Liam,' she said.

Harper smiled at her. 'I knew you would remember.'

'But why?' she asked, her face a depiction of puzzlement. 'Why did you come back here?'

'To find something in the house and like I said, to kill you.'

'Why kill me? I don't understand.'

'For the longest time, Elaine, I hated and resented you. The fact you were sent back here and I was hidden away like some dirty little secret. All I did was try to protect my big sister when nobody else would. I presumed you'd gone on to have some fantastic life and dismissed me from your thoughts like everybody else. Now I discover you were manipulated to forget Liam and that you're just like me – him.'

'I haven't killed anyone, so no – I'm nothing like you,' Elaine retorted.

'Let's just say you haven't killed anyone yet, but how far would you go, Elaine? To protect yourself, your children, to be with them again? What would you do if it were possible to make that happen?' he replied, insinuating she was indeed capable of such a thing.

'Why did you kill PC James?' she asked, turning the conversation away from herself.

'He found me in the barn. I couldn't let him take me in. They would have sent me back to the hospital.'

'Hospital? You mean – you're not free?' Elaine enquired.

'I'll never be free,' he laughed. 'It took a while but I had to escape and end it all. I told the doctors at Rampton what they wanted to hear, gained their trust and became friends with a member of staff who sympathised. I couldn't have escaped without help.'

'And what do you mean, end it all?'

'I need it all to end. Father was the first to die the night the police raided the barn. The police report said it was a heart attack.'

'You mean it wasn't?'

'Not at all,' he smiled.

'How did he die?' Elaine asked, mystified.

'They said I ran up behind him and rammed an old hay fork through his neck while they restrained him. I sometimes wish I hadn't given him such a quick death. Then again, it may well have been the only chance I'd ever get. Just wish I could remember more about it.

'All these years I've wanted to bring to mind the memory of killing our father. How I'd love to repeat the sensation of that moment again – and enjoy.

'Mr Denley Parker, on the other hand, is still very much alive, living in a luxury retirement home. He and the other three men were never charged for what they did that night. God knows how many more lives they went on to destroy.'

'Never charged?' Elaine said, horrified.

It was inconceivable such atrocities could have been deliberately swept under the carpet without punishment. The only people to suffer for their wicked crimes were her brother and her.

'Nope, they all got away with it. I know some are still alive and one by one, I'm going to hunt them down and kill them. When it's over, I shall take my own life. Only then, will Liam be free.'

'What about Ashton, the policewoman, and Dr Brown? Why did they deserve to die, what did they do?'

'I'm assuming Ashton was the piece of shit that hit you and was about to rape you. Need I say more! The policewoman, again, wrong place – wrong time. If she hadn't found me searching for Dad's secret hiding place, she'd still be alive.'

Outside, Chloé crept around the barn, listening to the muffled voices from inside. At the back of the barn, she came across Elaine's damaged car and Tom's police car. Calm but so confused, Chloé inspected the panels, searching for a gap to see what was going on inside. She found the same loose wooden slat Liam had spied through all those years ago.

Harper returned to his seat and picked up the folder. 'As for Dr Brown, he was bringing this file to you for a reason, and by the letter attached from a certain ...' He pulled the letter from inside to check the name, 'Dr Graham Walker, I reckon someone hadn't told their new doctor everything about herself. He was likely here to confront you, to find out why you'd kept everything from him.'

Harper placed the letter back in her records and waved the folder at her. 'Your history will follow you everywhere as long as these exist. Usually, with doctor/patient confidentiality, the patient supplies written consent or requests their files to be passed on if they change psychiatrist.'

He pulled out a different letter from the folder. From its discoloured and worn appearance, it was plain to see the letter had been written many years ago. 'Not in your case according to this court order. It's signed by a top professor of mental health and a high-ranking judge, recommending you be monitored throughout your life.' Harper placed the note on her lap for her to see. 'They saw you as a danger, Elaine.'

Elaine read the letter, astounded. 'But why? I would never hurt anyone.'

Harper placed a list of three names in front of her. 'I found Dad's secret hiding place. These were the other men in the barn that night. What's familiar?' he asked her.

Elaine studied the names.

Alan Whitehall.

Malcolm Hayes.

Edward Horner.

'Horner! One of these men has the same surname as the judge.'

'Judge Horner is the father of one of the men involved that night, one of the men who violated me. He would have done the same to you.'

Stunned, Elaine said, 'That's despicable, but I don't understand. I've never been a danger to anyone.'

'You still don't get it, do you? You weren't monitored as a danger to society, Elaine. You were monitored because you were a threat to the people involved in our abuse. They were never going to let something like this come out,' he explained. 'For me it was different, they were worried about what I'd remember, names, faces and such. You were an outside risk they were prepared to take a gamble on. I, on the other hand, was not. Their faces are as clear to me now as they were all those years ago. They will have aged but I know I'd recognise them. I knew Dad had a hiding place for his secrets somewhere in the house, so I came back to see if I could find anything to help me, and obviously, I did.'

'And to kill me!'

'That was the plan. Until I came across this file, I wanted to destroy your life and kill you. I had no idea how much suffering you've gone through.'

'And that's a good thing?'

He leaned forward and removed the piece of paper from her lap, placing it back in the folder. 'Not at all. What you have to understand is, for the longest time I had this belief you'd come back to get me one day – like a big sister should – but you never came. As far as I knew, you'd written me off like the rest of them. Now I know that wasn't the case. They'd brainwashed you to forget what went on and to forget your brother ever existed.'

Elaine's mind was a tangled web of uncertainty, not just about her past, but about her brother too. There didn't appear to be any set limit to what Harper Darmody was capable of. Why, oh why, if he'd changed his mind about killing her, did he feel the need to reveal all these horrendous pieces of her mixed-up life in such a tormenting way?

'So if you're not going to hurt me, why was all this necessary?'

'You needed to know who you are and what happened to you and Liam. I had to break you down. You'd never have come into the barn voluntarily – I'd already tested that. You wouldn't have seen the past for how it was and, well, you would never have remembered anything or believed me.'

He wasn't wrong. Her subconscious would have fought against him every step of the way. She would never have given him a chance to explain or have allowed him to bring her into the barn, a place that filled her with a compulsion not only to get out of there but to burn it to the ground.

For every question answered, she had a hundred more to ask. Elaine's attention reverted to the victims, all murdered by the man sitting in front of her. He may have been her brother, but this man was a psychopathic killer, thinking of only one thing, vengeance. He didn't care who got in his way. She empathised with the appalling life he'd had and his yearning for retribution, but there was no way she could excuse him for the murders of PC James, PC Morgan, Dr Brown or even Ashton, even though the latter was a tough call.

'What happens now, Liam?' Elaine asked, exhausted and withdrawn.

'Harper – I told you, Liam died a long time ago. There is barely anything left of him inside me,' he explained. 'Now, I go and finish this for you, and for Liam,' he said with a steely, determined look.

As much as Elaine wanted those involved to pay for what they'd done, she didn't want any more innocent people to die along the way. But what could she do about it?

'Are you going to untie me now?'

'I think it's best for you to stay like that until the police get here. That way you'll be fine, you've done nothing wrong. They'll be chasing a ghost until they connect all the pieces, hopefully by the time they do, this will all be over.'

As he finished speaking, he rushed from his chair over to the door of the barn and peered out. A car crunched up the drive, approaching the house.

'So why, Harper? Why did I need to remember all of this misery?'

He walked back to her. 'Because somewhere inside you, I bet you've always known something far deeper was wrong. Just from reading your file, I could see it. You can't erase the past, Elaine. Even if you forget it, it will always be somewhere inside your head. By knowing who you are, you'll become the person you should've been.'

Before Elaine could respond, he placed the cloth back in her mouth and reapplied the tape.

'Whatever happens, play dumb. Don't tell them you remember your past or your brother. If I fail, you need to finish this, not only for yourself but for Liam. Those monsters cannot go unpunished.' He picked up the folder and waved it in her direction. 'You need to either hide or destroy this, especially the court order. With that now in your possession, you are completely free. They didn't put everything on computers back then and this folder could well be the only link between us that's not buried away in some forgotten box.' He paused for a second and smiled, 'Do you remember the hollow?'

The fond memory came straight away and she nodded.

'That's where the folder will be. Remember, if they ask any questions, tell them nothing. Tell them you have no memory of anything before your mother hanged herself. I have to go now.'

Harper leaned down, placed both hands on either side of her face, and kissed her on the forehead.

'I didn't mean what I said about your son. I had to say whatever it would take to break you down. I'm truly sorry about what happened to him. When you find the man responsible, and believe me, you will – make him pay.'

Harper backed away and disappeared behind her, filling his pockets with the remaining cartridges and placing a large hunting knife behind his back, tucking it inside his duty belt. Seconds later, he came back into view with the long-barrelled shotgun in one hand and a police cap in the other. Harper opened the barn door and took one last glance at Elaine.

'When you do come across our so-called father's hiding place, you'll find a small, wooden red box. Everything you need to know is contained within and things will make more sense.'

Their eyes connected, communicating the sadness of all that had been lost between them.

'It was good to see you, Elaine. Liam loved you, very much.' He stepped outside the barn and closed the large door.

42

Robert parked next to Chloé's car and was incensed she'd felt the need to visit Elaine and interfere. Now he had two uncomfortable conversations to face. He knocked on the front door, to no avail. He called Elaine's mobile; it went straight to voicemail. Robert tried Chloé and heard a recorded message saying the number was unavailable. He tried again and got the same response.

Chloé managed to yank some wooden slats free from the barn and squeezed through the gap. She rushed over to Elaine, whose dishevelled state highlighted she'd been through a hellish ordeal. She dropped the tyre iron on the floor, ripped the tape from Elaine's mouth and pulled out the cloth.

'What's going on?' Chloé muttered.

Elaine gave her an evil glare for ripping the tape away so fast. 'Just untie me, I haven't got time to explain.'

'Who is that policeman?' Chloé asked as she attempted to disentangle the knot in the rope.

'He wasn't a policeman,' Elaine replied.

Chloé paused for a second, waiting for her to elaborate. Elaine remained silent, so she resumed her struggle with the rope. 'This knot is hard to undo,' she said, her overlong false fingernails getting in the way. Chloé's phone rang. The display said it was Robert and she answered.

A little way from the barn, Harper stopped in his tracks to look back. He could have sworn he'd heard a ringing sound coming from that direction. Squinting his eyes in the sun, he listened hard, but couldn't hear a thing. Harper turned his attention back to the house in the distance.

Robert didn't understand what Chloé said over the phone. Her accent and the poor reception did not help. He walked up and down the porch to find a better signal.

'Chloé, I can't hear you. I don't understand what you're saying, you keep breaking up – I said you keep breaking up! Hello, hello. Chloé!' The connection dropped. He tried again and she answered instantly. 'I still can't hear you properly, try moving somewhere else,' he said.

With one hand, Chloé fiddled about with her phone attempting to speak to Robert, while her other hopelessly toyed with the tight knot.

'Robert, I'm in the barn,' she said. 'The signal is useless in here!'

She heard him tell her to move elsewhere, so headed for the barn door.

'Chloé, where are you going?' Elaine asked. 'Chloé – no, come back and untie me. Don't go out there!' Her whisper grew louder as the distance between them increased.

Chloé ignored her and stepped outside. She moved away from the barn searching for a better signal and felt a sharp tug on her hair, viciously pulled back, extending her long, elegant neck. Then came the deft slice that eased across her pale skin. Chloé's mouth opened, she gargled blood in the back of her throat. Her combined expression of shock, fear and pain would be her last. Her legs gave way, her body eased to the ground by Harper.

Frantic, Elaine wiggled and jiggled her hands and arms to free them from the rope loosened by Chloé. The barn door closed and she stopped breathing, praying Chloé had gone for help. She didn't want to think about the consequences if Harper had found her. She carried on with the struggle to free herself, her wrists marked, reddened, and raw.

The phone signal died again and Robert was livid. He stormed to the rear of the house to see if Elaine had left the back door unlocked, confronted by the smashed glass panel.

'Bloody hell,' he uttered, not knowing what to think.

Carefully, Robert crawled through. He caught his bare arm on a shard still secured to the timber beading on the door. 'Fuck!' he shouted, seeing the laceration on his forearm.

Inside, Robert grabbed a wet tea towel from the worktop and held it against the cut. 'Elaine!' he called out as he wrapped it around his arm. 'Chloé!' His voice echoed along the hall. He tried Chloé's mobile again but it went straight to voicemail.

Robert made his way to the end of the hall, where he saw the metal door keep on the floor next to a splintered piece of wood from the architrave. Someone had forced the front door open and bolted it shut from the inside. He walked into the living room and recoiled in horror at the shocking sight of the two police officers. Distressed, he backed out of the doorway and into the hall.

'Chloé!' Robert yelled before charging upstairs to find her. He searched all the rooms, further alarmed to see the front bedroom door hanging off its hinge. Robert ran back down to the front door, sliding the bolt across and pulling it open. He rushed outside, already tapping 999 into his phone. About to press call, he looked up to see a police officer standing at the bottom of the steps with a shotgun.

'Oh, thank God, there are two dead police—'

Elaine jumped in her seat at the thunderous bang in the distance. She recognised the sound. Adrenaline surged through her, spurring her on to get free. She tried to squeeze her hand through the taut loop, shedding the skin from her wrist and the side of her hand. She grimaced and let out a fierce scream through tightly gritted teeth. One bloodied hand was almost free as the rope seared her skin. If she could pull it ... a little further.

*

Detectives Fuller and Pierce turned off the road onto Elaine's drive, an Aston Martin and a Mercedes convertible parked ahead of them.

'Christ, either she's been shopping, or she's got friends with money,' said Fuller, his mouth almost salivating over the Aston Martin.

DCI Fuller was still eyeing up the cars as he prepared to park. DI Pierce, on the other hand, was more focused on the blood trailing down the wall from the body of a man slumped on the porch.

He pulled at his DCI's arm, 'Gaffer, there.'

Fuller, blinded by the sunshine, shielded his eyes to peer through the windscreen. No longer concentrating on his driving, the car crunched into the side of Robert's Mercedes, causing them to jerk to a halt.

'Shit!' Fuller shouted. 'Call it in and get some backup out here, fast,' he ordered Pierce.

Fuller flung his door open and appeared more upset about crashing the police BMW than helping the gunshot victim. He shook his head in annoyance and trotted to the house.

While calling for backup, Pierce saw a uniformed officer walk through the wide-open front door. There was blood on the officer's shirt. Something didn't feel right.

Fuller stooped to examine the man on the porch: he was still alive but unconscious. He then clocked the police constable. 'And you are?' he enquired.

'PC Kell. I think you need to see inside, sir,' Harper answered. Looking grim and troubled, he led the detective inside.

With the call made, DI Pierce scanned around for a police car. 'Strange,' he said, suspicious of how a constable was in the middle of nowhere without transport. DI Pierce climbed from the car, closed the door behind him, and walked to the house.

Fuller followed the constable who stopped by the living room door. The DCI walked past PC Kell and entered the living room. Fuller reeled at the sight of two dead police officers. He was even more shocked to see one of them was Tom Burgess. He cast an eye over PC Morgan, noting the strangulation marks on her neck. He'd seen some bad things in his time, and this wasn't the worst, but it was so unexpected to see two fellow police officers, slain in such a brutal way. He needed air and made a hasty exit, barging past the constable.

Pierce had ascended the steps to assess the wounded man on the porch when Fuller rushed through the doorway, resting one hand on the doorframe as he doubled over.

'You all right, Gaffer?' a concerned Pierce asked, wondering what his DCI had seen inside the house.

Fuller lifted his head to the DI. Weak, dizzy, he tried to catch his breath and keep from vomiting. He straightened up, holding onto the frame, his eyes wild and wet, his skin pale and clammy, his mouth moving soundlessly.

Behind DCI Fuller in the hall and out of DI Pierce's view, Harper, casual as you like, reached a hand behind the front door for the shotgun he'd hidden there when the detectives arrived. At close range, he raised the weapon, aiming at the exposed side of Fuller.

The young DI's patience dwindled as he waited for Fuller to pull himself together and explain. He stepped forward, ready to find out for himse—

A deafening blast rang out. Instinct brought his hands up to his ears. DCI Fuller's body thudded to the floor. Speckles of blood peppered the dumbstruck Pierce, who stood mouth agape.

Red drops sprinkled like rain onto the recently painted white floorboards and the body of his dead colleague. The side of Fuller's blue shirt, in shreds, a chunk of his flesh replaced by a crimson lake from which two white pieces of fractured ribcage jutted out.

43

Free at last, Elaine winced at the sight of her hands weeping from the abraded skin. Another shot *roared* in the distance. She untied her ankles with shaking hands and rushed over to the barn door, shoving it open. Chloé lay face down, the ground beneath her soaked in blood, already scorched by the intense rays of the hot sun. Elaine knelt beside Chloé and rolled her over. She gasped at the sight of the gruesome slash to her neck and her wide, petrified eyes. She rummaged around Chloé's corpse for the phone. Elaine entered 999 and pressed Call. Nothing. No signal bars. After another failed attempt, she ran to the house.

The long barrel of the shotgun emerged through the open doorway, followed by the blood-soaked uniformed officer. DI Pierce knew he should run for cover, but his fight-or-flight response failed to kick in. Pierce stared at the man in front of him, glowering into the ice-cold eyes of the killer. Pierce turned, ran, and dived head first over the steps of the porch as the weapon fired, the shot striking his left calf. He hit the ground hard and rolled onto his back, yelling at the explosion of agony.

The gunshot reverberated as an exhausted and frantic Elaine ran. One thing was clear to her: Harper had to be stopped. He was no longer seeking retribution alone; he was on a murderous rampage. She had no idea what it would take to stop him or even if she could. He might kill her too.

Parked off the road in front of a closed gate to a field full of sheep, Police Constables Alfie White and Sean Norris sat in a police car pouring coffee into plastic cups from a flask. Both in their thirties, with Alfie pushing the big Four-O and Sean at the lower end.

'Well, at least we've discovered it wasn't an accident, your Mrs really can't make coffee,' said Sean.

'You're right, it is pretty bad,' Alfie laughed. 'I'll be glad when your Andrea gives birth and we can get back to normal.'

'Anytime now, Alfie. I doubt she'll be back making our coffee yet, though. What with the baby and all.'

'I bet if you took this shit back for her to taste, she would,' Alfie stated.

'You could be right there,' said Sean. 'I'm only joking. It's not that bad.' He took another sip and looked appalled. 'No, it is that bad. In fact, I don't think I've ever tasted anything worse.'

He emptied his cup out of the car window. 'Sorry, mate, I can't drink any more.'

'Can't say I blame you,' Alfie replied, slinging his out the window as well.

Looking back at the porch steps, Pierce tracked the line of blood from his leg wound. A steadfast Harper came into view above him. In trouble now, he couldn't get to his feet and run for it. Pierce watched as Harper pointed the shotgun at him. His life about to end and there was nothing he could do about it. Pierce closed his eyes and waited for death. He heard the distinctive click of the trigger and then – nothing. His eyelids flicked open in disbelief. The fleeting inevitability of death, relieved by an adrenaline rush of life itself, he scrambled to his feet, limping and hopping as fast as he could to the car.

After inadvertently toying with his prey, a calm and composed Harper let the barrel and forearm fall forward, releasing the spent shells. He reached into his pocket, pulled out a couple more and loaded them into the breech, all the while keeping one eye on the detective making his escape.

'Do you think they get bored?' Sean asked Alfie, who stood next to him as they both gazed straight ahead.

'Wouldn't you?' Alfie challenged.

'I suppose it depends.'

'On what?'

'Well, if you had a couple of mates to hang about with or even a bird, it might not be so dull,' said Sean.

'They look quite unsociable to me.'

'What do you mean?' asked Sean.

'Well, it's not like there's much talking going on.'

'Hmm, I suppose not.'

'You set on any names yet?' Alfie quizzed.

'For the sheep?' Sean asked, puzzled, as both men gazed straight ahead into a field, full of the woolly things.

Alfie looked at Sean, 'No, you dickhead – the baby,' he said, turning to zip up his fly. They'd been taking a leak. 'Why would I ask you to name a bleeding sheep?' he said, as he walked to the car.

'I thought that's what we were talking about,' said Sean, shaking himself before turning and zipping up.

'I worry for this baby, mate, I really do.'

The radio on Alfie's shoulder called for emergency assistance to Sablefall Farm. They'd visited the place once before to search with the detectives. Alfie responded immediately, telling them they were on their way.

'Come on,' Alfie called to Sean, 'that's not too far from here.'

DI Pierce threw himself onto the driver's seat, closing the door behind him. A harrowing realisation clobbered him: the keys weren't in the ignition. Enraged, he thumped his clenched fists on the steering wheel over and over. Through the windscreen, a frustrated Pierce beheld the armed man approaching.

'Shit.' He knew his one chance to get away had gone.

Harper bore down on him and stared through the open window into the detective's eyes. He raised the barrel to Pierce's head but held fire, distracted by another car pulling into the gravel drive.

Panting, Elaine crawled double-quick through the hole in the back door, unconcerned about the fragments of glass that pressed into her hands and knees. She let out a shriek as a shard of glass lodged in the palm of her hand. Her eyes fixed on the splinter under her skin, Elaine stumbled to her feet, Chloé's phone on the floor. She plucked the shard from her hand and set off through the kitchen and along the hall, passing the living room without a second glance.

She surfaced through the open doorway to be greeted by DCI Fuller's body sprawled out in front of her. Elaine stepped around him, missing Robert's body to her right, her eyes drawn to her brother aiming the shotgun at DI Pierce. Beyond him, a car sped up the drive: Lenny Grey's black Renault.

Lenny had come to see if Elaine had mulled over his offer and found himself in the middle of a war zone. It was clear he was heading right into the thick of it. Instinct told him that despite the uniform, the man with the shotgun was no police officer. He put his foot down, gripped the steering wheel, and sped up the bumpy driveway, headed straight for him. Lenny saw the man swivel on the spot and re-focus his attention towards his onrushing car, taking aim. Pedal to the floor, Lenny hoped for the best.

*

'Liam!' Elaine screamed.

Harper turned to her, their eyes bonding, his attention diverted. The ground rumbled as the black Renault speeded towards him. Harper unlocked his gaze and focused on the oncoming car – but he was too late. On impulse, Harper leapt onto the bonnet as the car ploughed into him.

The shotgun flew from his hand and landed on the grass. Lenny's windscreen shattered as Harper hit and tumbled over the top of the car and onto the gravel drive. Harper's body rolled over and over for a good few feet as the car came to an abrupt halt.

Lenny leaned over the passenger seat, opened the glove compartment, and pulled out an M1911 pistol he'd brought back after a spell as a correspondent during the Bosnian war. It was a gift from a former U.S. Marine who'd been fighting for the Bosnian Serbs. Lenny's tendency to rub people up the wrong way made it sensible to carry some form of protection.

He scrambled out of his car, glanced back at the man face down in the dirt, and slipped the gun into the small of his back. He saw a man struggling to get out of his car and went to his aid.

'I assume you're a detective?' said Lenny.

'DI Pierce.'

Lenny offered his shoulder, 'Come on, let's get you back to the house.'

Elaine stared over at her brother's battered body on the drive and then back to Lenny and DI Pierce. About to help, the sight of her ex-husband anchored her up. Barely a few feet away, his back against the rendered wall, his head hung low, one hand by his side and the other in his lap. In utter dread, she fell to her knees next to Robert, placed her hands either side of his face, and lifted his head; Robert's eyes steadily opened. As he forced his lips apart to speak, a trickle of blood left the corner of his mouth, making the short journey down his chin.

'Don't try to speak. I'll get help,' she said.

She searched herself for Chloé's phone and remembered leaving it on the kitchen floor. She hurried to her feet and rushed back inside the house to fetch it.

Lenny helped pierce up the steps to the bench. He glanced at the bodies on the porch. 'What a fucking mess,' he said.

Lenny pointed to the slumped body on the porch. 'Who's this poor sod?'

'Don't know him, but that's my DCI over there.'

'Well, he ain't your DCI anymore,' Lenny quipped. 'Have you called for help?'

'Yeah,' the DI muttered as he leaned forward to examine his leg. 'Should be here soon.'

'What the hell happened here?'

'I have no idea,' said Pierce.

Lenny stepped over the dead detective and entered the house to find Elaine. He walked along the hall and took a passing glance into the living room, and went inside for a closer look.

'Fuck me,' he said in disbelief.

44

'Elaine!' Lenny shouted as he went back out into the hall. He was about to yell again when he heard her voice. He marched along the hallway and found her in the kitchen, pacing near the back door, talking on the phone. He placed his pistol on the kitchen table just as Elaine hung up.

'Emergency services are already on their way,' she said to Lenny.

'Jesus Christ, Elaine – what's going on here?'

She beheld him with tired eyes and shrugged, conveying there was far too much to explain. Instead, she went straight to the sink to get some water. She downed an entire glass and turned to face him. She struggled for words, manifestly weak, overwhelmed, and exhausted. On her last legs and unsteady, she tilted, ready to keel over.

'Easy, girl,' he said, as he moved forward and saved her from falling. He eased her to the floor by the sink and poured her another glass of water.

*

A police car tore up the gravel track, blue lights flashing, siren raging.

'Is he one of ours?' asked PC Alfie White, nodding at an officer lying face down on the ground ahead of them.

'Shit, yes,' replied PC Sean Norris.

They parked up a little way from where he lay, donned their stab vests and raced over to their floored colleague.

Alfie stooped in front of the man to check if he was still alive. 'I can feel a pulse,' he said to Sean, who did not reply.

He looked up to see Sean staring straight ahead, transfixed on the house. Alfie rose to his feet to find out what he was looking at and saw the white rendering on the porch, covered in blood.

'Oh fuck,' said Alfie, taking a couple of steps forward. 'Right, you stay with him,' he added, before running ahead to the house.

Sean knelt down and rolled the injured PC onto his back, astounded to see so much blood. The PC lay still, eyes closed.

'Can you hear me, mate? It's going to be all right. An ambulance is on the way,' said Sean, leaning over his colleague as he analysed the bloodstained shirt, trying to figure out where the officer had been hurt.

Harper's eyes flashed open.

PC Alfie White scaled the steps to the porch, bewildered and alarmed. He looked at the detective sat on the bench.

'I'm DI Pierce,' he said, producing his warrant card.

'I know. We've met,' the constable answered, casting his eyes in horror over the grisly scene.

'The bloke on the drive – is he dead?' asked Pierce, urgency in his voice.

'Is that DCI Fuller?' Alfie asked.

'Never mind that,' said Pierce, pointing to the drive. 'Is he dead?'

'No, he's still alive,' Alfie responded.

'Then get some fucking cuffs on him and quick. He's not a police officer,' Pierce exclaimed.

'What are you talking about?'

'He's a fucking psycho!'

Alfie spun around and ran back towards Sean, shouting.

Bloodied saliva drooled from the constable's mouth. Sean's eyes bulged, his face, a picture of confusion and anguish.

'Shhh – let go,' Harper whispered softly as he twisted the sharp hunting knife further into his stomach, right between his vest and duty belt.

Sean heard the knife slice across the base of his belly and watched his innards drop from the savage wound and envelope his killer's hand.

Harper observed the other policeman heading his way and shoved Sean's body off to the side. Harper sat upright; his scheming eyes fixed on the advancing officer. He rose to his feet, shaking his arm free of torn flesh and entrails.

Alfie came to a standstill, visibly aghast.

Harper smiled at the officer's terrified reaction. He bent over, clasped a hand around the handle of the knife, and withdrew it from the dead constable. Thick blood dangled grotesquely like red string from the end of the blade as he walked towards PC Alfie White, menace emanating from every pore.

Alfie fumbled to release the Taser from his duty belt. He took aim, but too late. Two small dart electrodes attached themselves to his neck. Harper had fired the Taser from his own belt. Alfie sank to his knees before he dropped to the floor in spasms, his muscles painfully contracting.

Blasé, Harper ambled over to him, the Taser falling casually from his grip.

Sidelined by injury and now a mere spectator, DI Pierce was well aware how useless he was. Even with the damage to his leg, he couldn't stand idly by and do nothing. He staggered down the steps, limping as fast as he could, grimacing with every painful step. Pierce's agony took its toll. He stumbled to the ground by Lenny's car.

Standing over Alfie White, Harper gloried in Pierce's pain as he hobbled and collapsed. Harper fell to his knees beside the incapacitated policeman, a cold-hearted and calculating look in his eyes. He eyeballed the detective, wanting him to observe. Without remorse or effort, he eased the sharp long blade deep into the police officer's collarbone, severing his subclavian artery.

Harper checked he still held the detective's attention as he removed the knife from the constable's neck. Harper relished his savagery as he progressively ascended to his feet. His eyes lowered to the rhythmical pumping from the fatal wound flooding the ground beneath him.

The DI, sickened by the display of butchery playing out in front of him, got to his knees and cast an eye around, searching for something, anything that could aid his cause. The indignant look on his face said it all: from the affliction of his injury to the fact he could do nothing as two fellow police officers were cut down in front of him.

Harper was on his way towards him. Blood cascading down his arm and sluggishly dripping from the tip of the large hunting knife. Ahead of DI Pierce on the grass, the shotgun. The spirited detective heaved himself up onto his feet and made an excruciating dash for the gun.

Harper's steady pace remained unchanged.

As Elaine carried out a glass of water and knelt beside Robert, Lenny gasped at the sight of two dead officers on the drive and the impending confrontation between DI Pierce and the killer. He saw Pierce launch himself to the ground, seize the shotgun, and raise it a fraction before Harper arrived calmly, and placed his foot on the long barrel, forcing it down. Lenny reached back to grab the pistol, only to realise he'd left it on the kitchen table.

DI Pierce rolled onto his back and glared up at Harper Darmody, who stared down with a feral grin.

'Third time lucky!' Harper mocked.

'Go on then, you mad fucking bastard. Do it!' Pierce roared, spittle ejecting from his mouth.

Harper lowered himself, a knee either side of the DI's head, and plunged the knife into the detective's chest multiple times. Blood rained on the grass every time the blade was withdrawn. Pierce's agonised howl faded to a hush until only the sickening whispered squelch of the knife tearing in and out resonated.

The glacial blue of Harper's wide eyes was in direct contrast to his blood-soaked face. He inhaled the overpowering metallic scent that surrounded him.

'Get in the house, Elaine,' Lenny said, after watching Harper reach for the shotgun.

Lenny raised his voice, 'Elaine – come on, get in the house!'

'Why?' she asked, finally hearing Lenny's growl.

'Because the bastard's coming for us, that's why.' Lenny had never been afraid of much in his life, but on this occasion, he was markedly unnerved. This wasn't just any man coming for them: this was an inhumane monster.

Elaine didn't know if she was relieved or afraid that her brother was still alive, perhaps a little of both. She let Robert's head drop and stood by Lenny. They both regarded the sight of the deranged murderer standing over the shredded body at his feet. Harper eased his head up and fixed his gaze upon them, so sanguine in colour, he could have been the devil himself.

Elaine knew he hadn't been born evil. He was man-made. He was her little brother, who'd suffered so much at the hands of others. Unsure whether her safety was guaranteed, she focused on Harper's impenetrable eyes and inscrutable countenance. His body language gave the impression of a man who enjoyed both the hunt and the kill of these people who had nothing to do with the vengeance he craved.

Lenny grabbed her hand, pulling Elaine into the house. He closed the door, bolted it, and scurried along the hall to the kitchen to get his pistol. Not the fittest of men, the sudden rush of activity made him cough as he checked his gun.

Elaine was by the living room door. Immobilised by the daunting spectacle in front of her. She drifted into the room, denying the evidence of her own eyes as she looked at the body of Tom Burgess. Engulfed by sorrow, her shoulders slumped. She liked Tom, and if she'd had any tears left, they would have been for him. With immense sadness, she turned and left the room to join Lenny in the kitchen.

As she left, Tom's eyes opened. He was in critical need of help and tried to call out, but didn't have enough strength to raise a whisper. With every passing second, he weakened. Tom lay inert, doing his utmost to hold on, his head moving sloth-like, searching for anything that could aid him to get someone's attention. He saw his phone on the floor by the skirting – but it was out of reach.

*

Numb and detached, Elaine seated herself at the kitchen table. With all that was going on, it was as though she was elsewhere, or at least her mind was. Thoughts of what had happened to Robert and seeing poor Tom circled: it was an awful lot to take in. Lenny's loud, gravelly voice brought her back to the present.

'Who's the nutjob, Elaine?' he asked, as he caught water from the tap in his cupped hands and drank it. He repeated the process, this time splashing his boiling and sweaty face with the refreshing cold liquid.

'My brother,' she said, her tone soft and low.

Lenny spun around sharp, glaring at her, his face, dripping wet. 'Your brother! Are you fucking kidding me?'

'It's a long story, Lenny. You can't tell anyone who he is. Not yet. I'll explain it all to you, I promise.'

'Yes, you bloody well will. Come on.'

'Where are we going?'

'It'll be safer upstairs. We'll sit tight 'til more police get here. They must be close.'

Lenny led the way as they rushed along the darkened hall. Nearing the bottom of the stairs, a thunderous blast split the front door. The middle of the old wooden door flew off in pieces. Rays of sunlight penetrated the gloom. Lenny glanced at his chest, startled to see a long spear-like splinter of wood embedded into it.

'Fuck it!' he said. His body lumbered backwards, like a felled tree. Elaine was quick to catch and ease him to the floor; only then did she see his wound.

'Come on, Lenny,' she said, straining to heave him back to the kitchen. Lenny rallied enough to help by using his legs to push himself along, but they weren't getting anywhere fast.

Still conscious, Tom raised his head in time to see Elaine dragging Lenny past the doorway. As his head slumped to the floor, he reached his trembling hand towards his pocket.

Harper kicked the bottom of the door away and ducked under the top half. Unflustered, he advanced, aiming the shotgun at Lenny. Elaine doubted whether any part of her brother remained within the man stood in front of them. Maybe he wasn't lying when he told her Liam was dead. It was possible that Harper Darmody was all that remained now, with only the tragic memories of a past life he intended to avenge – no matter the cost.

The man who'd shot him stood by the living room door, targeting Lenny and Elaine. Tom retrieved some tissue from his pocket. His fingers fumbled around, trying to locate the gold pocket watch he'd found at the pond. He manoeuvred the chain through his blood-encrusted fingers until it was tight in his palm. Using his thumb, he flipped the top of the watch open. The musical tone began to play.

Harper turned his head abruptly and frowned at the police officer he'd presumed was dead. Defiant, Tom scowled back at him.

*

Taking advantage of this unexpected opportunity, Lenny lifted his shaky right hand and fired the pistol. The bullet entered the left side of Harper's stomach. Stunned, Harper glared down at the wound and raised the barrel.

Elaine, fearing Lenny no longer had the strength to keep his aim steady, placed her hand under his arm to add support. A second shot left the pistol, hitting Harper high up in the shoulder. Stock-still, Harper's eyes engaged with Elaine's. Lenny fired again, the bullet striking the left side of Harper's neck. Elaine let Lenny's hand drop, his head in her lap. Harper let the shotgun fall from his grasp and clatter to the floor. He held Elaine's gaze, blood *oozing* from his neck.

Distant sirens broke the silence. Harper put a hand over the hole in his neck to stem the flow. He calmly turned, ducked under the door and stepped out into the unrelenting sun. Elaine watched on as Harper's legs disappeared from view. She laid Lenny down and ran to Tom's side. She stroked his cheek as he regarded her with a weak smile, happy she was okay.

'Hold on, Tom – hold on,' her words soft and meaningful. 'I'll be right back, I need to check on Robert.'

Elaine left Tom and headed to the front door. She ducked and peered through the hole to see if it was safe, and then stepped outside. Her brother was nowhere in sight. She doubted he'd get too far with those wounds. Harper's body would be found sooner or later, somewhere. Through the trees along the front, several police cars and an ambulance announced their arrival, sirens blaring.

Elaine turned to Robert who had slumped over onto his side. She knelt in front of him and shifted him onto his back. He was still alive but his breathing was noticeably shallow. She waited with Robert until she heard the footsteps of the police and paramedics. Elaine turned to them, wiping her eyes, pleading for them to help. She moved out of their way and urgently guided another paramedic into the house to assist Tom, then she went back into the hall to check on Lenny.

Seated at the kitchen table. Lenny lit a cigarette as she walked in, seemingly unbothered by the large splinter embedded in his chest.

'What are you doing, you fool?' she asked, taking the cigarette from his fingers after he'd taken a long puff.

'Hey, if I'm gonna die – I want one last smoke. So give it back,' Lenny tone facetious, trying not to reveal his discomfort.

'You're not going to die, Lenny. People like you never do.' Elaine handed the cigarette back to the brazen and grinning Lenny Grey. She went to leave the room to check on Tom, a subtle smile on her face, secretly pleased Lenny was going to be all right.

'Ere, Elaine. I don't suppose I'll be getting my ten grand now, will I?' he asked.

She paused, looked back and said, 'Oh, I reckon we can come to a better arrangement. Just don't mention anything to the police about my brother. There's a story here, Lenny, and I'm going to need your help to tell it.'

Her poise, so different from less than five minutes ago. Perhaps a combination of the adrenaline still pumping through her veins and the realisation this ordeal was finally over. Maybe even relief that the hidden chapters of her life had been opened up to her, no matter how uncomfortable those unveilings were. There would be no more hiding from her past. A dark truth needed to be told and Lenny Grey could help her do just that.

Elaine glanced into the living room: the paramedics were doing all they could for Tom. She hoped and prayed it wasn't as bad as it looked. A police officer removed the top part of the front door as another medic entered the house. Elaine sent him to the kitchen to see to Lenny. She went back outside and took in the chaotic spectacle of so many police cars and ambulances, emergency personnel dashing between victims, checking for signs of life – of Robert, as paramedics used a defibrillator, trying their best to resuscitate him.

One of the paramedics stared up at her, words unnecessary. Robert was dead. Elaine was sad but bereft of tears. The medic hurried to her assistance, helping her over to the bench. He sat her down and assessed her wounds.

It had been a terrifying, traumatic, and tragic day. Sadly, it wasn't the only one she'd experienced in her life, and in all likelihood, wouldn't be the last. All she wanted right now was to sleep and return to some kind of normality. She watched Lenny Grey driven off to the hospital, followed not long after by Tom in an air ambulance. Elaine would be following shortly. For now, she stayed behind to give her statement and help with the investigation. Of course, she'd leave out some details, the events involving Ashton, for example, and her discovery of the police car in the pond. They didn't need to know every single detail. Some things were best left unsaid.

On the bench, Elaine was in the middle of giving her statement to DCI Rhona Hart when the detective received a phone call from an officer at Scarborough General Hospital and excused herself. The DCI walked behind the swing bench to the end of the porch, several feet away. Elaine's ears pricked when she heard the mention of Dr Neville Brown. It sounded as though he was conscious but in a very frail state. It surprised her to learn he was still alive; she'd expected Harper to have been more thorough. He'd been moved from intensive care to a ward, which the detective repeated as she made a note in her pad.

Time passed and the glow of daylight appeared to diminish earlier than usual. Clouds resembling shredded orange peel hung above the inconceivable crime scene at Sablefall Farm. There was much work ahead for the forensic examiners and detectives, which would, no doubt, go on for some days to come.

As the police helicopter carried Elaine to the hospital, she glanced over her property, reminded of being on the Ferris wheel the night Charlie was taken from her. The headlights and flashing multi-coloured lights from every emergency vehicle you could imagine almost resembled the fairground. Further along the road, vans and cars containing news crews and journalists tried to find a way past the roadblock that had been set up around the perimeter. Carnage on this scale was big news. The site of a massacre in a quiet little town like Helmsley would be broadcast to the world. People would talk about this for years.

45

Thursday, 17 August

The corridors and wards at Scarborough General Hospital were quiet, as they should be, during the small hours of the morning. A doctor considered it necessary to keep Elaine in for observation after her knock to the head, even more so after she'd mentioned feeling dizzy and faint. It would be easy to attribute it to fatigue after such a harrowing day.

Lying in the hospital bed, head bandaged to cover the stitches, her eyes opened. For a brief spell, she wondered where she was. She quietly yawned and speculated about the other bed in the room, the curtains pulled all the way around it. Exhausted, she hadn't noticed much when she arrived. The doctor finished checking her over, she rested her bandaged head on the pillow. Her whole body needed a decent rest.

Breaking the silence, a little boy sniggered. Through the curtains, she saw the outline of a small figure. Someone whispered, telling him to shush. She pulled off her covers and walked to the other bed. A second profile appeared, the shadow of a much larger person. She assumed it was a father and son and turned back. Elaine heard more childish laughter and smiled, thinking it was cute.

Then she heard the whispered words, 'Shush, Charlie. She'll hear us.'

Elaine's face paled. With dread in her eyes, she headed back towards the bed and took one uneasy step after another. With an outstretched hand, she whipped the curtain across the rail. Charlie sat cross-legged on the bed, smiling at her. Close by – Harper Darmody, dressed in the same blood-drenched police uniform. At the head of the bed, the sadistic and malevolent crimson creature from her nightmares, only now, something about him was different.

'Hello, Mummy,' said Charlie, holding a string attached to a yellow balloon which hovered above his head.

'Hello, dear sister,' Harper said, looking around with a grin, the bullet hole in his neck apparent.

The insensitive eyes of the beast glowered at her, his red lips parted, revealing his jagged, yellow teeth. 'We've been waiting for you, Elaine. Why don't you join us?' he said, his voice rough and raspy.

That voice, the familiarity of his features, it all started to make sense. A deathly chill swept over her shoulders. The beast *was* the embodiment of her father. Charlie released the balloon; Elaine watched it float up to the tiled ceiling – *Bang*! She jumped.

Harper snatched her arm and pulled her onto the bed.

'Don't be afraid, Mummy. It won't hurt – *for long*.'

Harper yanked the curtain across. The silhouette of the monster's big hands swooped down, tearing into her; shadows splattered the snow-white curtains as she screamed in terror.

Elaine woke to find a concerned nurse standing over her.

'You're fine, you were dreaming,' she said, and passed Elaine a glass of water.

The nurse gone, she tried to settle again, relaxing her head back on the pillow. For a while, she lay still, thinking about her children and how they'd take the news of their father's death. The gentle chiming of her phone alarm went off beside her. She swiped it to silence. It was two-thirty in the morning. She moved to the edge of the bed, put on her slippers and blue dressing gown, grateful the detectives had been kind enough to let her collect some personal things.

Going to another ward, the nurse on duty knew all about the incident and what Elaine had been through, and allowed her to enter. News of the massacre had spread like wildfire. The nurse directed her to the end of the ward and went back to her paperwork behind the desk.

Elaine stood over a bed, watching for a minute. Lenny was fast asleep, his chest heavily bandaged. Earlier, she'd found out which ward he was on. She dipped her fingers into a glass of water on the bedside cabinet and flicked it onto Lenny's face, and repeated the process. The water splashing eventually woke him with a start.

'Fuck me!' Were the first words from his mouth as he smiled and hauled himself upright, wiping the water away. 'This is a turnabout. First, you don't want me near you and now you're visiting me in hospital.'

'Still here then?' she said in a hushed tone so as not to disturb anyone.

'Yeah, ain't easy to get rid of me.' Lenny's gruff cockney tone was anything but hushed.

'Don't I know it,' Elaine quipped as she thought about the run-ins they'd had. 'I suppose it's not all bad you're still breathing, Lenny. We have lots of work to do together.'

'And why would I wanna work with you?'

'Because you need me, and sadly – I need you. Furthermore, there'll be plenty of money in it for you.'

'What a charming bedside manner you have,' he joked.

'Anyway, I only came to see how you're doing and I can see you're fine. I'll leave you to get some beauty sleep.' Elaine started to walk away.

'Oi, Elaine!'

She paused, her eyes signalling she'd never get used to the way he said her name. She turned to face him.

'For most of the night, I've been lying here thinking. Why *were* you gonna give me the ten grand?'

'Why were you asking for ten grand?'

'Well, what with that missing copper, I didn't think you'd want it coming out about your suicide attempt and timeshare in a mental health hospital. I thought you'd want to prevent any unwanted attention coming your way. Now though, I ain't so sure that was the reason you were going to cough up.'

She gave a subtle smirk and as she left the ward said, 'No – you were right, that was the reason.'

Lenny lay back down. 'Lying cow,' he smiled to himself.

Elaine did need Lenny's help and not just to tell her and Liam's story, but to help catch the man who'd killed her son.

*

Late morning and dressed, Elaine perched on the edge of the bed appearing somewhat reinvigorated, despite everything that had gone on, comforted because she'd soon be with her children. Michael and Emily were currently in the care of Robert's parents, who'd already made their grandchildren aware of the dreadful news. Elaine would see them as soon as she left Scarborough General, which she was almost ready to do.

First, there was someone she needed to see. Standing over a hospital bed with an affectionate smile, Elaine greeted the patient as he opened his eyes.

'Good morning, Tom,' she said contentedly. 'I didn't think you were going to make it.'

'I didn't think so either,' said Tom, very happy to see her. 'I feel like I've been ten rounds with the Hulk,' he joked. 'I am glad you're okay.'

'Don't you worry about me, I'm fine.' She smiled and placed her hand on Tom's arm.

'I heard they haven't found your brother yet,' he said, much to Elaine's surprise.

'H-How do you know about Liam?'

'I might not be a detective but I'm not stupid. I did some digging, plus I already knew things about your past.'

'Tom, I don't want it to come out—'

'Hey, stop now. I'm not going to say anything about him being your brother.'

'He's not, Tom. Well, not any more. Liam died a very long time ago and this so-called Harper Darmody, he isn't my brother. It's just the name he was given to hide the sins of others. The man he is now, or was, as the case may be, is the person he created to survive. A caged little boy full of anger for all those years, dreaming and thinking of nothing but vengeance. If he is still alive, he won't quit until he gets it, and God help anyone who gets in his way.'

'I can vouch for that,' he gestured with his eyes to his heavily bandaged torso.

Tom knew so much more about the old case from his father's notes. He'd found them in the attic when clearing out the house after he'd passed away. Tom knew all the wretched details about that despicable night and her father's death. One day, if she wanted to know more about what happened, he would be happy to pass them on to her. But that was a discussion for another day.

'The detective informed me they found poor Andrew in the boot of his police car. The coroner still has to do a full post mortem, but the early signs are, he drowned,' said Tom, a mournful look on his face.

Elaine looked horrified. 'But that means he was still alive when the car went into the pond.'

Tom gave a subtle nod of his head in response.

'Just get yourself well, Tom,' she said, noting how weak and tired he looked. She turned to leave when—

'Wait,' Tom said as he eased forward, his discomfort plain to see. He leaned over, opened the drawer at the side of his bed, and pulled something from it. As he settled back in the bed, he stared at Elaine. His hand opened to reveal the gold pocket watch resting on his palm. 'Do you know who this watch belongs to?'

'It's Robert's. It's been in his family for years. He told me he'd lost it,' she answered.

'I found it out by the pond. Anyway, I'm sure he'd have wanted his son to have it,' he said, placing it in her hand.

She flipped it open to play the quaint tune that had possibly saved her and Lenny's life. In all the commotion, fear, and panic of the moment, it hadn't occurred to her it was the tune from Robert's watch that distracted Harper. She closed her hand around it, leaned in to plant a kiss on Tom's forehead, then left him to rest.

46

Saturday, 26 August

Little over a week later, Elaine was permitted to return home. She'd had to wait until the detectives and the forensics team had finished with her property. For now, the children remained with their grandparents. It would give her a chance to sort out a few things. With Robert and Chloé gone, the property developing business was her responsibility. She still knew many of the staff and for the time being, placed someone she trusted in charge.

Elaine also had the task of getting the house ready for the children, and with a workforce at her disposal, the clean-up and refurb had already started. She considered boarding up the property and moving away, but her desire to finish what she started remained, or perhaps something deeper kept her from doing so.

Over the past week, there had been some much-needed rainfall, though the last couple of days had seen a return to the punishing sunshine. There had been no sign of Harper Darmody. She knew if they hadn't found his body by now, there was every chance he was still alive. He was probably out there somewhere, recovering from his wounds, biding his time until he was able to strike back at those responsible. As of yet, Elaine hadn't located her father's secret hiding place, so had no clue what Harper had left for her to find.

Elaine approached the oak tree. The rope swing lay on the floor having already been taken down. She stared at the trunk and then brushed the ivy aside to reveal a small hollow about waist height. Reaching inside, she pulled out the folder Harper had placed there. Also inside were various seashells, one of which was a brown spindly cone about three centimetres long. She recalled her teacher telling her it was an Auger shell. Elaine then pulled out Liam's favourite toy car: a black Batmobile, and considering how many years had passed, it was in remarkable condition. The tiny Batman and Robin figures were still seated inside. Smiling, she put the shells and the car back in the hollow and walked away.

Stood about ten feet back, Elaine glared at the old, shabby barn. She pulled a box of matches from her pocket, struck one, and tossed it to the floor in front of her. The match hit the ground and ignited a straight line of fuel running through the open barn door. The wood caught alight easily as the fire spread rapidly throughout the barn. She hoped burning this God-awful place of unspeakable memories to the ground was some form of closure. It wouldn't take away her past suffering, but at least she understood why she'd been so troubled throughout her life. Suppressing the abhorrence of her early years hadn't helped her at all. It had merely confused and scrambled her mind further; always knowing something wasn't as it should be. Now, back on her medication, she was feeling better in every aspect of her life. Soon, her children would join her and everything would be as close to normal as possible.

The barn burned and crackled as plumes of smoke filled the sky. Its demise constructive. The heat intensified, far too dangerous to stand so close. She bent over and picked up the folder. Edging away, she took a last glimpse of the barn and saw what was left of the roof cave in, blowing the fire outwards and the smoke upwards. The side of the barn collapsed and she saw the bed, consumed by flames.

Turning her back to the fire, Elaine strode to the house, leaving the past to burn behind her. She opened the folder that contained her mental health history and information about Liam. Also in the folder was the handwritten court order, hopefully, the only copy in existence. Whoever her brother had become and whatever Harper Darmody had done, this was a parting gift from the small piece of Liam that lingered.

As she walked on, with the fire roaring in the background, she recalled the conversation with Harper in the barn. "You're just like me," he'd said.

"I haven't killed anyone, so no – I'm nothing like you," she'd replied.

He came back at her with a sentence that would irrefutably have truer meaning now:

"Let's just say you haven't killed anyone yet, but how far would you go, Elaine? To protect yourself, your children – to be with them again. What would you do if it were possible to make that happen?"

Those words. He did know her after all, and exactly how far she'd go to do exactly that.

47

Thursday, 17 August

When Elaine's alarm went off at the hospital at half past two in the morning, it wasn't by mistake. It was the precise time she'd set it for, and going to see Lenny wasn't the primary reason for being in that particular ward. In one of the other multi-occupancy rooms near Lenny was another man she needed to visit.

Prior to being airlifted to the hospital, Elaine overheard the phone conversation between DCI Rhona Hart and the hospital. She'd not only learned Dr Neville Brown was alive, she'd learned what ward he was on thanks to the detective repeating it aloud as she wrote it down in her notebook. As luck would have it, she'd found Lenny to be on the same ward.

Standing over the bed, he looked peaceful in his sedated slumber. He knew too many things about her from the file he'd been sent by Dr Walker, who'd now retired abroad. Dr Brown could ruin everything for her. The new start with her children she so desperately craved would never happen if the contents of the file ever came to light. Had there always been a darkness dormant within her? A string of tragic events in her life bringing it all to the fore. Lenny Grey once told her he could see a darkness behind her eyes. Elaine wasn't going to let this man stop her from being with her children. Nobody was going to ruin her chances now.

She walked across to the bed opposite and without disturbing the elderly gentleman, eased a pillow out from underneath him. Returning to Dr Brown, she stood over him, resolute. She leaned forward, and with a firm hand, placed the pillow over his face. Weak, heavily dosed, there wasn't much of a struggle as she smothered him. She held the pillow until his body stopped half-heartedly fighting against her and fell limp. To be sure, she kept the pillow in place for a little longer before taking it away. She gazed at his lifeless body for a minute.

'I'm so sorry, Dr Brown,' she said, and shifted his body onto its front to make it look as though he'd suffocated.

Elaine returned the pillow, lifted the elderly gentleman's head and placed it beneath him. He stirred for a brief moment but soon drifted off again.

Wednesday, 16 August

The deaths of eleven people were eventually attributed to Harper Darmody, six of those being police officers. Although credited with every single death, Harper was only responsible for nine of them. One of those he didn't kill was Dr Brown.

At some point during the pandemonium on the day of the massacre, Elaine saw an opportunity. A clear picture developed in her head of what she needed to do. It had come to her right before Lenny told her to get inside the house because Harper was alive and coming for them. Kneeling and holding Robert's head up, he was still breathing. Her mind, with startling clarity, what a bastard he'd been to her. All the lying, all the cheating. A betrayal by the man she'd chosen to have a life and children with. Now he had the children, her children, and she had no chance of ever getting them back. Why hadn't she seen all this before? God only knows what else he would have eventually taken from her.

After Lenny shot Harper, Elaine went to check on Tom. She heard the sirens approaching and went outside to check her brother had gone; she saw how close the emergency services were. This was her chance, her only chance, and she had to take it. She dropped down in front of Robert and pulled him away from the wall, shifting him onto his back. She glanced over her shoulder to make sure what she was about to do would be concealed from the oncoming ambulance and police car. With the palm of one hand placed over his bloody mouth and a finger and thumb securing his nostrils, she blocked his airways. It was feasible Robert would have died anyway, but for Elaine, it wasn't a risk she was going to take. Robert's eyes opened, he looked up at her, in shock and disbelief. Elaine, unwavering as she glared down at him.

'I know everything, Robert,' she said in a quiet and chilling voice. 'All about the cheating, the affair with Chloé, and how you thought I was crazy. Guess you could be right about that,' she said. 'I also know you as good as killed our son while you were busy fucking that French slut. Do you know what today is, Robert? I bet you don't. It's exactly five years to the day since Charlie was murdered. How could you have done that to me, to our children? You left him all alone.'

Robert's eyes expressed not only his guilt and shame, but also his desire to live.

'What did you think would happen, Robert? Did you think you'd have me tucked away in an institution and get my business, my money, and more importantly – my children?'

Robert tried to struggle, to fight back against her, but he was far too weak. His efforts did not last long.

'Serendipity, Robert, that's what I call this. Oh, and by the way – Chloé is dead.'

Elaine watched and felt him make one last-ditch attempt to push back against her.

'Shhh – let go,' were her last words to him. Without knowing it, she'd used the same words as Harper when he'd buried his knife into the stomach of PC Sean Norris. It took only a few more seconds before any life loitering within him faded away as she watched on, unfeeling, unemotional.

In that instant she knew Harper was right, she was like him. It didn't matter if it was for different reasons. Harper merely pointed out that she was indeed, capable of murder. Elaine held her hands in position for as long as possible. When she heard the paramedics approaching her, she turned to face them, wiping her fictitious tears and pleading with them to help, before guiding another paramedic into the house to save Tom.

48

Tuesday, 12 September

Work on the house had progressed well during the last two weeks. The children's rooms were now ready and furnished with all their favourite things. The hall, stairs and landing looked bright and fresh. The living room and kitchen completely refurbished and the porch redecorated – *again*. With the tree swing gone, she'd had a small, safe children's play area installed with a couple of swings, a large climbing frame, and a slide. The drive, completely resurfaced with gravel looked great and the parking area tarmacked. And let's not forget the newly fitted front door. Elaine had really gone to town with the place and had more plans in store.

All she needed to complete her dream were her children, and she expected their grandparents to arrive with them any minute. She knew it wouldn't be easy for them at first, especially Michael, but she was determined to do everything in her power to help them settle in and make it work.

Brimming with excitement, Elaine saw the car carrying her children pull onto the drive. She had seen the kids often since the day she left hospital but this was different; they were coming home. As George switched off the engine, Emily was desperate to get to her mother and was first out of the car. Elaine also couldn't wait and hurried down the steps to greet them. She dropped to her knees as Emily launched herself into her mother's arms. Michael followed with a broad grin. She stood to greet him, her fears unfounded as he protectively hugged them both. Her babies were home at last. George watched on sympathetically as Elaine held her children close to her in such an emotional and overwhelming moment. Emily spotted the climbing frame and, in her excitement, broke away and made straight for it. Michael couldn't wait to check out his new bedroom and rushed inside the house.

'Am I going to get left out?' said George, as he approached her with a loving smile.

'No, Dad. Come here.' They embraced each other.

From the first moment Robert had introduced them all those years ago, they'd developed a close bond; she adored her mother- and father-in-law. They weren't at all happy when Robert ended the marriage, and they also knew about their son's infidelities. They never approved of Chloé; well, not so much approve, they just didn't like her.

Elaine couldn't see her mother-in-law. 'Maggie didn't come?'

'She wasn't ready, not with this being where Robert died, but she'll come round.'

'Everything looks fabulous from out here,' said George, taking in all the work she'd had done to the place.

'Yeah, it's been hard, but the guys have been fantastic. I'll show you around in a bit.'

Emily came running back to them. 'Mummy, can we take Grandad to the pond and show him the ducks?'

'I'm afraid the pond isn't there anymore. It's been filled in,' said Elaine.

It was true; the farmer who owned the next field over had never worked that far down because of some confusion with boundaries on the property deeds. He had no idea about the old pond being there or even that it belonged to him. He'd had it filled in so he could make use of his newly gained land.

'But what about the ducks?' Emily asked.

'Take Grandad's hand and come with me.'

Elaine guided them around to the back of the house and showed Emily the new pond she'd installed to re-home the ducks.

'Now, whenever Grandad comes to see us, you can bring him out here and feed the ducks like you used to do with Daddy.'

A tearful George put an arm around Elaine's shoulder as Emily went closer to make sure the ducks were happy with their new home.

After their first evening together, Elaine prepared for bed and wanted to do a last check on the children. It was an exhilarating feeling for her to be doing what she enjoyed the most, taking care of the two people she loved and cared about more than anything in the world. First, she checked on Michael. He was in bed on his laptop, chatting with his friends. She went over and kissed him on the forehead.

'Don't stay up too long.'

'I won't, Mum.'

She knew full well he'd still be awake in two hours. She entered Emily's room to find her sound asleep. She stroked the hair away from the side of her face and leaned over to plant a kiss on her cheek. Emily was hugging Matthew, Charlie's old teddy bear. She smiled and caressed the bear, thinking of her cherished son. She switched off the bedside lamp, left the room, and closed the door behind her.

Elaine stood outside the door for a few seconds, happy and content her children were here with her. She then ambled along the landing to her bedroom.

A loud noise downstairs disturbed Elaine's sleep. She checked her mobile phone for the time: it was almost 2.30 a.m. Elaine climbed out of bed and went to investigate. As she tiptoed down the stairs, she heard another loud thud from out on the porch. The return of Harper Darmody would remain a constant concern to her. Until they discovered his body or found him alive, there would always be that uncertainty.

She unlocked her new front door, pulled it open and wandered outside. There wasn't anything to see out there except for the swing bench swaying in the light breeze. She turned, about to go back inside.

'Mummy,' a soft voice called after her.

'Charlie!' There he was, sitting on the swing bench.

'Sit with me,' he said.

Unsure whether this was another cruel nightmare, Elaine walked over and sat beside him on the bench, her eyes searching for the malign beast that had haunted her for so long.

She gazed into her sweet boy's eyes. 'It is you?' She put her arms around him.

'You have to let me go now, Mummy.'

Her eyes welled up. 'But I can't – I don't want to.'

'If you let me go, the monster can't hurt you anymore,' he said, in his sweet and gentle young tone.

'I don't care what he does to me in these dreams, not if it means I get to see you,' Elaine declared.

'If you let me go, he can't hurt me.' Charlie's sentence pulled at the strings of her heart. How could she be so selfish if it meant her son would be free of anguish? She now knew she would have to let him go, realising, at last, she was responsible for their lingering torment. It was time, time to let him be at peace and put an end to these awful nightmares.

She wept as she kissed him on the lips and put her arms around him, holding him tight. 'Okay, Charlie. You go now, but wherever you are, I'll always love you.'

'I'll always love you too, Mummy,' her beautiful boy whispered.

She stayed in the same position for a few seconds, but to her, it was as if time stood still. As she pulled away, Charlie vanished from her arms. A tearful Elaine swayed gently in the bracing air of the early hours. A faint smile broke through her sadness. The ache she'd held onto was gone, replaced by relief as the weight of grief she'd carried for so long lifted. She would never be entirely over it. She would never come to terms with losing a child, but she now believed she could at least manage her pain.

Elaine woke and glanced at her phone by the side of her. It was 2.45 a.m. She remembered her vivid dream, but it had been so different from the kind she was used to. Perhaps it was her minds way of dealing with the trauma and setting her free of heartache. She lay there content, loving these new emotions as she drifted serenely off into a long-awaited and gratifying sleep.

The next time her eyes opened, it was almost seven in the morning. Elaine felt magnificent as she stretched on her bed, smiling. She glowed from the inside, a sensational comforting radiance about her, a new beginning at last. Elaine climbed out of bed and checked in on her sleeping children, before heading downstairs to start breakfast. With no idea why, she had an urge to open the front door and go outside.

The sun was already illuminating the sky above. Yet another gorgeous day lay ahead. According to the weather reports, it wasn't going to last much longer and they'd told everybody to make the most of it. She sauntered to the edge of the porch and leaned against the post, relishing the freshness of the new morning. As she turned to re-enter the house, she caught sight of Charlie's teddy bear on the bench. It should have been upstairs with Emily. There was no way Emily could have brought it out here. She couldn't have opened the front door. Elaine picked up the bear, somewhat troubled.

'There you are, Matthew.'

Elaine turned to see Emily standing near the front door in her nightie. A feeling of reassurance engulfed her. She sat down on the bench with the bear on her lap, smiling.

'Come here, you little monkey,' she called to Emily, who ran over and jumped onto her mother's lap, taking Matthew from her.

Elaine didn't want to think of an explanation for how the teddy bear came to be outside on the bench. Was it a sign from Charlie he was at rest, or a sign of *something else*?

Michael then emerged from the house. 'What's for breakfast?' he asked, settling himself down next to her.

Blissfully content, with one child on her lap and the other next to her, Elaine placed her arms around them, bringing them both closer. Together on the swing bench, they all looked happy and at home. At last, Elaine had what she'd wanted all along, but at what cost? Only time would tell. For now, everything had fallen into place.

49

October
One Year Later

Crasten Hall was once a considerable mansion belonging to Lord Giles Crasten. He'd had the lavish house built in 1784 for his teenage French bride, Adelina Bujol. They'd spent some happy years there, or so Lord Crasten believed. One horrific night in 1806, Giles returned home during an abysmal snowstorm to find his wife in bed with another man – his nephew, Gideon. Adelina and Gideon declared their undying love for each other. Of course, Lord Crasten was outraged and sickened by this inappropriate act of betrayal.

Many a tale was told about what happened next. The favoured being that Giles beheaded his wife in front of his nephew and had him cursed by a witch to live forever with the image. He went on to burn down the house with himself and Gideon still inside. Gideon survived the fire and knew the curse to be true. Most of the property was destroyed, but much later rebuilt to the original plans by a man who wished to remain anonymous. For decades nobody knew who was in residence at the mansion. The rumours persisted, with many people suggesting it to be the cursed Gideon himself.

Over time, the building again fell into decay until 1974, when it was purchased and redeveloped into luxury accommodation for the elderly, where only those wealthy enough could afford to live out their remaining days in luxury.

'Anything else I can get for you before you turn in, sir?' the butler enquired of an elderly gentleman seated in his velvety green, comfortable armchair by the fireplace.

'No, thank you, Malcolm,' the man replied, reaching for his late-night glass of dry Fino Inocente from the silver tray. 'That will be all.'

'Goodnight then, sir.' The suited butler removed himself from the room. No reply came. He knew that once the gentleman had finished his sherry, he would return to put out the fire that roared in the huge marble fireplace. This was their nightly ritual and had been for many years before they moved here.

The man put his nose over the glass, as he always did, taking in the qualities of the pure Albariza soils, chalky, with a dusting of breeze from the Atlantic Ocean. Lightly salted almonds with more than a few hints of fruit, and a gentle touch of vanilla.

He took his first sip and savoured the full-bodied elegance, how he loved to taste the oak from the barrels. Every evening at ten on the dot, he took great delight and pleasure in these moments. By ten-thirty it would be over and he'd be tucked up in his four-poster bed. But for now, he would relish the minutes with his sherry. It was the one thing he looked forward to every night, never knowing when it would be his last.

A sudden noise made him look around at the door.

'Malcolm – is that you?' he frowned.

It was evident the gentleman didn't like to be disturbed during these quiet times to himself, one of the only pleasures left in his life. When no reply was forthcoming, he went back to his sherry and sighed. He would have words in the morning. But for the light of the fire and a dim lamp beside his chair, the room was comfortably dark and glowing with a radiant warmth.

The door behind him closed and the elderly gentleman glanced around in his armchair.

'Tut, Malcolm! What are you playing at?' he shouted in displeasure.

Again a quiet stillness greeted his query. He returned once more to his glass, staring into the burning kindling, contemplating life and the approach of the end of his days. He often wondered how many moments like this he would reap before his time was up.

He shuddered all over as if a cold breeze had blustered over him, but he knew it was something else; a fate he always knew might one day catch up with him.

'I've been waiting for you. You've taken much longer than I'd anticipated. Nevertheless, here you are,' the old man said with confidence, knowing exactly who'd entered the room.

'Well, come on – no need to remain in the shadows. You can't sneak up on a man who's been expecting you,' he said.

A waft of cold air swiped the side of his face as the dark figure moved past him to take the seat opposite.

'Well – I must say, I am slightly taken aback it's you and not your sibling.' The man sipped his sherry, engulfed with smugness. 'I would offer you a glass of this fine sherry, but I'm sure you don't want to keep me from the fate you have in store. After all – it has been a long time coming.'

There were no comebacks or vengeful comments. The old man was ready for the reckoning, but the hushed calmness had an unnerving influence on him.

'Have you nothing to say?' he asked the composed person sitting in front of him.

'What do you want me to say, Mr Parker?' Elaine responded.

'I don't know. Do you have questions or a need to know why?'

'I don't care about the why. As for questions, I'm not sure you'd have any answers or if indeed I'd even want them.' With her latex-gloved hands resting on the arms of the chair, Elaine pulled herself forward.

'Well, don't expect an apology,' he muttered insensitively. 'I'm not sorry for any of the things I've done, especially to you or that pathetic little brother of yours. It must be said though, certainly had spirit that one, and like a wild horse, his spirit had to be broken. Unlike you, gullible and eager to please, like a little whore,' he smirked, revealing the gap in his yellowed teeth.

Inside, she wanted to rip him to pieces for his discourteous words, but it wasn't time yet, there were ways of dealing with men like this, and she wasn't going to give him the easy way out.

'The fact you're here and not your brother would suggest he must be dead, and from what I heard – practically by your own hand. You've always had it in you to be a killer. I recall seeing a look in your eyes the moment you rammed that fork into your father's neck. Nearly took his head clean off,' he laughed.

This was a new revelation for Elaine. Her brother had told her that he'd killed their father, though he had admitted he couldn't remember doing it.

Denley Parker judged from her reaction this was new information to her.

'Ah, I see you still don't recollect every single detail, deary. How lovely for me to bring something new to the table.' No longer was he unnerved, in fact, he was quite the opposite. He accepted he would die this night, but now felt a superiority over Elaine and the occasion.

Her stare drilled into him.

'There it is, that's the look, those wonderfully dark, devilish eyes – how delightful. I almost feel like I helped create you.'

A smile spread over Elaine's face.

'I'm glad you find this all so amusing,' he remarked, not expecting her to be so casual. Denley felt the tide turning again, his dominance waning.

'Oh, I do, Mr Parker, I do. You are under the illusion you are in control of this situation and of your fate. Perhaps you believe it will be swift. You can try to goad me into giving you a quick death all you like, but it won't work. I want to make you suffer for your crimes against Liam and me. Not to mention those that came before or after. No, no, Mr Parker – I'm afraid you have no sway over how you will die tonight. There is nothing left to say. Any more words would be inadequate. You did what you did, and now it's time for us to make you pay.'

'Us?' Denley asked, flustered and confused.

A smirk and a nod from Elaine to someone standing behind Mr Parker took him entirely by surprise. A gloved hand reached over his chair and covered his mouth while the other injected something into his neck. As a weak, elderly man, it wasn't difficult to restrain him.

'You have been given a neuromuscular blocking agent, so just sit tight for a minute or two, the effects will soon take hold,' Elaine explained.

Mr Parker had expected this to be over swiftly, or at least that's what he'd hoped. His posture drooped as his muscles were forced into relaxation. The person holding Denley stepped out from behind the chair, into full view. Mr Parker's eyes exhibited the terror that the muscles in his body could not. He knew the other person was her brother. One of them eventually coming for him had always been in the back of his mind, but both of them was something he had never envisaged. Now he was at their mercy, of which there would be none, and he knew it.

'I'm sure I don't have to tell you who this is,' said Elaine. 'He is going to have a little time to reacquaint himself with you.'

Harper immediately punched Denley hard in the face, breaking his nose. Pain ripped through Mr Parker.

Harper straightened Parker's head and punched him over and over. So much hatred he felt for this man who had sodomised, beaten, and humiliated Liam Bennett beyond comprehension.

If Harper had his way Parker would be dead already, but Elaine was more methodical, she knew what was needed here for both of them. Revenge certainly, but also closure, an emotional need to resolve the trauma suffered by two young children.

'Harper!' Elaine called out.

He stepped back and gazed at the bloodied face of the merciless monster. He sank to his knees in front of him. Elaine appeared relaxed in the chair as she supervised. Harper grabbed hold of Mr Parker's slippered foot and twisted it until the ankle snapped, the noise horrendous, and just like Harper, Elaine was unflinching. Peering into Denley's eyes, she savoured the agony behind them. Tears seeped down his face. His nose bent out of shape. He heard his bones break, felt the unbearable agony, but no emotion or movement was possible.

Harper backed away without saying a word as Elaine climbed out of her chair and walked over to the open fireplace. She browsed through the small pile of logs to the side and picked up the poker.

'There is something that goes beyond pain when you can go through all the physical and mental emotions but can do nothing to prevent it. It's indescribable. What you are feeling right now is not even on a par with the atrocities you committed in your lifetime,' she said aloud, a clarion call describing what Liam and she endured all those years ago.

'Considering your age, we probably don't have enough time to drag out the agony for as long as we would have wished.' Elaine poked into the slowly diminishing flames to spread out the kindling and stacked the couple of logs she'd selected neatly into the fire to make a platform. She turned to Mr Parker. 'The drug you've been given will shortly make your breathing extremely difficult. If you're lucky, it may even suffocate you, which may be agonising, but much better than what awaits you if it doesn't.'

She looked at Harper and nodded to him. They both grabbed Denley Parker, wrestled his dead weight from his comfy armchair, and dragged him over to the fireplace. They rested his head down on the log platform she'd built. Denley Parker's eyes suggested he felt the intense heat from the fire on the top part of his body. Desperate mumblings emanated from the back of his throat, but even if he'd found a voice, there were no words that would have prevented them from moving ahead with their plan. Harper took the seat forcefully vacated by Parker, while Elaine gathered up some smaller kindling, placing the pieces on the fire to help it blaze up once more.

She stood over him, wanting to see the look in his eyes as the intensity of the pain from the heat built up. The logs began to catch; slowly the flames rose up the platform, the hairs on the back of his neck and head singed, his skin blistering. A sickening acrid, sulphurous scent filled the air in the room.

Were Mr Parker able to scream, no doubt he would. His grey hair seared and withered away. Denley's eyes shifted to one side, his ear scorched by the flames and melting. The skin on the side of his face, bubbling. His horrified eyes gazed up at Elaine. Harper stood by her side for one last look at Denley Parker. The unsympathetic pair watched on, glorying in their own brand of justice, which would soon be handed out to others responsible for the crimes committed against them.

'How do you feel?' asked Harper.

She took her time, thinking about her answer, not once averting her eyes from the flaming head of Denley Parker.

'Fucking great.'

OUT NOW
Godless Creatures

Turn the page for a preview of the sequel to The Mother of All Things and continue the story . . .

Three years have passed and life has slowly returned to normal in the aftermath of the tragic events at Sablefall Farm. Elaine and Harper continue to exact their brutal vengeance against those responsible for the crimes against them.

Investigative journalist Lenny Grey is hired to track down the man who murdered Elaine's son eight years earlier, and when a detective friend reaches out following the discovery of two dead boys, they suspect they're looking for the same killer. It soon becomes apparent they are dealing with something far more sinister than imagined.

With another young boy missing and events taking a dark turn, Elaine, Harper, Lenny and Tom form an unlikely alliance to stop the depraved child killer.

1

Wednesday, 13 February

'I think even you can deduce the cause of death here, DCI Baxendale. If it wasn't the rope around his neck, you can be sure the castration and disembowelment would have done the trick,' said Arthur Potts, forensic pathologist.

The two men, wearing white protective suits, gloves and plastic overshoes, stared up at the naked body suspended over the stairway of the large, impressive entrance hall, his innards scattered over the wooden steps and parquet flooring. A second, younger detective appeared behind them looking a little worse for wear. He'd already removed himself from the scene once, and after a second glance at the crime scene, his cheeks swelled like a blowfish and he was out of the front door like a whippet.

'The youth of today,' said the detective.

'I quite agree.'

'He was the same a couple of months back, when you were away,' said Baxendale.

'Ah, yes. The body on the bed force-fed hydrochloric acid. I recall the pictures: a particularly nasty business. My esteemed colleague said it made *her* feel queasy, and believe me, Olivia has a much stronger stomach than I do.'

'I didn't fair too well on that one either,' Baxendale admitted.

They turned their attention back to the dangling corpse.

'What's with all the holes in his body?'

'Not holes, detective. Nails,' said the pathologist. 'It's not easy to tell from down here, but those are nails. Six-inch nails to be precise, hammered into his body. If you follow me, I'll show you some more grisly findings.'

The pathologist led the detective down the hall and through the kitchen to another, smaller staircase. They climbed the stairs and walked along the landing.

Arthur pointed to the parquet floor. 'As you can see from the trail of blood, the body was dragged from this room along here: the study.'

Baxendale glanced over the bannisters to view the body directly below, sickened at the sight of the man's entrails. He thought back to the aforementioned crime a couple of months earlier and whether the two could be connected. Gruesome murders so close together, gentleman of similar age; it could not be disregarded.

As they entered the bright and airy study, Baxendale was blinded by an abundance of light permitted by the wall-to-wall window. Long teal curtains dangled either side, matching the paintwork surrounding the huge, intricately carved antique wooden fireplace. Overstuffed bookshelves lined the walls from floor to ceiling. His eyes adjusted and he focused on the large wooden desk in the centre of the room. A luxurious leather swivel chair was positioned in front of the desk. Blood covered the dark oak floorboards beneath.

Arthur Potts explained the scene. 'The man was stripped and forced to sit in the chair, his arms splayed out behind him across the desk and secured with six-inch nails driven through his hands. With his feet *pinned* to the floor, nails were hammered into various parts of his body. From the amount of blood pooled here under the chair at the edge of the seat, I'd say this is where he was castrated. As you can see, the nails are still in place, so when his hands and feet were removed, they were viciously ripped away. He was then dragged along the landing and down the stairs. This was torture of the most extreme and we both know, nobody goes to this much trouble without good reason.'

'No. That's very true,' replied the detective. 'So, where are his nuts?' he asked, looking around the floor.

'Good question. As yet the man's testicles remain missing.'

The detective stepped out of the room onto the landing. 'So why not hang and drop the body from up here?'

'Another good question and I can only think of one reason: an agonising and slow death.'

'So they dragged the man downstairs, put a rope around his neck, disembowelled him, and pulled him up gently so as not to strangle and kill him too quickly?'

'Seems that way. I think the killer wanted to watch him suffer until the end. It's highly likely the victim would have lost consciousness from the strangulation rather than from the loss of blood.'

'How long?'

'Somewhere between eight and twenty seconds, I'd have thought.'

'And how long before death?'

'Ten to twenty minutes.'

'Jesus Christ! What kind of person does this?'

'Well, that's your job, detective, but I'll state the obvious and say revenge. This attack was premeditated, brutal, and heartless, done by someone who held one hell of a grudge, and in my experience, anyone who kills in such a methodical way will rarely leave trace evidence.'

Baxendale nodded in agreement and said, 'I'll keep my officers out of your way and let you finish up.'

'Detective, I'm sure you've already alluded to the thought, but do you think there is a connection between this and the acid murder?' Potts asked.

'Could be. Two different but very extreme deaths. I doubt it's a coincidence.' The detective took another look over the banister and walked along the landing towards the back staircase.

Outside the mansion, the officers chatted, smoked cigarettes, and drank steaming takeaway tea to help stave off the cold February morning as they waited to investigate the crime scene. Detective Chief Inspector Harry Baxendale made a quick call to update his superior and then approached the men, quickly noticing the young detective constable with the temperamental stomach had removed his protective clothing.

'Who told you to take off your body-suit?'

'Nobody, guv,' he answered, clearly intimidated.

Harry didn't follow up, but instead scrounged a cigarette. He was about to take a puff when a uniformed officer informed him the pathologist wanted to see him.

'I'll be right there,' he said, drawing in a long puff before stomping it out on the ground. 'You! Get your body-suit back on and be ready to get your arse back inside the house,' said Harry.

'Yes, guv.'

Baxendale entered the house. The body lay on the floor of the hallway, taken down by the forensic team. Potts leaned over the body as Harry wandered up behind him.

'What is it, Arthur?'

'Balls, DCI Baxendale!' said Potts, glancing up at Harry.

'Come again?'

'Balls. You wanted to know the location of the gentleman's testicles – well, I've found them.'

'Where were they?'

'If you look here,' he said, opening the mouth of the man. 'At some stage during his torture they were stuffed into his mouth, and going by the teeth marks on the one testicle I *can* see, I'd say they made him eat them. The meaty looking remnants in his mouth are quite likely to be the other.'

Baxendale grimaced at the thought and instinctively guarded his own testicles as Arthur Potts continued.

'I'll retrieve this one when I get the body to the morgue. I'm fairly confident I'll find pieces of the other either in his oesophagus or in the contents of his stomach on the steps over there.'

About the Author

Gabriel enjoys writing psychological thrillers with plots that twist and turn and leave you wanting more. Born in London, he now lives on the Kent coast of England with his wife and cats.

He left school early to work in the building trade as a painter/labourer, and went on to become a carpet fitter, postman, and a multi-tradesman, but not all at the same time.

Books that inspired him to write were Salem's Lot by Stephen King, Flowers in the Attic by Virginia Andrews, and The Rats by James Herbert.

You can find out lots more about me, my books, and other exciting info on my website:
www.gabrielblake.com

To be the first to receive updates about future releases, exciting news, and special offers, please subscribe to my occasional newsletter:
https://tinyurl.com/Subscribe-to-Gabriel-Blake

It would be fantastic if you joined me on Twitter:
https://twitter.com/GabrielBlake_

Follow me on Instagram:
https://www.instagram.com/gabrielblakewriter/

Thank you for reading. If you enjoy my stories, please know that it means the absolute world to me. You can show your support for my writing by leaving a rating or better still, a review wherever you can. Subscribing or following me on social media is also a massive help.

Lightning Source UK Ltd.
Milton Keynes UK
UKHW010010301021
393062UK00005B/1273